THE EDEN STORIES

THE GREAT WALL OF VEN-US

Terry Toler

The Great Wall of Ven-Us
Published by: BeHoldings Publishing

Copyright @2020, **BeHoldings, LLC**
Terrytoler.com
All Rights Reserved

Unless otherwise noted, all Scripture quotations are taken from the Holy Bible, New Living Translation, copyright © 1996, 2004, 2015 by Tyndale House Foundation. Used by permission of Tyndale House Publishers, Inc., Carol Stream, Illinois 60188. All rights reserved.

Cover and interior designs: BeHoldings Publishing
Editor: Jeanne Leach

For information, address support@terrytoler.com

Our books can be purchased in bulk for promotional, educational and business use. Please contact your bookseller or the publisher at sales@terrytoler.com

For booking information email: booking@terrytoler.com
First U.S. Edition: November, 2020
Printed in the United States of America
ISBN 978-1-7352243-2-9

The Great Wall
Of
Ven-Us

OTHER BOOKS BY TERRY TOLER

Fiction

The Longest Day
The Reformation of Mars
The Great Wall of Ven-Us
Saturn: The Eden Experiment
The Late, Great Planet Jupiter
Save The Girls
The Ingenue
The Blue Rose
Saving Sara
Save The Queen
No Girl Left Behind
The Launch
Body Count
Mercury Protocols

Non-Fiction

How to Make More Than a Million Dollars
The Heart Attacked
Seven Years of Promise
Mission Possible
Marriage Made in Heaven
21 Days to Physical Healing
21 Days to Spiritual Fitness
21 Days to Divine Health
21 Days to a Great Marriage
21 Days to Financial Freedom
21 Days to Sharing Your Faith
21 Days to Mission Possible
7 Days to Emotional Freedom
Uncommon Finances
Uncommon Marriage
Uncommon Health
Suddenly Free
Feeling Free

For more information on these books and other resources
visit TerryToler.com.

Based in part on true events.

PART ONE

The more things change, the more they stay the same.
Jean-Baptiste Alphonse Karr

1

Two hundred years after the garden of Eden fall on Ven-Us (Ven-te 200)

The sun was about to set on Ven-Us bringing slightly cooler temperatures and a magnificent colorful sunset. Eve walked through the encampment where hundreds of tents were set up, enjoying a cool breeze out of the south. A welcomed respite from the day's hot sun.

A noise stopped Eve in her tracks. A woman. Crying. Moaning. Coming from Terah's tent.

Eve called out to her friend. No answer. She opened the inner flap and looked inside. Terah was sitting on the edge of a makeshift bed, doubled over. Sobbing. Seemingly in agony.

Was she sick? Did someone die?

"Why are you crying?" Eve asked.

"My husband is with another woman," she said between sobs.

Eve couldn't believe the words she'd just heard. Terah and her husband, Hamm, had been married for seventy-five years.

"What? That's not possible. I know Hamm. He wouldn't do that to you."

"It's true. He's with her right now."

"Who... Who is she?"

"Raga."

Eve's mouth flew open in amazement. "She's young enough to be his granddaughter!"

Raga was the daughter of one of Terah's best friends. Eve and Terah had helped deliver Raga. A beautiful girl. Twenty years old. Never been married. One of the prettiest and nicest girls on Ven-Us. Girls outnumbered boys or she'd already have been married. When

Raga's mom died in childbirth, Terah took her in as her hand-maiden.

Raga worked faithfully for Terah. Cooking meals. Fetching water at the well. In exchange for basic necessities. Hamm was old. Something wasn't making sense.

"Are you sure? How do you know they're together? Maybe it's not what you think."

"I'm sure... I'm the one—"

Eve interrupted her in mid sentence. "Where are they? I'm going to go get Adam. He'll talk some sense into him. I'll talk to Raga."

"You can't. It's not Hamm's fault," Terah said, trying to regain her composure. She dug her fingernails into her arm so hard, blood oozed from the nail marks. Because Ven-Us was the second planet closest to the sun, with a hot climate, God made human beings with very thin skin that cut easily.

"What do you mean it's not his fault? Of course, it is. He can't just cheat on you and get away with it." Eve stood to go get Adam.

Terah motioned for her to sit back down.

Eve stayed standing, ready to leave and determined to right this wrong.

"I told Hamm to lay with her," Terah confessed. "It was my idea..." she said, barely able to speak the words from the obvious feelings of guilt coming through in her voice.

Eve sat back down in stunned disbelief. "Why would you do that?"

Terah started talking so fast Eve had trouble understanding her words.

"Slow down. Start from the beginning," Eve implored.

"You know how God told Hamm he was going to give us a son?"

"I remember. You laughed when he told you."

Terah managed a slight grin. "I didn't mean to laugh. It just sounded crazy. I'm too old to have kids."

Terah was ninety. Hamm was three years older. Terah was barren. A few years before, God had numbered man's days at one hundred twenty. For whatever reason, God had allowed Adam and Eve to live beyond that lifespan. After that proclamation from God, women quit being able to have kids around age sixty.

Before his encounter with God, Hamm had accepted never having a child. He said on more than one occasion that it didn't matter to him. He loved his wife and would accept their fate. If God wanted them to have children, he would've given them some. Eve thought they were fine with it.

One night, God led Hamm outside and told him to look at the sky. God said his descendants would be like the stars. He'd have a son. Excited, Hamm rushed back to tell Terah. They both believed it by faith, or at least Eve thought they had. Ten years had passed though, and some hope had faded.

"We've all been praying for you. If God said he was going to give you a son, he will. You just have to be patient and wait," Eve told Terah for not the first time.

Terah bit her upper lip, then covered her eyes with her hands in obvious shame.

"I know. I felt so bad. So ashamed. Like I let Hamm down. I think it's my fault we can't have kids. And... he wants a son so badly."

Eve nodded in understanding. They'd had this conversation before. Adam and Eve had encouraged them to keep trusting God and to not give up hope. No matter how long it took.

Terah continued. "I talked to Raga. I asked her if she would lay with Hamm and try to give him a son. On one condition. She had to let me raise him so I can have a family." Terah paused. Remembering. Obviously regretting it. "She refused at first. But I was able to persuade her."

"I can't believe Hamm agreed to it," Eve said.

"Me either. I mentioned it to him. He was all for it!" Terah balled her fists, the anger was apparent in her words as the tears stopped momentarily. "Why wouldn't he be? He gets to lay with a young girl," she added.

"I understand why he would do it, but why would she?" Eve asked.

"Hamm is the richest man in all of Ven-Us," Terah explained. "I said to her, 'Give him a son. The son will become an heir. You'll be rich like me.'"

"I guess... for the wealth and prestige," Eve said, answering her own question as more came to mind. "Is Hamm going to marry her?"

"I told him he couldn't. That she could only be his mistress."

Eve nodded in understanding.

"But what if he does... make her his wife?" Terah asked anxiously. "He could throw me out and let her raise the boy. I'm not young and pretty anymore... Like Raga," she said with disdain. "I'm old and wrinkled." Terah raised her arms and flapped the skin back and forth which had sagged some with age.

Eve couldn't help but notice how remarkably beautiful Terah was for her age. "Stop saying that. You're beautiful," she said.

Ven-Us was close to the sun and the days were very hot. However, God had thickened the atmosphere of Ven-Us. He filled it with water which reflected much of the sun's rays away from the planet. Most of the women had soft, alabaster skin with very few wrinkles. Eve was more than a hundred years older than Terah but barely looked it. Only slight wrinkling of the arms and hands was the only way anyone could tell they were older than Raga.

"Maybe Hamm is tired of me," Terah continued. "He might want someone new to be with. He's never said anything or acted like he was tired of me." She had a faraway look. Confused. Dazed. Obviously in shock. Her whole world was turning upside down.

Terah's eyes widened. "What if Hamm was wrong? What if it

wasn't God who said I would have a son? What will I do?" she asked, wringing her hands and rocking back and forth on the bed.

Before Eve could say anything, Terah blurted out, "What if he doesn't love me anymore? He'll leave me."

"That won't happen. Hamm loves you," Eve said assuredly, although she wasn't sure what to believe at that moment. "Remember this wasn't his idea," Eve added. "In his defense, you encouraged him to do it."

"That's true. I have to keep remembering that. Maybe I'm overreacting. We've been married for seventy-five years and Hamm has not once ever mentioned wanting a mistress or another wife. We've always been faithful to each other. He could've had more wives. But he never wanted to."

At that moment, the tent flap opened, and Hamm walked in. Eve bolted up from her seat.

"I'd better go," Eve said, glaring at Hamm as she left.

Hamm had a distant look on his face.

Good luck. You're going to need it.

Eve hurried to tell Adam.

* * *

Two thousand years later (Ven-te 2200)

"Dean Church-Well. Did Hamm have sex with Raga?" a student asked me.

As dean of Western Ven-Us Theological Seminary, I wasn't often in the classroom. Teaching was my first love, so I filled in for my professors whenever I could. One happened to be absent, so I jumped at the chance to teach her class. The graduate students in the *Old Testament Biblical Studies* class were enthralled by the story of Terah, Hamm, and Raga, and I spent the first half of the class relating the salacious details to them. A story of sex, deception, and betrayal captured their interest as I shared more detail and background than they'd probably ever heard before.

"First of all, you can just call me Dean Row." Rowan was my first name. When my little brother was first learning to talk, he had trouble pronouncing it. The only thing audible was the first syllable, Row. My parents picked up on it. So did my older brother. The nickname stuck.

"To answer your question, yes he did. Hamm laid with Raga much to the regret of his wife."

"Did she get pregnant?" another student asked in follow up.

My style of teaching was open discussion, question and answer, rather than lecture. The students were asking questions in rapid fire. I was firing answers and my own questions back at them just as fast. And loving every second of it.

"She did. She had a son named Nary," I answered.

A light bulb must have gone off in one student's head as he said more of a question than a statement, "That's where the Naryans get their name?"

The Naryans were the ones who constantly threatened us with war. A war that could destroy all of Ven-Us.

"Yes," I replied. "They are descendants of Nary." The Naryans lived on the east side of Ven-Us. The Christians lived on the west side.

"What about Terah? Did God ever give her a son?" someone asked.

"That's what makes this story so fascinating," I answered. "She was actually pregnant when she asked her husband to take on a mistress."

Loud laughter went through the classroom as they considered the irony.

"Had Terah simply waited a week or two and trusted God, none of it would've happened," I explained. "Nary would've never been born. The Naryans would not exist."

I paused to let those facts set in.

"Terah had a son and named him Casik. The name means *promise*. This is a great lesson on patience and waiting on God to fulfill his promises. If God says he's going to do something, he will, if we wait on him."

Several students nodded in understanding. To me, this was why God gave us the Bible stories showing us the characters in all of their faults. These were teachable moments. We could learn about God and how to relate to him by looking at their failures. Unfortunately, this failure by Hamm had devastating consequences for generations to come. Even for us today.

"That one act changed the whole course of the history of Ven-Us," I explained further.

I stood from behind the teacher's desk and walked over to a large writing board on a side wall and wrote the words *Consequences of Hamm's Actions.* "Let's make a list of everything that has happened on Ven-Us that wouldn't have happened had Hamm not had a child with Raga and there were no Naryans."

"The wars," a student shouted out.

1. Wars.

I started the list on the board and then asked for more clarity. "Which wars?"

"Really all of them," a young woman on the front row replied. "The seven-day war. The World War. Crusades. The Religious Wars. All of them have been between the two factions. Especially the religious wars. Really, every one of them has been a religious war at their foundation."

"Good," I affirmed. "Every single war for the last two thousand years can all be traced back to the conflict between the descendants of the Naryans and the descendants of Casik."

One student raised his hand to speak even though it wasn't necessary to do.

I nodded to him to go ahead.

"The Great Wall of Ven-Us," he said hesitantly.

"You are correct," I said, sensing his uncertainty.

2. *The Great Wall*, I wrote in big letters.

"The wall was built to separate the two civilizations," I explained. "To keep us out of the east and to protect those of us who live in the west."

I could see several taking notes. Emboldened, I continued without hesitation, not wanting the class to get bored.

"The Naryans are intent on our utter destruction. Their leaders continually call for the annihilation of the western pag-anites as they call us. So, a Great Wall separates the east from the west. It spans around the entire globe. Armed guards patrol both sides, and very few people are allowed through the main gate which is right in the center of the wall. Virtually no one is allowed out of the east. Almost daily, someone is shot to death trying to escape the horrors of life on the east side while trying to get to the relative freedom of the west."

I paused to let the notetakers catch up. "What else?" I asked.

I waited a few moments as the students struggled to come up with another answer for the list.

I thought I'd help them out and wrote: 3. *The Mount of the Rock.*

"Sal-Am," the young woman on the front row added, the rock obviously sparking her memory. "He would've never been born. Sal-Am is a descendant of Nary." She was sharp. One of the best students in the class, seemingly.

4. *Sal-Am.*

"How are Sal-Am and the rock related?" I asked.

She answered without hesitation. "The Naryans say the rock is where Sal-Am ascended into heaven without dying. The Christians believe the rock was where Jesus was killed. Also, where Hamm sacrificed his son Casik."

Not a difficult question. The rock was a holy site for Christians and for Naryans, and these students had likely visited it many times. Most of the information I was relating would sound familiar to all of them.

"Fortunately, it's in our control," I said.

The rock was on our side of the border. A large glass bullet-proof wall separated the two sides. A fact that created tremendous ongoing conflict. The peace was kept only by the barrel of a gun. Not so much a peace as a stalemate. Christians could visit and touch the rock anytime. Naryans could only see it through a glass partition, except for one week a year when they were allowed to come on our side and view the rock. A major issue in the ongoing conflict.

"The Quan-di," the front row young lady added with a confident look. I made a mental note to learn more about her. She had potential.

"What's your name?"

"Sarah Hatch-Ard" she replied.

"Sarah, what is the Quan-di?" I asked, testing her knowledge.

"The Quan-di is a book written by Sal-Am. The Naryans consider it their version of the Bible."

"How is it different from our Bible?"

"Sal-Am considered Jesus to be a prophet and not the Messiah. He claimed he was the *Messiah* for Ven-Us. The Quan-di is full of heresies."

5. *Quan-di*.

I sat back down and began speaking in a more serious tone. "Excellent observations, class," I said affirmingly. "This is an important lesson on cause and effect. Every action you take in life has the potential to affect the rest of your life and possibly even the lives of generations to come. Hamm had no idea his one act would still affect us two thousand years later."

At that moment, a message came across my air-line overriding the hold on my notifications. The message was marked *Urgent!* I instructed the class to read pages 1.23-1.25 in their textbooks and then stepped out of the room.

One hour. Usual location. Confirm receipt.

A bolt of adrenaline shot through my body. One hour was the least amount of time I'd ever been given to make a meeting. Something significant was happening. I confirmed and stepped back in the classroom. The students were diligently reading their assignment.

"You can leave after you finish the reading assignment. I'm dismissing the class early. I have somewhere I have to be," I said as I gathered my things.

Sarah raised her hand. I called on her.

"Dean Row, I have a question. Why do the Naryans hate us so much?"

"That is a long story," I said. "I'll have to come back and explain it to you another time."

I have a feeling that's the same question I'm going to have to answer in one hour.

2

Before (Ven-te 200)

"Why do you hate me so much?" Raga asked Terah, her voice barely above a whisper. Both women held their sleeping infant sons in their arms.

"Your son has no right to my husband's birthright. My son is the legitimate heir," Terah replied angrily, the intensity present, even without the volume.

"My son was born first," Raga said in a softer voice, seemingly trying not to raise Terah's ire any further. "Nary is the first-born child. The first-born is the heir of inheritance by law."

"Your son was only born an hour before mine," she retorted a little louder.

Terah didn't know she was pregnant when she implored Hamm to lay with Raga. Even then, Casik should've been born before Nary, but she was late, Raga early. Both women went into labor on the same day. There were anxious moments in both tents as the race to deliver first was on. Neither lady had any control over the outcome. As fate had it, Nary was born an hour earlier.

"The god's have spoken, and my son was born first," Raga reiterated her position.

"There are no gods other than the God of Hamm," Terah said emphatically. "God spoke to Hamm and said his descendants would be like the stars. Casik is the son of promise. Your son is the son of a prostitute."

Terah immediately regretted the words. A fire of hatred raged inside her. Almost to the point of uncontrollable anger.

I don't have to be mean.

Still she was torn and kept going back and forth between blaming herself and blaming Raga. Really wanting to blame Hamm but knowing it was her idea.

Tears formed in Raga's eyes. Terah felt compassion for a moment until Raga's tone turned accusatory.

"It's not my fault. You told me to lay with your husband."

"You didn't have to do it. Why would you lay with another man who's not your husband? Don't you have any morals at all?" Terah turned her back to Raga as Casik started to stir.

"I did it for you. You wanted a child," Raga retorted. "You're the one with no morals. Asking another woman to lay with your husband. What kind of wife are you? You couldn't satisfy your husband. But I could!"

Terah turned back around and slapped Raga across the face, waking both babies as the sound hung heavy in the tent.

"I didn't know I was pregnant," Terah said with intense hatred building for Raga. "You shouldn't have done it. You shouldn't have listened to me. You did it so you could steal my husband. You wanted to be his wife and have access to all of his riches. You took advantage of me. Now you're trying to steal the birthright. I'll not stand for it. Casik will have what's rightfully his."

The babies were crying at the top of their lungs. The women screamed at each other above the din.

"You'll never have the birthright. It's my son's!" Raga shouted angrily.

"Then I will banish you from the camp!" Terah said, raising her voice to a scream so she'd be even louder than Raga.

"You can't do that. I'll talk to Hamm."

"Hamm's gone. He's out gathering the flocks. I'm in charge of the camp. Give me the birthright. Swear to it, and you and your son can live with us here in the camp. If you don't, I'll send you into the wilderness alone with your child."

"You wouldn't dare!"

"Don't tempt me."

"Not even you can be that cruel."

"Give me the birthright," Terah said, grabbing Raga's hair with her free arm.

"Never. I will not," Raga said as she slapped Terah's hands off of her easily, being younger and stronger.

"Then from this day forward you are banned from this camp," Terah stated. "You must leave tonight. Go gather your things. If you refuse, I'll have the guards throw you out of the camp."

Raga stormed out. Terah followed her. She got two of the watchmen to come with her. When they arrived at Raga's tent, they found her sitting on her bed refusing to get up. The baby was screaming. Raga tried to console him. Terah instructed the watchmen to remove her.

"No!" Raga screamed. "Let go of me," she said as they grabbed her arms and dragged her outside. The commotion caused several people to come outside as well to see what was going on.

"I will not leave," Raga said emphatically.

Terah's rage boiled to the surface and exploded like a volcano. "Escort her several miles away from the camp out into the desert," she said to the men. "If you see her come back to the camp, kill her and bring the baby to me."

"At least give me a tent," Raga pleaded. "And some food and water. How am I supposed to survive out in the wilderness with a new baby on my own? There are wild animals out there. I'll need a weapon."

Terah told the watchmen to guard her. She left and returned a couple minutes later with a skin of water and some food.

"This is your last chance, Raga. Give me the birthright, and you won't have to leave."

"Never."

"You have your orders," Terah said to the men. She gave Raga the food and water—about two day's supply—then turned and walked away, trying to drown out the screams of Raga and her baby as they were escorted out of the camp.

* * *

Hamm returned several days later from a successful trip and called for a great feast. Everyone in the camp attended, and much celebration filled the camp for God had blessed their livestock and would provide food for them all for another year.

Later that night, Hamm and Terah were in their tent. Hamm held his son, Casik.

"Where was Raga and Nary tonight?" Hamm asked. "I didn't see them."

"Why do you care?" Terah asked sarcastically.

"I just wondered. I thought she'd be there. I wanted to see my son."

"I don't know," she said. "Am I my handmaid's keeper?"

Nothing more was said for a few minutes. Hamm wasn't sure what had escalated the hostility. A confrontation must have happened while he was gone. He decided to drop it. He'd find them tomorrow.

Terah broke the awkward silence with an even more awkward question. "What was that night like for you?" she asked, bringing up a topic that had never been discussed. Something that had been avoided at all costs.

"What do you mean?" Hamm knew but thought the best approach was to play dumb.

"That night with Raga. What was she like?"

"I did what you asked me to do. Nothing more." An answer he had rehearsed in his mind for this moment, which surprised him that it hadn't come sooner.

"How was she?"

"I don't think we should talk about this."

"Was she better than me?" Terah asked with anger rising in her voice.

"Different. She was different."

Terah slammed her hand against the water bucket, knocking it over spilling water in the tent. Wrong answer, he thought.

"You have no idea how hard this has been for me," Terah said, as she fought back the tears. "I've replayed the night in my mind over and over again. Pictured you with her. The images have haunted me for months. I cry myself to sleep every night. Remembering... Trying desperately to forget."

Hamm wasn't sure what to say. Anything he did say would probably only make it worse.

"Don't you have anything to say for yourself?" Terah asked.

"What do you want me to say?" Hamm asked with anger rising inside of him. *This wasn't my fault.* He felt tremendous guilt and regret. He wished it'd never happened. All he had to do was trust God, wait a few weeks, and they would've learned Terah was pregnant. He'd been stupid. Nothing he could do about it now. He wanted to express those thoughts to Terah but didn't think it would help.

"Do you love her?" Terah asked.

A question Hamm had asked himself hundreds of times. "No. I haven't been with her since."

"You must have some feelings for her."

"I love my son," Hamm said gently. "It didn't mean anything. Except she gave me a boy, and he's my first born."

"Casik should be the first born," Terah said strongly. "He's the son of promise. He's the one who deserves to be your heir. I'm your wife. She's just a tramp. Her son is illegitimate. You must declare Casik as your heir."

"I can't unless his birthright is sold by him or by his mother."

Hamm had thought about this dilemma on more than one occasion. He couldn't change the law to suit his own ends.

"Or she's no longer around..." Terah said, her voice trailing off.

"What have you done?" Hamm asked, standing up from the bed. She looked away.

"What have you done to Raga and Nary?" Hamm asked more emphatically. He walked over to Terah, grabbed her shoulders and turned her so he could look directly into her eyes.

"I sent them away into the wilderness," she said, still not making eye contact.

"Alone? How could you do that?"

"I banned her from the camp."

"Why?"

"She wouldn't sell me the birthright."

"Did you give her any provisions?"

"Two day's supply."

"How's she supposed to survive in the wilderness? Alone? Carrying a newborn? With only two day's supply? You have to get her back."

"It's done. I don't know where she is. She's a long way from here by now. Probably in somebody else's camp selling herself to them."

Hamm paced back and forth in the tent.

"I have to leave again and see to our crops or I would go look for her myself. If she comes back, I want you to restore her to the camp. He's my son. My first born. You had no right!"

"You're still in love with her, aren't you?" Terah asked with more fear in her voice than anger. Afraid of what the answer might be.

"It's not about her. It's about Nary. I told you what to do. You have to fix this. If she comes back, give her food and water. I command you."

Hamm stormed out of the tent.

* * *

It doesn't matter. She's not coming back. No way she survived the wilderness this long. Terah shuddered at the thought. She'd already regretted sending Raga out alone with a baby. Now, Hamm would never forgive her if something has happened to his son.

* * *

Raga wandered in the wilderness near Baar of the Rocks. Her food and water were gone along with her hope. She settled under a small tree and laid down to die.

"I can't sit here and watch my son die," she said to herself as Nary began to cry. As she sat there, she began to sob.

What do I do? If I go back to camp, Terah will kill me. Better to die there than here in the wilderness.

I don't even have enough strength to make it back to camp.

The thoughts swirled in her mind as she wondered if she was even thinking clearly anymore.

An angel of God appeared to her from heaven and said to her, "What is the matter, Raga? Do not be afraid. God has heard the boy crying as he lies there. Lift up the boy and carry him back to camp. He will not die. I will make him a great nation."

God opened her eyes, and she saw a well of water. She went and filled the skin with water and drank. Strengthened, Raga walked back toward Hamm's camp not knowing what to expect when she arrived. She stumbled into camp with barely the strength to walk, having not eaten for several days.

The watchmen stopped her and led her to Terah's tent. A meal was brewing. The smell permeated outside of the tent. Raga's insides ached at the smell of the food. Hunger stabbed her like a sharp knife.

Terah rushed to Raga as soon as she saw her enter the tent. Perhaps she felt sorry for Raga and the baby. She took the baby in her arms.

"I've been so worried about you," Terah said sincerely. "I'm sorry I threw you out of the camp. I've had many restless nights worrying about you and Nary. We searched for you but couldn't find you anywhere. I thought maybe you'd been eaten by wild animals."

"Have mercy on me," Raga said. "Can I have some stew?"

Apparently sensing an opportunity, Terah said, "Will you sell me the birthright for some food?"

"I'm about to die. So is my baby. Do you not have any compassion?"

Terah gave the baby back to Raga and stirred the stew again, sending waves of aroma through the tent.

"What good is the birthright if your son is dead?" Terah asked.

Raga was torn. *What should I do? Terah's right. What good does the birthright do if my baby is dead? Terah is so evil, she doesn't care. She'll let my son die.*

"Okay," Raga said with disdain. "I'll sell you the birthright for a bowl of stew."

"Swear to it!"

"I swear."

Terah dished out a bowl of stew and handed it to Raga, making it official. The watchmen witnessed it. Raga scarfed down the stew, her hatred building for Terah and her son with each bite.

3

Now (Ven-te 2200)

Five minutes late for the meeting wasn't bad, considering the four levels of security I had to go through to get to the most secure room in the most secure building on Ven-Us. Fortunately, a staffer met me at the entrance of the *Red-Ford Building for the Security of the Free Land* and ushered me through, which made it easier. If not, I might've been much later.

The six people in the room didn't notice my entrance, or if they did, they didn't acknowledge it. Probably the words, "catastrophic consequences," spoken as I entered by Ted Cole-Man, the Director of Freeland Security, captured their undivided attention. A large screen at the front of the room had a picture of the atmosphere of Ven-Us and a rocket penetrating its protective layer. The visual made it easy to figure out what the catastrophic consequences were and why we were meeting in the first place. The only question was why I was summoned to it. I figured I'd find out soon enough.

"Do we know for sure the Naryan missile will even penetrate the atmosphere?" someone I didn't recognize asked. The room was set up classroom style. Large tables with chairs were set up in four rows. I was in the back. The others were dispersed around the front three rows. Ted stood at a lectern just to the right, my left, of the screen behind him.

"Let me turn this part over to Pat and let him explain," Ted said. Pat Walk-Er stood and walked to the front of the room. I recognized him immediately. Arguably, one of the foremost scientists on Ven-Us.

"As you all know from basic science, Ven-Us's atmosphere contains oceans of water," Pat explained while pointing at the picture of clouds holding water. "The water protects us from the sun's rays. Without the water and with our close proximity to the sun, the temperature on Ven-Us would be around 864 degrees. Obviously, life could not exist."

Pat took a deep breath. The room seemed to collectively do the same.

"This protective layering, called the Jo-zon layer," Pat said, "keeps our temperature around ninety-five degrees during the day and seventy-two at night. It's a marvel of nature. It holds the water in the atmosphere at just the right thickness to keep the water from breaking through, yet it's thin enough to allow the sun's rays to get to the surface. Remarkable really."

Several people nodded in acknowledgement. I remembered this from my basic science classes. The layer was like a water balloon. It held the water in place by a thin layer. Scientists had been concerned for centuries about penetrating that layer and releasing all of the water. Not unlike if a pen was stuck into a balloon. All the water would pour out of even the smallest hole. Everyone on Ven-Us would drown. If anyone managed to survive the flood by some miracle, they would burn up by the excessive heat no longer blocked by the Jo-zon.

Environmentalists had been claiming for years humans were causing the layer to thin, and manmade pollutants were going to cause the catastrophe. One noted scientist recently said we only had eleven years before it would happen. I believed they were sounding a false alarm. There was no evidence that Ven-Us was warming because of anything man was doing. I mostly kept those opinions to myself and out of the raging debate. Clearly, man penetrating it with a missile was a more immediate concern.

Penetrating the Jo-zon layer inadvertently had been a worry for years. Technology existed for travel in the atmosphere and even into space, but any aircraft would penetrate the layer and release the water. Only small, low flying craft were allowed in the sky, and they had to fly at a low altitude.

Several years ago, someone invented what were called SCCs, Space Communication Craft. These spaceships could be launched into our orbit with the ability to manage communications. We couldn't even release SCCs into the orbit around Ven-Us. Shooting them into space would break the seal and kill us all. The SCC wouldn't survive the excessive heat in the orbit anyway. It would burn to a crisp. So, we had to find other ways to communicate. The west had a sophisticated communications land system; the east was years behind us but catching up by stealing our technology.

Pat paused to take a drink of water, and I took the opportunity to pour one for myself as he began to speak again. "Literally, if the layer was one foot thicker or thinner, it wouldn't work. It's exactly perfect." Pat added, "It's amazing how perfect it is."

I knew God was the only one who could've created it so perfectly, although I wasn't sure who else in the room agreed with me. Some scientists had concocted a theory years ago to try to explain creation without the existence of God. While I didn't know if Pat had bought into that theory, I suspected he did. I thought the theory was so implausible it bordered on the absurd. However, it had somehow become mainstream and made it into school textbooks being taught more as fact than theory. Of course, *our* school taught God was the source of all creation, including the Jo-zon layer. To me, the layer couldn't have developed with such mathematical accuracy on its own. It had to have a creative design. By a designer. God.

"All this was put in place during the great explosion millions of years ago," Pat said, confirming where he stood on the subject.

The purpose of the meeting was not to debate science and creationism, so I didn't say anything. My purpose for being there wasn't clear yet, but it definitely wasn't to start an argument. Ted didn't give me the chance anyway.

"If the Naryans shoot off a missile and it penetrates the Jo-zon layer, all of the water in the atmosphere will come crashing down on Ven-Us, and everyone will perish," Ted said, emphasizing the word *perish* for effect.

A man raised his hand but asked the question without being called on. He sat next to a woman who looked vaguely familiar.

"Why would the Naryans shoot off a missile if they know they will die as well?"

My purpose for being there. To answer that very question.

"They want to usher in the end times," I spoke up without being called on. The other members of the room turned around to see who was speaking. I nodded my head as if to say hello. The woman smiled at me familiarly, distracting me momentarily.

When I recovered, I said, "The Quan-di predicts a great flood in the end times. The Quan-di is the Naryans' equivalent of our Bible. The Bible says God will never flood the world. The Naryans, of course, reject the Bible. More concerning, they believe paradise awaits them when they destroy the infidels. Infidels being us."

I noticed a couple of people change positions in their chairs as if what I was saying was making them uncomfortable. Something that had concerned me for years and which I had expressed to Ted many times, which was why I was part of the V-7 team and why he called on me in times like these.

Ted waved for me to pause so he could introduce me and explain my credentials. "Dr. Rowan Church-Well is the Dean of Western Ven-Us Theological Seminary," Ted said. "He is the foremost expert on Naryan theology and religious beliefs. He's also the most deco-rated V-7 operative in history."

It seemed to me like everyone already knew who I was, so I con-tinued with only my nod of the head. "The general population of Naryans aren't anxious to destroy the world," I said. "It's the far-left radicals who control the political and religious institutions who are hell-bent on destroying us. They don't care if they destroy themselves in the process. They think they are following god's plan for Ven-Us."

I probably wasn't telling them anything they didn't already know, but I said it in my teacher's voice anyway.

"We don't think they even know about the Jo-zon layer," Ted said.

"Or don't believe it," I corrected Ted.

His lips curled into a slight frown and he ignored my comment, probably not interested in starting a debate either. "The Naryans have been trying to acquire missile technology for a long time," Ted said. "They want to attach bombs to the missiles and shoot them at us. Kill us as Dr. Church-Well has said. They probably don't even know they might flood the whole world by penetrating the Jo-zon."

An eerie silence filled the room.

"Whether they know or not," Ted said looking directly at me with a stern look, "it's my job to stop them."

"Does the V-7 know where the missiles are?" the man sitting next to the woman asked.

Ted was the director of V-7. The United Ven-Us States (UVS) was a collection of thirty western states who came together a couple hundred years ago to form one nation. Although each territory was autonomous and self-governing, the UVS provided limited government services. Primarily defense. Ted was in charge of our entire defense structure. Seven different branches of forces, hence the name V-7.

Some pushed for increased contributions from the states to the government and more national control over things like education, health care, and human services. So far, the people had rejected giving the collective states too much control over the individual ones. Probably only a matter of time before the nationalists won out. Centralized power and control were too big a temptation to resist for the powers that be. As the national budget increased, so did its power.

I was called in occasionally because of my expertise on the Naryans and understanding the Quan-di and their religious beliefs. And twelve years of experience as a special forces spy, ten of which I lived undercover in the east. That gave me a unique perspective no one in the room likely had. Except maybe the man and the woman who were clearly operatives.

After my wife and daughter were killed by a suicide bomber during my last year of seminary, it became my life's calling to wage war against the Naryans and to spread the gospel of Jesus to combat their teachings. Volunteering, being accepted, and going through two years of training along with my extensive knowledge of their religious beliefs made me a perfect candidate for operating on the other side of the wall in the east. The missions were so successful, they lasted for ten years. I won many commendations for my performance. Secretly. My identity couldn't be known to the Naryans.

Now I was a consultant, and was called to the meeting to offer my perspective. Although I didn't know the people in the room, they had some purpose as well, which I expected Ted to get to fairly soon.

As if on cue, Ted said, "Let me get right to why I have called you here today." Ted distributed a folder to each person. The outside read in bold red letters, *V-7 Special Ops, The Garden of Eden Operation.*

My mouth flew open. What did the garden of Eden have to do with missiles? How did the five of us fit into the operation? I wondered what Pat thought of the title. Pat certainly didn't believe the garden of Eden ever existed. To him it was a myth. A legend. A fable. What was his role? Surely more than to just explain the science. Who were the other people in the room? The man and woman sitting to my left in front of me were definitely special operations. I spotted that fact the moment I entered the room. They were probably going to go into the east and destroy the missiles. Who was the other man and what was his role? Thoughts and questions were swirling in my mind like an eddy in a river.

"To answer your question," Ted said after everyone had a folder, "we don't know where the missiles are. That's the mission of this team. To find the missiles and destroy them."

I was reading ahead, trying to discern my role and figure out what the garden of Eden had to do with it. Ted explained it just as I got to the corresponding page in the folder.

"On page eight, you will see actual transcripts from communication intercepts. Don't ask me how we got them," he said dismissively. "That's classified."

I quickly read the first intercept. A conversation between two of the highest leaders of the Naryans talking about constructing missiles at the garden of Eden site.

Construction on the missiles have begun on the garden of Eden site.

My mind wanted to lead me to figure out how they got the intercepts, thinking about my time on the ground and how I'd relayed similar intercepts over the years. But the mention of the garden of Eden had me perplexed.

No one knows where it was.

The Naryans couldn't possibly know. Things were making less sense.

"They believe they've discovered the original site of the garden of Eden based on the writings in the Quan-di," Ted explained. "They are building the missiles on that site. Dr. Church-Well's job is to figure out where the garden of Eden was."

What?

A wave of panic pulsed through my veins as my breathing quickened and my heart raced. The gravity of the situation hit me all at once.

The entire fate of Ven-Us rests on my ability to find the garden of Eden?

Impossible!

4

Before (Ven-te 212)

"What's wrong, Adam?" Eve asked. "You've been quiet tonight."

Eve sat up in their bed. She had recently put out the fire, and the time had come to go to sleep. Inside and outside the tent was pitch black. As she lay in the comfortable darkness, she thought, as she often did, about what God had told her when they used to have conversations in the garden.

God had told them back in the garden he made the moon and the stars. Ven-Us was so close to the sun, it had no moons so there was nothing to reflect the sun's light into the night sky.

"What is a moon?" Adam had asked since they didn't have one as a point of reference.

God explained it to them. Even though they couldn't see any moons on the other planets, they accepted what God said as fact.

"Why don't we have any moons?" they asked God.

"Because they would be so small, they would be pulled into the sun's gravity."

"What is gravity?"

God laughed. "One day, you will have children, and this is what it will feel like. They will ask you lots of questions. There are some things you will just have to discover on your own."

God had explained to them how he created life on many different planets. On each was a garden of Eden, an Adam and an Eve, and a tree of the knowledge of good and evil. They had many more questions of him in the garden about other planets, but the fall happened before all of them were answered. Eve often thought back to her time in the garden, although she never really talked about it with Adam.

Recently, Eve noticed Adam becoming increasingly moody. Introspective almost. Sad which was unlike him. Usually he was outgoing, funny, laughing, and joking around most of the time. Adam generally was warm and affectionate. Now, he was withdrawn. Even from her.

"It's nothing," he said, kissing her on the forehead. "Let's go to sleep." Adam turned, facing away from her and pulling the covers up around his head.

Having been with him for more than two hundred years, Eve knew when something was wrong, and that she'd have to pry it out of him. A characteristic she noticed in most men in the camp. Usually, if she just didn't say anything, he would get over it on his own or eventually tell her what was wrong. Letting it go was not in her nature. A characteristic she noticed in most women in the camp. Too often she'd let it go, and then explode in anger a few days or even weeks later because she resented him not telling her. Solving it right away was always better. Something that was not easy for Adam to do.

"Did I do something to make you mad?" she asked, making sure she had a little tone of consternation in her voice.

"You didn't do anything to make me mad," he said with a chuckle.

Wrong response. Adam still hadn't learned the best thing to do was to tell her. He probably wasn't going to get any sleep until he did. Laughing about it was only going to make Eve mad.

It did.

"Fine!" she retorted. "Don't say anything. Eventually you'll tell me why you're mad at me." Eve turned her back to Adam and pulled the covers over her head, making sure she pulled them slightly off him.

Fuming.

Nothing was said for several minutes as they played tug of war with the covers. Eve adjusted her position in the bed several times to let Adam know she wasn't asleep and to make sure he wasn't going to get to sleep either. Several loud sighs sent him the desired signal—she was mad.

She knew her husband well. He would ignore her and pretend he was sleeping, hoping she would drop it. She might drop it for now, but he'd pay a price later.

God had told them to never let the sun go down on their anger. A principle they had not always followed and usually regretted when they didn't. Even after all these years together, they didn't resolve conflict well. Adam still didn't understand her.

A myriad of thoughts flooded her mind.

Does he not care about my feelings? He doesn't appreciate everything I do for him. Cooking. Cleaning. Taking care of his kids and grandkids. Typical man. Makes decisions without me. I don't have a voice. Spends more time with his friends than with me. Works too much...

Now Eve regretted even bringing it up. Maybe nothing was wrong. He might just be tired or had a bad day out in the fields. Why did she have to get mad at him and blow it out of proportion?

I should apologize.

Why? I did nothing wrong! It's not my fault. Why do I always blame myself? He's the one being insensitive. All I did was ask him what was wrong. What's wrong with that?

Something was definitely wrong. Why couldn't he just tell her what it was? Why couldn't men express their feelings like women can?

God made me his helpmate. I'm trying to help him. He's such a fool sometimes.

A battle was raging inside of her. Eve contemplated what to do. It would take her hours to get to sleep when she was like this.

Should I tell him how I feel? Or let him sleep. Why should he get to sleep while I lay here with my feelings hurt?

"I've been thinking a lot about Eden," Adam said in little more than a whisper startling Eve.

"Oh..." she muttered, not sure how to respond. Eden was a topic Eve desperately wanted to always avoid. A wave of guilt flooded through her at the mention of a past they'd tried so hard to forget. They fought about it for years after it happened.

Blaming each other. Regrets. Shame.

Then they made peace with it, years ago. Or at least she thought they had. Not really peace. Just acceptance. It happened. Nothing anyone could do about it. They'd decided they were both equally wrong. A convenient truce was formed and they didn't bring it up.

Now she was suddenly afraid of where this conversation might lead.

"I miss Eden," Adam said, his voice cracking.

Eve immediately regretted being angry at him. She felt the same way and desperately missed Eden too. Everything about it. Eve understood why he didn't want to talk about such a painful hurt buried deep inside of him. She avoided the pain as well and didn't fully share her own feelings about it. Eve turned over and placed her hand on his back shoulder. She couldn't tell for sure, but he might be crying. He rarely let her see him cry. Probably why this was coming up in the dark.

This must really be bothering him. *I didn't know.*

"I miss it too," she said sweetly while stroking his head.

"I remember falling asleep one day," Adam said. "When I woke up, you were there." God had said it was not good for Adam to be alone. One night, he put Adam into a deep sleep. The next morning, Adam awoke with a pain in his side and Eve lying next to him.

Eve laughed, relieved he wasn't bringing up eating from the tree. "That must have been a real shock. Seeing me there."

"I couldn't believe my eyes," Adam said as he turned over and faced her. "You were so beautiful."

Eve was thankful for the dark so Adam couldn't see her blushing, as her face suddenly felt flush. "That's so sweet," she said.

"Really. You were the most beautiful thing I'd ever seen. A lot better than the hippos and elephants." They both laughed. "God gave me you. I'm so glad he did. I wouldn't want to be married to a giraffe. How would we fit in this bed?"

Eve was glad to see Adam's humor had returned.

Eve responded warmly. "Me too. I'm glad he gave me you. I wouldn't want to be married to a rhinoceros. His horn would be poking me all night long. I'd never get any sleep."

Adam didn't laugh. Eve could tell he was fighting back tears.

"After we left Eden," Adam said, his voice cracking and his tone serious again, "I thought I might lose you."

Eve thought "left Eden" was a strange way to say it. They were thrown out by angels with swords. The worst day of both of their lives. God was so mad they ate from the tree they thought he was going to kill them so they ran and hid ashamed of their nakedness.

"You weren't going to lose me," she said assuredly. "Where was I going to go? You were the only man on Ven-Us." A slight chuckle did not lighten the mood.

"I was afraid I would," Adam continued. "Things were really rough between us those first few years."

"I know. But we got through it. I love you. I can't imagine life without you." It was Eve's turn to fight back the tears.

"Why are you bringing this up now?" Eve asked. "Are you afraid of losing me now?"

"No," Adam said with a chuckle. "You're stuck with me now." Adam kissed Eve on the lips.

"I guess I am. I've put up with you this long. It would be really hard to train another husband," she said sarcastically then kissing him back more passionately to let him know she was kidding. "Besides, you need me. You'd never find another wife as good as me."

"I'm glad I'm not Hamm," Adam said, half serious, half joking. "A wife and a mistress. What a disaster!"

"Do you want a handmaiden? I can arrange one for you," Eve said playfully.

"Not a chance. Hamm's life has been hell ever since he laid with Raga. The boys have been at each other's throats. I swear they're going to kill each other if Hamm doesn't kill them first."

Eve remembered the conflict between their two boys. One of their sons killed the other. Another topic they avoided. They'd blamed themselves at the time. Both of them thought it was somehow their fault. Burying their son was another one of the worst days of their lives.

The conflict between Hamm's two sons was a painful reminder. She'd wondered if it brought back those same haunted memories in Adam. She'd bring it up another time. If at all.

Instead she said, "I know. Same with Terah and Raga. I have to always keep them apart. They're constantly fighting. If I turn my back for one minute, they're at each other's throats about the smallest things."

"It's not a good situation," Adam said. "I don't know what to do about it."

"Nothing we can do," Eve said, her voice trailing off. For years, they'd blamed themselves for everything bad that happened on Ven-Us. Knowing they were ultimately responsible because they brought sin into the world. Many times, Eve had imagined what life would be like if she hadn't eaten the fruit.

God never brought up the garden or the sin to them again after the fall. He never tried to punish them further or make them feel bad. Still, they had to live with the curses. They were used to living under them. That didn't make it any easier. Childbirth had been torture. Adam had to toil almost every day for their food.

"Like I said, I'm glad I have you," Adam said, holding Eve closer and interrupting her dark thoughts.

"Maybe, we should go back there," Eve said.

"Where? You mean Eden?" Adam asked.

They hadn't been back since right after they were thrown out. They went back the next day, but angels were guarding it and wouldn't let them in. A few days later, everything was gone. They got as far away from there as they could, relocating more than a five days journey away. Thinking out of sight, out of mind. Didn't work that way, but it did help. Not something they would ever totally forget. Neither had ever suggested going back.

"Why not? We're not getting any younger. I'd like to see it again."

"I don't know if we could even find it. There's nothing left of the garden."

"I can find it. Remember the big rock. We wrote on it."

"I remember."

God placed a large rock right at the site where the tree of the knowledge of good and evil once stood. Adam and Eve carved "Adam and Eve were here" on the side of the rock. Afterward, they sat at the rock sobbing uncontrollably for hours and holding each other. Feeling all alone. Abandoned by God. Trying to get used to the skins God had made for them to wear. Get used to feelings they'd never felt before.

Shame. Guilt. Fear.

"I don't know if it's a good idea. It might bring back too many memories," Adam said.

Eve put her hand on his chest and pushed him away somewhat playfully. "You men. Always afraid you might feel something. I think it would be good for us. We should take our kids. Let's take Hamm as well."

Hamm had asked them many questions about Eden. He even asked them to take him there. They had refused. Although they did answer his questions. As painful as it was, they felt everyone should know what happened. The good and the bad.

"I think they should know where Eden was so they could pass the information on to future generations," Adam said. "It's a part of our history. The history of mankind. Seems like we have an obligation to let our kids know where it was. Remember how God said he gave every planet what he called a Bible so they would know the history of the planet and know God's ways?" Eve nodded, then mumbled yes, realizing he couldn't see her. "They need to put our story in the Bible."

"I agree. Let's do it. We'll start making arrangements tomorrow. We'll break camp and take everyone there. The rock can become a memorial."

"It's settled then," Adam said as he started kissing Eve passionately.

They both felt better a few minutes later.

5

Now (Ven-te 2200)

The Great Wall of Ven-Us was one of the most impressive architectural feats in history. Except for the purpose of its existence and the reminder of the hate between the east and the west, it would be the most impressive. I stood on top of the wall, unable to look any direction without painful reminders of memories I wanted to forget. It had been nearly ten years since I'd been there and had no idea why I was here today.

After the V-7 meeting ended, instead of turning west and driving the thirty minutes to my home, I turned east and drove straight to the wall as if something or someone was drawing me there. Now I found myself walking on the top, almost numb, wandering around with no purpose apparent to me. The observation area about a hundred paces wide and packed with tourists gave me plenty of space to wander aimlessly with my thoughts.

Even distracted by the memories, I found myself in full operation mode. My skills quickly returned even though I hadn't used them in several years. Scanned every face. Looked for anyone or anything suspicious. Slowed down. Sped up. Changed my patterns. Noticed only those things that were important. Blocked out distractions.

Eyes... Clothes... Anyone wearing anything not appropriate for the weather. Bulky clothes that hid weapons. Bulges in places they shouldn't be. Nervousness. Spies had a certain manner. So did terrorists. A man or woman getting ready to blow themselves and others to pieces would be understandably nervous. Easy to see in their manner and eyes.

Seeing the same face several times was another sure tell. Once or twice was not unusual. Three times was a sure sign of a tail.

Relax. No one is tailing you.

If nothing else, practicing my skills had some value. It made me feel alive. Important even. Like I knew something no one else around me knew.

I had my own nervous habits that returned as well. I constantly touched the gun on my belt just under my shirt which I was now required to carry with me at all times. My handlers had tried to break me from that habit. A "tell" as we called it. A giveaway to an enemy operative who might also be looking for anyone or anything suspicious.

Not that I was worried about being seen. I knew with my superior skills I'd see them before they saw me. So, I didn't try to control my nervous tics. Besides, the likelihood of any hostiles on the wall was very remote. Especially anyone looking for me. I'd made enemies in the east, but they had long since forgotten about me. The bigger concern was someone wanting to harm the tourists. The wall had become more effective over the years in keeping them out but the danger still existed.

Nevertheless, touching my gun made me feel better. More secure. Knowing I had the weapon and the ability to deal with any situation I might come across in the unlikely event something bad happened.

Why am I even here? What does it have to do with my mission? There were dozens of guards around tasked with protecting the wall. Nothing was going to happen. I needed to focus on why I was there.

For some reason I'd felt drawn to the rock. When first entering the tourist area, it opened into a large foyer. A holy place. Men had to remove their hats. Women had to cover their shoulders and dress appropriately. In the center of the foyer was a large rock encased in glass. Tradition said, there, on the rock, God told Hamm to sacrifice Casik.

Many scholars also believed the rock was where Jesus was killed. I had no reason to doubt them. Naryans believed Sal-Am was miraculously carried up into heaven without dying at the rock. That, I didn't believe.

The holiest site for both religions in all of Ven-Us was within those four walls. The rock was on the western side of the wall. Thankfully. In our territory. Controlled by the west. Many wars had been fought over that site, and the west now had control. Something they were determined not to cede.

The Naryans could visit the rock. However, they had to stay on the east side behind a large bullet proof, but see-through, partition. On our side, Christians could bend down and reach in an opening in the glass enclosure and actually touch the rock, which thousands stood in line for hours every day to do. It was a source of great consternation for the Naryans. Once a year for a week, they were allowed in to touch the rock during their holy days. It almost always involved some type of confrontation. However, the gesture prevented all-out war.

I'd just come from taking a number of pictures of the rock with my air-line. An air-line was our way of communicating. A wireless device used to make calls and send messages. Mine was issued by the V-7 and had a sophisticated ability to capture images in real time. I could actually view the photos on my air-line immediately after taking them. I didn't bother. I'd pull them up on a bigger screen later.

Something about the rock...

For some reason, I felt like the rock had something to do with my mission to find the garden.

An instinct. Gut feeling. Those had served me well in the field and had saved my life many times. Sometimes I felt like God or the Holy Spirit was directing my steps and protecting me. Many times, I was saved from great harm by following those instincts.

After I finished taking pictures, I exited the rock exhibit area and took the stairs up to the top of the wall. Now standing on the top of the wall, I wished I was anywhere else. From there, every direction invoked a painful memory from my past.

I look out to the east to the land of the Naryans. Seen only through the barbed wire and armed guards stationed every fifty paces. It was a stark reminder of my years spent as an operative, years trying to exorcise demons, and missions to exact revenge. Which I did. But not with any satisfaction. Other than knowing my part made us safer, if only a little, my main consolation was that I did what I could.

Even if I never killed Qary.

To the north and south was wall as far as the eye could see. It was less painful to look in those directions. Most people believed the Great Wall and its branches spanned more than 10,000 mil-ead. A mil-ead measured by a thousand paces or the length of an average person's foot times three. The truth was that the entire length of the wall was only about 3,100 mil-ead. A fact I knew from personal experience having walked some of it. Ran some when I escaped from a torture camp where I'd been held for three months.

Desperate, I had searched for a way to get over the wall and back to the safety of the west while avoiding the detection of the soldiers guarding it. The east side of Ven-Us was mostly flat and desert like. There were not many places to hide. Somehow, I managed to make it to the tunnel that brought me home safely. It was the last time I'd been in the east.

Will I have to go back there on this mission?

I doubt it.

A sudden pain in my arm reminded me of the days spent with my arms tied behind my back. My shoulder dislocated and required three surgeries to repair. Something I was reminded of every morning as I struggled momentarily to get out of bed from the pain in my legs which were restrained for long periods of time as well.

Getting out of bed was something I was more than anxious to do. The pain in my body was easier to deal with than the pain in my mind. The nightmares haunted me every night. Not from the painful memories of the east, but those from the west.

Freed-Om Square.

From my vantage point on the wall, I could see it perfectly, although I refused to look that way. The square consisted of a large tourist center where several thousand people a day checked in to visit the wall. Immediately to the right was security where tourists stood in line to pass through metal detectors before entering the House of the Rock and the Great Wall. I easily passed through security by simply flashing my V-7 credentials and bypassed the line altogether.

In the center of the square stood a beautiful memorial with the names of the victims of a suicide bomber who, twenty years before, had taken the lives of 234 people, including my wife and daughter. The reason I hadn't been to the wall in ten years and why I couldn't bear to look at the square. The reason I'd spent ten years in the east hunting the man responsible.

My wife had begged me to go with her to the wall that day. *Perhaps if I had...*

Another reason I didn't want to come to the wall today. Too many regrets.

I started walking to the north after carefully scanning the crowd again, blocking the pain with purpose. I kept moving so as not to draw attention to myself. From what, I had no idea. Somehow, I felt better, familiar, to be operating again. If only in my mind. No one was paying any attention to me. I went back and forth between focusing on the view and my silly desire to act like an operative.

Focus. On what? What am I looking for? I still had no idea why I was there.

To the north of the House of the Rock was the Burg-Ess Gate, and I was standing right over it. The gate was the only entrance point between the east and the west and was heavily guarded on both sides. A limited number of people were allowed to go through the gate on any given day. No one was seeking entrance on either side, and the guards looked bored.

Suddenly I saw a familiar face. Ahead of me, walking my way, out of place, older, but definitely him. I looked away so he didn't see me. A man I'd tracked for ten years in the east and almost had him on several occasions. The man who planned the attack that killed my wife and daughter.

Would he still recognize me? I was older too.

They said he was dead.

Why was he on the wall? How did he get past security?

He's very much alive.

Qary Raa'be Mal-Am looked back over his shoulder after he passed me. Something an operative was never supposed to do. A sure tell. The Naryans weren't well trained in evasive techniques, from my experience. That gave me an advantage. He hadn't seen me but looking back gave me a good look at him, confirming my suspicions.

Rage rose inside me. The desire for revenge had driven me for years and suddenly returned like a flood. I tamped it down, like I'd learned to do over the years. Ten years was a long time to be away from it. I'd found peace at the seminary, almost forgiveness. It was amazing how fast the anger, resentment, unforgiveness, and bitterness could return. I needed to think clearly, so I ignored the feelings.

Qary stuck his hand in the pocket of his long black coat. Another tell. Too warm for the coat. His nervous habit. Touching his gun like I did. I wanted to reach and touch mine. I resisted the urge. Now I was in complete control of my emotions, even as strong as they were. My nervous habits disappeared. I'd do nothing to be spotted or to let him know he'd been marked. I followed closely behind but not close enough to be identified. Close enough to react if he was foolish enough to pull his gun.

He wouldn't. He always went for what would make the biggest splash. No doubt, just there for reconnaissance.

I quickly thought through my options. I could alert the guards, but I dismissed that thought. Qary was one of the most dangerous men on the planet and was well trained in combat if not spy techniques. A guard might get trigger happy and try to take him down on his own. Qary was too good. The guards were not well enough trained. He'd never escape the area alive, because there were too many guards and he'd be outnumbered. But he could kill a lot of people before they got him.

I could take him down myself. I dreamed of this opportunity years ago. I felt a pained look come on my face. A dilemma. Too many innocent women and children were around to start a gun fight.

What about all the people he would kill in the future? Certainly, more than would die today. But what if he somehow killed me? Who would find the garden of Eden?

The decision was made. I had to let him go. If I kept following, he'd eventually recognize me. As far as I knew, he probably hadn't thought about me in years. I was out of the game. No longer a threat to him. I wanted him to keep thinking that.

We neared the House of the Rock. As Qary disappeared into the crowd, I made another decision.

I'm going back to the field. I'll find him and kill him.

* * *

I quickly left the area to avoid any possibility of Qary spotting me. Back in my car, I stared at the wall and contemplated the events of the day. What started as a normal day, teaching a class, filling in for one of my teachers, had turned into one of the most consequential days of my life.

Qary was alive.

More importantly, I had to find the garden of Eden. All of Ven-Us depended on me. That had to take priority. As much as I wanted to hunt down and kill him, finding the garden was more important.

"What a mess" I thought as I glared at the wall. The very bane of my existence.

Then another thought occurred to me. Why did God bring me to the wall that day? My gut instinct was right. It couldn't be by accident. There must be a divine purpose.

Was it to see Qary? It couldn't be a coincidence.

Still, "vengeance is mine" says the Lord in the Bible. God wouldn't bring me here for me to exact revenge. He'd been working on me for ten years to let the anger and hatred go. I couldn't let Qary become a distraction.

It had to do with the wall. The search for the garden of Eden somehow was related to this holy spot. What was the correlation?

Another thought. Why this spot? Who drew the line between the east and the west? The division between the two religions goes back centuries.

How did the dividing line come into existence?

6

Before (Ven-te 225)

The journey to find the original site of the garden of Eden should have only taken five days. Instead it took more than three months. The logistics of moving an entire camp including women and children, livestock, supplies, tents, and historical artifacts proved more challenging than Hamm had thought it would be. When Adam and Eve first approached him with the idea, it sounded good. Now he wasn't so sure.

Adam and Eve found the site easily enough walking right to it. Both broke down in obvious pain upon seeing it. They said the wave of memories flooded their minds with the good and the bad. Memories of life in the garden and the pain of having it all taken from them in the fall.

Hamm couldn't imagine what it must be like to carry that weight of what might have been, what was lost. The consequences they must still feel having brought sin and death to the entire world.

The trip had been almost more than Hamm could bear. Physically and emotionally. Complicated by the constant fighting between the two boys who had grown in stature and were reaching the age of taking a wife. Several times they came to blows. Hamm considered letting them fight it out but was convinced they wouldn't stop until one or the other was dead. Keeping them separated was the best strategy but nearly impossible, considering the close proximity of their living conditions.

Members of the camp had taken sides and divisions were running deep as Hamm had lost much of his respect among several of the families and relatives he had supported all those years. They didn't say so publicly, but Hamm heard some of what was said privately, behind his back. The constant fighting between Terah and Raga made things worse as they didn't even try to hide the animosity anymore.

Things were slightly better since they arrived at the site and set up permanent camp, although Terah and Raga constantly came to Hamm with their disputes. He spent more and more time in the fields to try and stay away from the ongoing conflict. He rued the day he had agreed to lay with Raga. Like Adam and Eve, he had his own regrets. It had been twenty-five years yet the trouble never seemed to go away.

He also sensed the end of his life was near. He would be one hundred twenty in two years. His eyes had not dimmed, and his strength had not abated. He felt as strong as he did when he was twenty. Yet, God had numbered man's days, and one night he would fall asleep and not wake up. His life would be taken from him. He worried every day about what would happen to his sons when he was gone.

A tremendous burden. There'd be no one to manage the conflict. The only one keeping them from killing each other was him. A nagging question ate at him every day.

Who do I give the firstborn blessing?

The argument raged inside. Nary was the firstborn and the blessing was rightfully his. But his mother sold it. Was the transaction really legitimate? Who would sell their son's birthright for a bowl of stew? Terah had manipulated the situation. A case could be made that she stole the birthright. Yet, birthrights were exchanged for something of value all the time and were negotiated like currency. Just because the value was minimal didn't mean the transaction wasn't valid.

The blessing was consequential in that the firstborn also received a double share of the inheritance. When Hamm died, all he had would pass on to his sons. Whoever he gave the blessing would also have significantly more wealth. The biggest problem was how his sons would feel. One of them would hate him. He could hardly bear the thought. He loved them both.

One son would resent him for the rest of his life.

He decided to ask God.

Sitting next to the Eden rock one evening, Hamm said to God, "Which of my sons deserves my firstborn blessing?"

God responded, "Casik I have loved. Nary I have hated."

Hamm stood straight up to his feet.

"Why do you hate my son?" he implored. "That's wrong."

"I will have mercy on whom I have mercy and compassion on whom I have compassion," God said.

"What did Nary ever do to deserve you hating him?" Hamm retorted. "He wasn't even born. His mother sold the birthright, not him." Anger rose inside of him as he said it.

"Is there unrighteousness with God?" Adam said to Hamm. He'd arrived at the rock just as the conversation started. "God forbid! When the children were born, didn't God say the elder would serve the younger?"

"The children not yet born, had done neither good nor evil," God explained. "I do not hate Nary as you understand the word hate. I love all my creation. Everyone including Nary. But Casik is the son of choice. The son of my election. I love Casik, not based on works, but on calling. My favor is not on Nary because he was not the child of promise. Casik should receive the blessing."

With those words, God departed.

Tears welled up in Hamm. God's words made sense but were hard to accept.

"Nary will hate me," he said to Adam.

"They are both your seeds," Adam replied. "God will make both a great nation. But they are only children of your flesh. Casik is the child of promise. The seed of the everlasting promise of God."

"I'm going to give the blessing to Nary. He's the one who deserves it."

"Nary doesn't deserve it," Adam said strongly, raising his voice. "Casik should've been the firstborn. Just because you chose not to believe God and made a son on your own disobedience, doesn't change God's will. Casik shouldn't lose what is rightfully his because of your unfaithfulness."

Adam put his hand on Hamm's shoulder and softened his tone. "I'm not judging. Far be it from me to judge. We're sitting right here at the very site where I ate the fruit from the tree. I've paid a great price ever since. I know firsthand what it's like to disobey God."

Adam looked to the sky and then looked around the area of the rock as if remembering.

"Have faith in God," Adam said. "He told you what to do. Make the right choice, my friend. Or you'll regret it."

"I don't know what I'm going to do," Hamm said. "I need the night to think about it."

Adam left without another word as Hamm buried his head in his hands, sobbing.

* * *

The next morning, Hamm sat in his tent on a mat with his legs crossed and his arms folded as Casik and Nary entered together, cautiously. Hamm motioned for them to sit across from him. They jockeyed to sit on the right side. Casik was closer but Nary pushed him away from behind causing him to fall on his side.

Casik stood with his fists balled.

Hamm grabbed Nary by his feet and pulled them out from under him. He landed roughly. Even at 118 years of age, Hamm was much stronger than either of them.

"I can still take both of you by myself," Hamm said in a joking tone meant to try and lighten the mood.

The boys were not grinning. Hamm had sent for the boys and instructed his servants to let them know it was about the firstborn blessing. Tension was already high between the boys as the long, anticipated day had arrived.

"As you know, I'm an old man now," Hamm said. "I don't know when I'll die, but it'll be soon."

The two boys nodded without looking at each other. They were keeping their eyes fixed on their father. Both were sitting forward.

Hamm heard a noise outside the tent. It sounded to him like Terah and Raga were listening through the outside flap. They seemed to be jockeying for the best position to hear as Hamm could hear them arguing.

Hamm took some bread, broke it and gave a piece to each son. Then he gave them each some wine to drink. "Let's eat one last meal together in peace," he said.

"Please come a little closer, both of you, and kiss me."

They each kissed Hamm on the cheek. He grabbed each boy's hands and put them together. They tried to pull them apart, but he was too strong.

"You are both my sons. I love you both equally. None more than the other. But only one can have my firstborn blessing. Promise me that no matter what happens today, the two of you will put aside your differences and live together in peace for my name's sake."

The boys would not agree. Hamm implored them several times, but neither would promise. Anger rose inside him, growing stronger each time they refused. Finally, he decided to speak the blessing and give them his reasoning.

"Nary, you are the firstborn. The blessing and the inheritance were rightfully yours from birth."

The boys were listening intently, their eyes wide as saucers. The din on the outside of the tent had stopped. Apparent that the women were listening with great anticipation as well. Only Hamm knew what he was going to do. He'd not discussed it with either of them.

"I never even thought I would have either of you. I was too old to have children. God spoke to me and told me I would have a son. Now I have two. He said my descendants would be like the stars in the sky. God is going to make a great nation out of both of you. I pray that you are able to resolve your differences and live together in peace regardless of what I do here today."

"Casik, you are the child of promise. From the dew of heaven and the richness of the earth, may God always give you abundant harvests of grain and bountiful new wine. Many nations will become your servants and will bow down to you. All who curse you will be cursed, and all who bless you will be blessed."

"What does this mean?" Casik said when Hamm had finished. "Is that the firstborn blessing?"

Hamm didn't answer.

"Nary, you will live away from the richness of the earth, and away from the dew of the heaven above. You will live by your sword, and you will serve your brother."

Nary stood to his feet. The firstborn blessing had gone to Casik. Terah let out a squeal of delight outside the tent.

"Father, I will soon be mourning your death," Nary said angrily. "After you die, I will kill my brother Casik. Out of respect for you, I will let him live today."

Casik, threw his chest back and lunged for Nary saying, "I will kill you today! You heard the blessing. You will serve *me*!"

The boys rolled around on the ground, each trying to get an advantage over the other. The food and wine were knocked over. Hamm tried to pull them apart, but the weight of the two knocked him to the back of the tent, stunning him for a moment.

Nary settled on top of Casik, momentarily getting the upper hand.

Hamm was unable to react. He shook his head from side to side trying to regain his vision.

Nary had a knife hidden under his clothes. He pulled it out and swung it toward Casik.

Casik grabbed his hand, stopping what would have been a fatal blow.

Terah and Raga rushed into the tent both screaming. They hesitated, clearly not sure what to do. Terah grabbed Nary from behind and tried to pull him off of her son. Raga grabbed Terah by the hair and pulled her away. They rolled on the ground and were biting, scratching, clawing at each other. Both spitting words of hate.

Hamm knew if he didn't react soon, someone was going to die.

Nary had the knife in his right hand, trying with all his strength to bring it down on Casik.

Casik held it away inches from his throat with both hands. Desperately trying to wrench it free. He could not hold out much longer. Eventually his strength would give out.

Hamm regained his bearings. Not taking the time to get to his feet, he crawled over to the boys and reached for the knife. As he did, the knife turned toward him and sliced open his hand. Blood poured from the wound.

The pain was excruciating. Hamm grabbed his hand and let out a cry of agony. A gaping wound from where the skin parted showed that the knife had sliced his hand all the way to the bone.

A loud slap reverberated through the tent as Raga backhanded Terah, temporarily stunning her and gaining the upper hand.

Hamm was unsure whether to help Casik or Terah. Or tend to his hand, now unusable.

"Enough!" Hamm shouted at the top of his lungs. The boys and the two women ignored him. The fight escalated even further.

Rage. Pent up frustration. Years of hate released all at the same time.

Hamm cried out again in pain, unable to do anything about it. Nary looked his way, as did Raga. The distraction was enough for Casik to throw Nary off of him. Terah as well. All four stopped to look at Hamm writhing in pain in the corner. Blood was everywhere.

"Father!" Casik cried out. "You're hurt."

"Hamm!" Terah screamed.

Nary went for the knife. Casik went to his father.

"You're hurt, Father," he said. "I'm so sorry."

Hamm was badly hurt. Terah ripped his shirt and wrapped it around his hand to try and stop the bleeding.

Nary stood at the corner holding the knife with a look of uncertainty on his face. Raga stood next to him. Adam and Eve walked into the tent at that time, obviously having heard the commotion. Adam took the knife from Nary.

Hamm was in obvious pain as Casik and Terah gathered around him. Nary and Raga remained in the corner.

"I want everyone to meet me at the Eden rock in thirty minutes," Hamm said. "I'll be all right. I must tend to my hand. Go tell everyone," Hamm said to Adam and Eve.

"Stay away from each other," Hamm said, sternly looking at Casik and Nary.

Raga took Nary by the arm and made him leave the tent. Terah stayed to tend to her husband.

Adam and Eve left to tell the camp about the meeting.

Hamm instructed Casik to stay with him as well. "It's not safe for you. Stay here with me," he said as Terah tended to his wounds.

"If we don't stop the bleeding, I'm going to die," Hamm said, crying out in pain when Terah applied pressure to the wound.

* * *

More than an hour later, Hamm stood and addressed the crowd that had formed at the rock of Eden. On the side of the rock, the words *Adam and Eve were here* could still be seen, only slightly faded.

Hamm's hand was wrapped in blood-soaked bandages. The crowd murmured when they saw Hamm was injured.

"Blessed are the people whose God is the Lord," Hamm began. "I spoke to the Lord at this very rock yesterday. Adam was a witness."

Adam nodded in agreement.

"The Lord said that Casik was the child of promise. He has received my firstborn blessing this morning." A cheer went up from half of the crowd. The other half jeered.

Hamm stepped down from the rock and picked up a large stick. He walked thirty paces on the other side of the rock. To the east. There he drew a line in the dirt. A river flowed a few paces further to the east.

"Everything to the east of this line belongs to Nary and his descendants. Everything to the west belongs to Casik and his descendants. The garden of Eden was the first promise made to man from God. That will remain on Casik's side. As the second born child by law, Nary is entitled to one third of my possessions."

"Go gather them now." Hamm said to Raga and Nary. "Gather what is rightfully yours and take them on the other side of this line. Cross the river. There you will live in peace. Any person who wants to go with them is free to go. Anyone who wants to stay on Casik's side can do so. Once you choose, then you will live with your choice. Nary, you are only to cross this line one more time."

Nary looked at his father with intense anger in his eyes. "When is that," he said with disdain.

"Cross it one time to bury me. Other than that, stay on the other side of the line. Casik, you and your descendants stay on this side of the line. I pray for peace between you after I'm gone."

"Go and get your possessions and leave here immediately," Hamm said and then collapsed from the loss of blood.

7

Now (Ven-te 2200)

A large conference table in my office was strewn with papers, books, and maps. Along with two copies of the Quan-di, the so-called Bible of the Naryans. A blasphemous book that denied the deity of Christ and elevated Sal-Am to a position of messiah to the Naryans. For the most part, Sal-Am merely copied the biblical stories, changed them to suit his own twisted and warped intentions, adding his own spin to them. As far as I was concerned, a madman really. The purpose in my mind was nothing more than to create a book that was self-serving to him in securing his position of prestige and power to people who desperately hated the west, Christians, and their Bible.

The Quan-di contained an account of a garden of Eden and an Adam and Eve. My primary concern at the moment was studying those passages. It'd been several years since I had looked at the Quan-di text. The story was changed in subtle ways to create Sal-Am's own narrative and to offset any accusations of plagiarism. He falsely purported that his account was the only true word of God, with he and his followers purporting that the Bible was the blasphemous book, even though he claimed to be the prophet mentioned several times in the Bible. Interesting how he denied the infallibility of the Bible when it suited his own designs but embraced it when it benefited him. He denied its validity when it diverted from his account.

Sarah Hatch-Ard, the student who'd shown so much promise in the class I taught, sat at the table, poring through the Quan-di looking for any references to the garden of Eden. I'd recruited her for the task, not telling her the full extent of what we were doing. As far as she knew, the project was a research paper for extra credit. Ted had signed off on me bringing her into the project as long as she never knew the real purpose. To conceal that, she thought we were going through an intellectual exercise of trying to see if we could discover from the Bible and the Quan-di the actual locations of the garden of Eden as written in each book.

To Sarah, this was more than an intellectual exercise. She'd thrown her energies into the project with the veracity of a hungry lion in search of a prey. We'd been working on it every day after class for a week, and I was more impressed with her by the day. Her knowledge of the Naryans and the Quan-di was beyond my expectations, and she was extremely helpful in research. Even then, it didn't seem like we were any closer to finding an answer. Sarah was undaunted.

I was frustrated.

Difficult for me to hold in my anxiety considering the stakes. As far as she knew, we were doing great. For me, the clock was ticking, and the missile could be launched at any time. Sarah and I were both obsessed with finding an answer, only for different reasons.

"Let's review what we know," I said, sitting across the table from her with a writing pad and writing instrument. "What have you found?" I asked with a sense of urgency she didn't acknowledge. She just matched my enthusiasm.

"The Quan-di says Adam was made from soil like clay," Sarah said. "I've researched the east and found there are twelve areas with dirt like clay. It doesn't narrow it down much, but it's a starting point."

"That's okay," I said and pulled out a map of the east. "What are the twelve areas? We have to start somewhere."

As Sarah named them, I circled them on the map.

"What's next?" I asked.

"A garden of grapes."

"Right. I remember that," I said with my hand on my chin, thinking.

"The Quan-di mentioned Adam tended a garden of grapes in Eden and ate freely from it," Sarah explained further.

"Did you find any areas where grapes grow?" I asked. Not remembering any off the top of my head.

She read through another stack of notes. "There are four areas."

"What are they? Let's see if any overlap the areas with clay."

Sarah named off the areas. Three of the four overlapped. Progress.

"The Quan-di mentions dates and palms."

"That won't help. Those grow everywhere in Ven-Us." I said it more sharply than I intended. I looked for any expression of hurt on Sarah's face. None manifested, which I was thankful for. She's not easily offended. A good quality for this type of work.

A puzzled look came on her face as she curled her lips and squinted her eyes in obvious confusion.

"What?"

"The Quan-di mentions streams underneath the garden."

"Maybe a spring," I said. "Some think he meant the garden was actually in paradise. Their word for heaven. Which would mean that he believed the garden was above the world and the rivers were on Ven-Us below them."

"I read some things about that controversy," Sarah said. "I always thought that was their prevailing belief."

Mine too, but the intercept was clear that they believed they'd found the garden of Eden sight on Ven-Us. I couldn't tell Sarah about the intercept, so I needed to keep her focused on finding it here on the Ven-Us.

I said, "For these purposes, let's assume it was here on the Ven-Us. The Bible mentions four rivers and actually names them. One river flowed from the garden and then parted into four headwaters. The Quan-di states all four rivers flowed out of Eden."

I paused for a moment to think about that fact. "The Bible, of course, is the accurate account," I continued. We don't know if the rivers even exist anymore. I think it would be a waste of time to search for rivers. Although..."

We had to think like the Naryans thought. They still believed the rivers and the spring existed. They would've looked for the spring. It might be worthwhile to look for rivers in the east, although there were a lot of them.

"The Quan-di says hills overlooked the garden," Sarah said. "The hills would still exist even if the rivers didn't."

"Good thinking. What are some hills in the east? There couldn't be many. The east is mostly flat." Hills would be easier to find than rivers that dry up and get diverted from their original paths.

Sarah didn't know I'd been in the east for more than ten years. Very few people in the west had ever seen the hills of the east. She pulled out a topographical map. She didn't need to. The only real hills were in the Push-on Valley. I looked at my map with the circled areas.

"Sarah, look at this." I turned the map toward her and pointed to a spot. "The Push-On Valley has soil like clay. Dates and palms grow there, but I don't remember any grapes."

I caught myself. "I don't remember reading that grapes grew there. Doesn't mean they couldn't. They are in the region where they could grow. I think this is the area to focus on," I said excitedly. I hated lying to Sarah, but it couldn't be helped. The main thing was we were making progress.

"Let me look and see if there are any springs in the region," Sarah said. "There would have to be if fruit grows there."

Nothing was said for several minutes. Sarah looked through books.

I searched my memory. I'd spent many nights hiding in the Push-On Valley where I ate the plentiful dates and palms and drank from the streams. I remembered a spring. The main river of the valley started from that spring.

The valley... a perfect place to hide the construction of missiles.

Clay. I had a memory of clay. I'd actually stepped in it. It got all over my shoes, hands, and clothes. A regiment of soldiers were searching for me in the area. I covered my body with the dark brown clay making myself nearly invisible to them.

Where was the spring?

I looked at the map, trying to pinpoint a location.

There.

The Iya-Basin. That's where the river started. The mouth of the river was in that valley. I remembered a spring with hills all around. I even vaguely remember eating grapes. But I couldn't trust that. Sometimes your brain imagines things to make all the pieces fit.

Still... That must be it. My brain was processing information like a spinning top. Was I missing anything? Could I have found it that easily? Was this the location mentioned in the intercept?

Yes. Has to be. We found it. I looked at Sarah with admiration. She saved me a lot of time.

"I have to make an air-line call," I said as I bolted out of the room, not waiting for a response.

A man answered on the other line. Ted Cole-Man, Director of V-7.

"I think I found where the Naryans are building the missiles," I said confidently.

* * *

Qary Raa'be Mal-Am sat in a tent in the Push-On Valley in the Iya-Basin. Several of his commanding officers sat in the tent with him. A spring flowed from the ground right outside the tent and fed a river that flowed through the valley and provided them with ample drinking water.

"The plan is going just as I knew it would," Qary said smugly.

"How do you know the pag-anites will look for the missiles here?" one of the men said.

"Have faith in god, my dear friend. I saw the infidel Row Church-Well at the Great Wall."

Qary had devised a plan to make the west think the missiles were being built in the Push-On Valley. He sent through a false message which he knew the west would intercept. A message that described missiles being built at the garden of Eden site. They had followed the message up with several more.

Knowing Church-Well and his background, Qary believed Church-Well would lead them right to the Push-On Valley. Qary had tracked him for weeks in the valley years before, and both knew it well.

The plan had come together several months before when Qary discovered that Row Church-Well was still alive. Word had gotten back to him of a professor leading a conference on Naryan relations at a western seminary. Row Church-Well was the man.

His nemesis. A name and face seared into his memory. A raging lion he had awakened when he ordered a suicide bomber to attack the Freed-Om Square. How could he have known his wife and daughter would be there? Fate. Determined by god. Not by him.

Nevertheless...

Church-Well had been obsessed and had tracked him for ten years. Several times Row tried to kill him and almost succeeded. They'd finally captured him, threw him into prison, and tortured him. He never broke. When the prison exploded and was destroyed in flames, Qary thought he was done with the man. Everyone thought all the prisoners were dead, including Church-Well.

Qary barely escaped the explosion with his life. The best part of the explosion was that the west thought he was dead. That's how he could travel back and forth to the west undetected. Qary winced from the several places on his body that still hurt from injuries he sustained at the hands of Church-Well. Now he knew Church-Well must have been the one who started the fire at the prison. The injuries were his fault. Something he would now avenge with even greater purpose.

"The pag-anites are so predictable," Qary said. "The message said the missiles were being built on the site of the garden of Eden. I knew the pag-anites would come looking for the missiles. Only one man in the west knows enough about the Quan-di to figure out the Push-On Valley site. I tracked Church-Well for weeks in this valley many years ago. He knows it well. He'll come here looking for the missiles. I'm sure of it."

A faint smile formed on the side of his lips. "Especially now that I've seen him at the wall."

Qary spotted him at the rock. At first, he started to run. Then he decided he wanted Church-Well to see him, so he walked right by him, in plain sight. The hope was that Church-Well would be the one to come looking for the missiles. To seek revenge. The hatred between them ran deep. He knew Church-Well wouldn't be able to resist.

A trap awaited him in the Push-On Valley. Qary would finish what he'd started there years ago. There were no missiles. The intercept was merely a distraction. So, the west would waste their time looking for the garden of Eden. The pag-anites didn't even know that the garden of Eden was in paradise and not even on Ven-Us. Adam and Eve were thrown down from paradise out of the garden. The pag-anites were so stupid. Believing Eden was actually on the planet.

"What do you want us to do?" another of his commanders asked, interrupting his thoughts

"We will set a trap for the pag-anites. Church-Well will lead them right to this location. When he does, we will rain down fire and fury on them. It will be our greatest victory. Prepare your men."

8

Now continued

A second meeting was called to discuss the potential location of the missiles in the Push-On Valley. Held at the same place in the V-7 building in the same room. Only four of us attended this time. Director Ted Cole-Man, me, and the two operatives who would go to the valley to search for and destroy the missiles. Eric and Lacy were the two operatives and sat confidently together, certain of their abilities to find the missiles and destroy them, assuming I'd correctly identified the location. Their last names were withheld for obvious operational reasons. They didn't even know each other's last names. A necessary precaution in case of capture and torture. Standard operating procedure for field operatives.

Ted described the operational plan. Eric and Lacy would enter the east through an underground tunnel to the north of the main gate. Once on the other side, they'd pose as husband and wife. For the most part, the people on the east looked the same as those in the west. The two would blend in without a problem.

They'd then travel by local ground transportation to the city of Ida-Mon where they would find an all-terrain vehicle parked in the garage of a V-7 safe house. Their supplies and munitions would be stored in a secret compartment underneath the spare tire. Ted didn't expect any trouble up to this point.

Things would get more dangerous once they left the city. They'd have to navigate several checkpoints and present papers and talk their way past them without raising any suspicions. The cover was a couple celebrating their anniversary, going to a remote cabin in the valley. Discovery of their weapons and munitions would blow that cover. Clearly, the biggest risk, at least until they reached the missile sight.

Assuming everything went well, they'd arrive in the Push-On region a couple days after entering the east. Once there, they'd detour off of the main road and hide the vehicle. Then hike five mil-ead through hilly terrain to an observation point, which I knew well and gave them specific directions to. Food and water would not be a problem. They'd have plenty of supplies in the jeep but would leave most behind, taking only what they needed for a day or two. Agility and flexibility were of the utmost importance. The munitions were heavy enough without being bogged down with unnecessary supplies.

A road would bring them closer to the valley, but the assumption was if missiles were being constructed there, the road would be heavily guarded. Ted made the decision along with Eric and Lacy that it would be safer to hike in. It'd take more time but leave less opportunity for detection.

After all the logistics were decided upon, a fairly heated argument ensued.

"I should go with them," I said emphatically.

"We've been over this," Ted said, dismissing my words with a wave of his hand.

"I know the terrain like the bottom of my foot. It'll go quicker if I'm there. If they run into trouble, I can show them where to hide."

"I need you here. Your research is vital. In case you're wrong, and the Push-On Valley is not the location of the missiles, we may need for you to find an alternate location."

"I'm not wrong," I said, raising my voice further. "That's where the Naryans believe the garden of Eden was located. It's the only place that makes sense. It has to be there. I'm the best person to find the missiles. There are any number of places in the valley where they could be hidden."

"You've been out of the field for ten years," Ted said.

"I can do it—"

"You're not going!" Ted said, angrily slamming his folder closed with a loud bang. "And that's final. Eric and Lacy are perfectly capable of finding the missiles and destroying the site."

I looked down at the table, hesitating. "I saw Qary."

I hadn't planned on divulging that information. I'd been holding on to it, waiting for the right moment. I might regret bringing it up.

"What? Where? What are you talking about?" Ted asked.

"He was at the Great Wall last week," I said.

"How can you be sure it was him? He's dead."

"I saw his face. I know it was him."

Ted stood from the conference table and began to pace the room. Obviously distraught from the sudden revelation of that important information. Exactly the reaction I wanted. He'd have to let me go now that he knew Qary was alive.

"Why didn't you tell anyone? Why did you let him get away?" Ted said accusingly.

"There were a lot of people around. I couldn't start shooting at him. I followed him, but he disappeared before I could do anything about it."

"And you waited until now to tell me?" Ted asked.

"I was waiting..." Whatever I said would be the wrong answer.

I thought Ted would let me go on the mission. It never occurred to me he wouldn't. I was the obvious choice to find the missiles. After finding the missiles and destroying them, my plan was to hunt Qary down and kill him without anyone knowing about it until after the fact. I calculated it was better for me to keep that plan to myself. It sounded like a good idea at the time. Now it seemed foolish, even in my head as I tried to formulate the words.

"I want to go and find Qary," I said.

"All the more reason you shouldn't go," Ted said with a softer tone. "You're too emotionally attached to this mission."

Eric and Lacy remained silent. I wasn't sure if they knew about my wife and daughter. I assumed they did but couldn't be sure. Their expressions didn't give anything away. They probably agreed with Ted. Emotions can get you killed in the field. There's no stronger emotion than revenge.

"We'll deal with Qary later," Ted continued as my heart sank. "I wish you'd told me sooner. Not that it changes anything. The missiles are the biggest concern for now. We might even find out Qary is behind the missiles."

I started to speak, but Ted wasn't finished talking.

"Get ready to go," he said to Eric and Lacy. "You leave tomorrow. Come by my office later so I can brief you on Qary." Ted abruptly turned and walked out the door without another word.

For a moment, no one said anything. Everyone was seemingly stunned at the sudden end of the meeting. I didn't know Eric and Lacy very well, but I stood from my chair and walked over to them and gave each a strong and warm embrace.

"Do you have any questions I can answer for you?" I asked.

They both nodded no.

"I'll be praying for you," I said. "Be careful. Expect the unexpected. Anything can happen over there. Watch out for Qary. He's a very dangerous man."

With those final words I left the room, very disappointed I wasn't going on the mission.

* * *

Before (Ven-te 225)
God decided to test Hamm.

He said to him, "Hamm!" in a loud and recognizable voice. So loud that it startled him.

"Here I am," he replied. Hamm sat in a shaded area under a tree drinking water taking a break from working in the fields. He was almost falling asleep from the warmth of the day and after a morning of hard work.

"Take your son, Casik, your only son, whom you love," God said. "Go to the Eden rock. Sacrifice him there."

Hamm didn't know what to say. God had instructed them upon arriving at Eden to sacrifice a lamb as a burnt offering on the rock. The first time any of them had ever done a sacrifice since Adam and Eve did one at the rock after the fall. Now God was telling him to sacrifice his son. Kill him in the same way they killed the lamb.

Casik... The son of promise.

Was he dreaming or making it up? He knew God's voice. There was no mistaking what God had said.

But why?

Tears formed in his eyes. He couldn't disobey God. Yet, he couldn't take his own son's life. He'd lost so much already.

Nary... sent away because of Casik. He hadn't seen him in over a year. Now, he would lose both sons. The loss would be more than he could bear.

He pictured the lamb struck by the knife and the blood that poured from the wound. Hamm remembered the lamb's last breath as the life left him. Then he pictured Casik being struck in the same way. The pain in his heart stabbed him like the knife he'd have to use on Casik.

How could I possibly go through with it? I don't have a choice.

He remembered what happened to Adam and Eve when they disobeyed God. How they were thrown out of the garden and cursed. Would God curse him if he disobeyed?

Adam had explained that it didn't make sense why they couldn't eat of the fruit. It seemed good to eat and was. It tasted better than any fruit in the garden. But the consequences were too great, and they shouldn't have eaten it. It would've been better to do what God said. It was clear to Adam now, after the fact.

The questions kept swirling in Hamm's mind. Why did God give him a son only to have him sacrificed on the altar? It didn't make sense. God said his descendants would be like the stars. The descendants of Casik. How would Casik have descendants if he was dead?

He went back to the camp, clearly distraught. Terah asked him what was wrong, but he didn't say. Couldn't say. How could he tell her what he was going to do? She would think he was mad. Maybe he was.

I can't do it.

Can't do what? Kill Casik or tell his momma?

Neither.

Hamm tossed and turned all night, tormented by the horrendous secret. He felt guilty when he kissed Terah goodnight. She had no idea she'd never see her son alive again. She deserved to know, but he didn't have the courage to tell her.

Early the next morning, Hamm got up and loaded his donkey. Terah was still asleep. Hamm woke two of his servants and instructed them to gather wood for an offering while he went to wake Casik. When Hamm and the young man returned, the wood was loaded on the donkey and the provisions were all in place.

"What is the sacrifice?" one of the servants asked.

"Casik," Hamm said in a quiet voice so his son couldn't hear.

The servant seemed stunned as his eyes widened and his mouth flew open.

"You're going to sacrifice your son?" he asked in a higher pitched voice. "Have you gone mad?"

"God told me to sacrifice Casik on the Eden rock as an offering."

The servant started to say something, but Hamm stopped him. "I must go at once and do as God has commanded me. Stay here. You are not to follow me."

Hamm, Casik, and the donkey set out for the Eden rock leaving the servants behind.

* * *

The servant who had asked Hamm about the sacrifice ran to Hamm's tent, burst in, waking Terah.

"What are you doing?" Terah asked, trying to make sense of why a servant was in her tent that early in the morning. She reached for Hamm, but he wasn't next to her. Still groggy and rubbing her eyes, Terah instinctively pulled the blanket up to her chin to cover herself.

The servant was talking so fast Terah couldn't understand him. "Slow down," she said. "What's this about Casik and Hamm? And an offering?"

The servant took a deep breath and started to speak more slowly. "Hamm took Casik to the Eden rock. He said God told him to sacrifice Casik on the rock. Like he did the lamb when we first got here."

"Hamm wouldn't do that!" Terah said as she bolted out of bed. The servant covered his eyes even though she was fully clothed in her bed garment.

"Yes, he will," the servant retorted. "He's gone mad. I tried to stop him. He told me to gather wood for the fire. Casik was there with him. They left to go to the rock. He's going to kill that boy. I know it. Somebody's got to stop him. He wouldn't let me go with him."

"You go to the rock and try to stop him. I'm going to go and get Adam. He's the only one who can talk some sense into him."

The servant didn't move.

"Quick!" Terah shouted. "Go. Right now. Hurry. Go to the rock and stop him. Or at least tell him to wait until Adam gets there. Hurry please. Don't let him kill my son."

Terah wiped away tears that were streaming down her face. She knew the servant wouldn't disobey Hamm and go to the rock. Adam was her only hope. Not bothering to change clothes, she slipped on her sandals and took off running to Adam and Eve's tent which was on the other side of the encampment.

She burst into their tent. Thankfully, they were awake, drinking a beverage, obviously startled by the sudden unexpected intrusion. There had been a lot less drama in the camp since Nary and Raga had left more than a year before.

Terah explained what the servant had told her. "Adam, you have to stop him," she implored.

"You stay here," Adam said. "Just in case he's already..." Adam stopped himself from saying anything further.

Terah was glad he didn't finish the sentence. She knew what he meant to say.

"Stay here with me," Eve said, putting her arm around Terah to comfort her as Adam quickly changed his clothes, put on his sandals, and rushed out of the tent.

"How could he do this?" Terah kept saying over and over again. "I hope Adam's not too late."

* * *

"Father?" Casik said.

"Yes, my son," Hamm replied.

"The fire and wood are here," Casik said, "but where is the lamb for the burnt offering?"

"God himself will provide the lamb for the burnt offering." Hamm was convinced God would raise Casik from the dead.

Hamm built an altar and arranged the wood on it. He told Casik to climb up on the rock and lay on top of the wood. His obedient son did what his father asked without a word. Willingly. Without questioning. Nervous though. His hands were shaking. Body trembling. Obviously not sure what was going on. Trusting his father.

Hamm bound his son's hands and feet and tied him to the wood. He took his knife from the sheaf and raised it in the air.

"Hamm, wait!" Adam called to him. "Thank God I'm not too late. What are you doing?"

"God has told me to sacrifice Casik on the altar."

Casik laid on the rock looking up at them with fear in his eyes. Sweat poured from his brow. All the color drained from his face.

"Are you sure? Why would God give you a son and then tell you to sacrifice him? That doesn't make sense."

"I know," Hamm said. "But I believe God will raise Casik from the dead."

"How can you be sure?"

"I just know it. I don't know how to explain it. If anyone should understand God's ways, it would be you. God spoke to you. Right here at this spot."

Hamm saw Adam wince. He hadn't meant to bring up the painful memory of the garden or compare what he was doing to what had happened to Adam. Still, the point was the same.

"God told you not to eat of the fruit," Hamm explained. "You know God's voice. So, do I. That probably didn't make sense to you either. 'Why can't we eat of the fruit,' you must have wondered. I don't blame you. But you know I have to do what God said for me to do. It will always work out for our good if we trust God. I have to do this."

A rustling in the bushes interrupted them. A ram was in the thicket.

"Look!" Adam said excitedly. "God has provided another sacrifice."

Too late...

Hamm had already plunged the knife into Casik's heart as Adam looked on in horror.

9

Now, (Ven-te 2200)

Eric didn't like the mission and had just told Lacy as much.

"What don't you like about it?" she asked.

They were well into the mission. Everything had gone smoothly as planned to this point. They made it through the tunnel to the safe house in Ida-Mon and were now in their vehicle halfway to the Push-On Valley. Something was bugging Eric, and he didn't know what it was and had no way to put it into words.

A feeling.

At first, he thought it might be related to her. This was Lacy's first mission into the east. Twenty-four years old, she was fresh out of training. Eric was thirty-two and had successfully completed dozens of missions to the east over the years. None as important as this one. Still, he had a lot more experience. Perhaps he was feeling anxious about working with someone so inexperienced for the first time.

If not in experience, Lacy matched Eric in her skills. At least, from their successes in training. Both were first in their respective classes. Lacy's credentials were even more impressive than his. He won most outstanding marksman. When it came to firing a weapon, Eric was as accurate and lethal as anyone on Ven-Us.

Lacy won most outstanding trainee in several areas, hand-to-hand combat the most notable. You wouldn't know it by looking at her. Five foot seven, a hundred and twenty pounds. From Eric's vantage point, all muscle. Not an ounce of fat. Yet, she consistently bested men twice her size. He'd heard about her tapping out a three-hundred-pound man in a competition, which she won. She confirmed the story that had made her a legend in the agency. Mostly, she simply brushed it off.

"Not that hard to do," she'd said. "He was big and slow."

Still...

Rumor was that no one had ever challenged her to a fight. In fact, she had trouble finding anyone to even spar with her. He'd never seen her abilities firsthand but had heard about them enough times to believe it.

Eric had seen her file. She'd no doubt seen his as well. If going into enemy territory where one's life was in danger, any agent would want to know who they're going there with. Lacy's was an impressive file. Most intelligent. Best problem solver. Second-best marksman. Her list of commendations went on for several pages as instructors raved about her. The best ever. A title he held until she came along.

Also, the most outstanding driver. Eric finished last in that area of training. He couldn't believe her driving test scores. On the last day of training, cones were set up in a complicated obstacle course. Each operative had to successfully navigate the course without hitting a wall or the cones. Lacy was the only operative in the history of the program to not hit a single obstacle. Very impressive. He couldn't even remember how many he'd hit.

As time went on, he had become more comfortable with her. Finally, he had dismissed his reservations about her. Lacy wasn't the reason for the angst concerning the mission.

"I don't know what it is," he finally answered. "Nothing specific comes to mind. Just a gut feeling."

Eric turned the car on to the main road leading to the Push-On Valley. The all-terrain vehicle had been waiting for them in the garage at the safe house in the city. While Lacy was the better driver, in the east, women were subservient to men. It would be out of place for her to be driving with her husband in the passenger's seat.

She agreed with the strategy. Besides, no one expected evasive driving skills to be necessary.

"Everything seems too neat and clean," he finally articulated his thoughts into words.

"What do you mean?" Lacy asked.

Eric hesitated. He'd never worked with Lacy before. So far, he was impressed with everything about her. Maybe he should keep his concerns to himself. He had no proof, no concrete reason for his concerns. Why create unnecessary anxiety in her? It might make her hesitate at the wrong moment. Freeze up if and when it came time to make a split-second decision.

Sensing his hesitancy, she said, "I think I know. The intercepts for instance. Wouldn't the Naryans know we're listening in on their conversations? Why disclose the location of the missiles in a call that might be overheard by the west?"

Eric was impressed. His observation exactly.

Lacy continued. "Also, checkpoints. Have you noticed there haven't been any? We're getting close to the valley. If they were building missiles there, I would expect there to be a lot more activity. Trucks. Construction vehicles. Armed convoys. We haven't seen another car in several mil-ead."

"That's what I mean," Eric said, glad now that he'd brought it up. Lacy was extremely perceptive. Refreshing to have someone to talk to about the mission. More often than not, he'd worked alone. He felt better being able to voice his concerns with someone who was an intellectual equal.

"It's almost like the Naryans want us to find the missiles..." he said as his voice trailed off.

"Could it be a trap?" she asked.

He shrugged his shoulders. "We have no way of knowing until we get there."

"Either way, we should assume it is and take every precaution."

"I agree. Always assume the worst-case scenario."

A loud bang!

Out of the blue.

They both jumped. It sounded like a gunshot.

The truck began to vibrate. Eric struggled to hold the vehicle on the road. He pulled off onto the shoulder.

"Speaking of the worst-case scenario," Eric said. "We have a flat tire. Maybe not the worst-case, but it's going to delay us."

Lacy started to get out of the car. Eric stopped her by touching her arm. He scanned the horizon. "Let's make sure someone didn't cause the flat tire," he said. "Remember what you said about a trap. This could be an ambush. Probably not, but—"

"But always assume the worst-case," Sarah said.

"Exactly."

They were out in the open. No trees or hills were around where someone could hide. The Push-On hills could be seen at a distance, but they were still a distance away. No cars were coming from either direction. Some hills were several mil-ead away. It'd take an impossible shot to hit a moving vehicle's tire from that distance.

Satisfied they were safe, they got out. Lacy saw the tire first since the back, right passenger side tire was flat. Eric inspected it to be sure it wasn't flat from a gunshot. It wasn't. The tire had an obvious defect on the inside where it had blown out.

Lacy scanned the horizon again to make sure there weren't any hostiles around. They'd be sitting ducks if there were. Their weapons were hidden in the car. Normally, they would be carrying them. However, if there were any checkpoints, it's possible they might be searched. Carrying a weapon wasn't feasible. Too difficult to hide in the event of a search. If they were found with a weapon, they'd be thrown in jail immediately. No questions asked. Tortured later. No one but the soldiers were allowed to carry guns in the east.

Eric had already opened the trunk and was pulling out the spare tire above the hidden compartment with weapons and explosives in it. Lacy kept watch.

"At least it's a full-sized spare," he observed. Eric positioned the jack to raise the truck enough to change the tire. He left the back of the trunk open just in case they needed to get their weapons.

Lacy checked the other tires while he worked. "The other tires look okay," Lacy said. "Hopefully, we'll only need one spare. I don't know what we'd do if we had a second flat."

"We'd have to abandon the truck and carry everything into the valley."

"Let's hope that doesn't happen," she said.

Eric suddenly stood up from where he was kneeling by the tire.

"Quick, cover your head," he said excitedly. Women in the east were required to have their heads covered in public. Lacy didn't question why. She just reacted and did it. A car was approaching. Not just any car. A Naryan patrol car.

Eric saw Lacy tense. A look of fear crossed her face as her eyes darted back and forth. Eric immediately regretted not closing the trunk.

"Just keep your cool. He's probably just checking on us to see if we're okay," Eric said as the patrol car slowed and pulled onto the shoulder next to them.

Here we go. We'll see how good Lacy is.

Dr. Church-Well had a saying that was famous throughout the V-7: The mission doesn't start until the first shot is fired.

Let's hope the mission is not about to start.

* * *

Western Ven-Us Theological Seminary

I sat at my desk, going over the mission plan one more time, deep in thought. Sarah sat at the conference table with a puzzled look on her face. Her eyes had a faraway look. The end of the writing instrument was in her mouth as she was also, deep in thought. My thoughts were on Eric and Lacy. I wondered where they were and how things were going. By my estimation, they should be arriving at the Push-On Valley sometime in the next few hours. Assuming they didn't run into any problems at any of the checkpoints.

We had no way of knowing if they ran into trouble, were arrested, or worse. The first we'd learn about any trouble would be if they didn't show up back at the tunnel in a reasonable period of time. We've had operatives who disappeared with no idea what happened to them. They didn't know where I was for three months until I escaped from the prison and showed up at the tunnel.

They had an air-line, but it wouldn't work in the Push-On Valley. They could only use it in the cities and only in the event of an emergency. The Naryans could potentially intercept the call and listen in. We didn't know if they had that technology.

I knew from experience they were isolated and alone. Two people against the entire armed forces of the Naryans. Highly trained, but at their most vulnerable point. I wish I was with them. Not knowing was the worst part. Working with Sarah had mostly kept my mind off of them. Nothing I could do about it anyway.

Sarah was working on finding the original garden of Eden from the Bible account. I'd brought her into the project on the basis of finding both. Since we found the Naryan version much quicker than I ever imagined, or at least I hope we had, she'd since attacked the Bible version with the same tenacity. I had little optimism she'd make any progress, but I enjoyed watching her enthusiasm. This was a topic researched by many people in the past with little success.

"What are you thinking about?" I asked.

"The garden of Eden," she replied. "I'm trying to figure out where it was."

I stood up from my chair, went to the conference table and sat across from her.

"What do you have so far?"

"The garden was in the east according to Genesis 2. Over where the Naryans live."

That spurred a thought in me. I was silent for a few moments while I thought about it. "Remember Ven-Us rotates the opposite of most planets," I said. "Counterclockwise. That wasn't discovered until a few centuries ago. It might be possible—"

"Maybe the east is actually the west in the Bible," Sarah said, completing my thought.

"Yes!" I said with excitement. "When God threw Adam and Eve out of the garden, he set the cherubim on the east side of the garden. What if they were really thrown out to the west? Or at least what we call the west today. Technically, it's the east because of the rotation of Ven-Us. We know that's where Adam and Eve and Hamm lived. They lived on this side of the wall. Hamm traveled to the wall from the west. That's where he sacrificed Casik. On the rock. So... Eden might be on our side of the wall as well!"

"Or at least closer to us than we originally thought," I mused. "Read the verse aloud."

Sarah opened the Bible and began reading. "After he drove the man out, he placed on the east side of the Garden of Eden cherubim and a flaming sword flashing back and forth to guard the way to the tree of life."

"Very interesting," I said. "That's just like God and why the Bible is always true. The Bible had the right direction because God knew how the world turned, even if we didn't. All this time, we've always believed that the garden was in the east. I'm beginning to believe it was in the west. Let's look at the other verses. But let's look at them from the perspective of being in the west."

"There's the river that broke into four headwaters."

"Theologians have looked for the rivers for years. To no avail. It says that one flowed out of the garden into the four. We should be thinking in terms of one major river that fed four others. What else do we know about the rivers?"

"The first river flowed where there was gold."

"Right. Where has gold been discovered on Ven-Us?" I asked.

Sarah opened a book and began looking through it. I pulled out my air-line and did a search for where gold had been found on Ven-Us.

An article popped up on my screen. My mouth flew open. I'd forgotten about what was reported in the article. Not sure I even really ever knew it. A vague memory suddenly came to mind.

"Read this article," I said.

Sarah began reading it aloud. *"Gold Discovered During Construction of the Great Wall.* In 1498, John T. Mar-Shall was employed to work on the Great Wall at the west branch of the river known as the New-Spring River."

"I'd forgotten that a river used to flow at the Great Wall," I said. "They purposefully dammed up the source so they could build the wall. Keep reading."

"While digging the footing for a wall, Mar-Shall discovered pieces of gold as they glistened in the sunlight at the bottom of the sluice." Sarah looked up at him. "What's a sluice?"

"It's a device that controls the flow of water. Like a gate. It's an old term we don't use much anymore. It's what stopped the flow of water so they could construct the wall."

Sarah continued reading. "Pieces of considerable size were taken from the dried river basin. Highly valuable nuggets were found. Word spread quickly throughout the region as prospectors came from all around to stake a claim. Construction of the wall came to a halt as eager men and women from mil-eads around came to the wall seeking their fortune."

"It goes on to say they let them dig because it helped them create the foundation for the Great Wall," Sarah continued. "Once all of the gold ran out in the area, the prospectors left, and the construction of the wall resumed."

Sarah paused as she scanned the rest of the article. Presumably finding nothing else of interest, she handed the air-line back to me. I scanned other articles on my air-line.

"There are three other places on Ven-Us where gold has been discovered," I said. "None of them are near the wall. They are way out in the west. All were around rivers, but none have four rivers around them."

"The Bible also says onyx was there," Sarah said. "I didn't see anything in the article about them finding onyx."

"Do you have any older maps of Ven-Us?" I asked.

"I don't know of any. Here's a modern map," she said, opening a book and handing it to me.

"Look at this," I said, standing up and walking around the table so we could look at it together.

I pointed to where the dam was in the south. "Look at the map. There are four rivers that flow away from the dam. The dam was built to stop the flow of the river that ran to the wall."

"Four rivers," I said tapping my fist on the map. "One that flowed to the Great Wall where gold was discovered."

"What does it mean?" Sarah asked.

"I wonder if the garden of Eden might have been near the rock at the Great Wall," I said almost to myself.

I wonder...

10

As soon as the sun began to set, I sent Sarah home, concerned about appearances. We'd been spending a lot of time together after school hours, and I took every precaution to make sure those meetings never gave the wrong appearance. I always kept my door open if she was in my office. Her professors were aware of the arrangement. If the assistant dean, whose office was next to mine, left for the day, Sarah left as well. I insisted we keep a level of formality in our relationship. She always called me Dean Row rather than by my first name. Our conversations were friendly, but always professional. Personal and emotional subjects were avoided. Probably even to a level unnecessary. Everything was strictly business. Though I admit it... I had grown fond of her.

Now that the lights were out in the building and everyone had gone home, I realized I missed her. Not in an inappropriate way, but in a professional way. Almost as a peer, because significant energy had been infused into our work when we discovered the possibility of the Garden of Eden being in the west, not in the east.

Not a peer, I suddenly realized. A daughter. Sarah was filling a void that had been missing for twenty years. My daughter would've been the same age. Maybe even a student at the seminary if she had such interests. Same dusty blonde hair. Same zest for life. Sarah was how I imagined Meg would be. Bright. Ambitious. Personable. Beautiful.

An intense sadness came over me. I suddenly felt the pain I'd been avoiding for twenty years. My ten years in the east, tracking Qary, was an attempt to replace the loss of my daughter and wife with revenge and hatred. The obsession allowed me to avoid the real hurt.

I'd thrown myself into the training, then the operations, driven by an intense desire to do what I thought was a good and noble thing—serving my country, ridding the world of bad guys. What I was really doing was immersing myself in the intensity of the hunt so I wouldn't feel the intensity of the hurt. Not realizing they were the same thing. Driven by the same emotion.

Ten years as dean was a continuation of the avoidance. More doing good. This time for the cause of Christ. What more noble a profession than shaping young minds to learn the Bible and then go on to successful ministries? I was good at what I did. An overachiever. The pain and loss were the underpinnings of that success and what drove me. Now I saw the success for what it was. The failure to come to an acceptance of the death of my wife and daughter. For a moment, I wondered if anything in my life was real. If all the effort had been wasted. Not wasted. But with the wrong motive.

Was there any difference?

Tears formed in my eyes as I realized what I'd been missing all these years. A woman's touch. A daughter's admiration and affection for her father. Growing old with my wife. Watching my daughter grow and mature and accomplish her own dreams. The pain was almost too great to bear.

The loss was irreplaceable. Was it really? God could replace anything. Maybe I was the one who wouldn't let him. Sarah could never replace Meg. But it would help, if I'd let it. I couldn't imagine how anyone could replace Mia, my wife.

I'd not been on a date since Mia died. Keeping everything appropriate with Sarah was second nature to me. I kept every woman at a distance. At arms-length. Safe. Even those relationships that would be considered appropriate. No one was allowed in. I was always appropriate. With everyone. All the time.

I realized how much I longed for one opportunity to let the walls down. Not so I could be inappropriate. There's nothing wrong with loving someone else, I suddenly realized. Nothing wrong with caring about Sarah as more than a student and mentoring her like a daughter. Nothing inappropriate about that. Nothing wrong with loving someone else besides Mia. I could love both.

The thought occurred to me that this was something I needed to change. As scary as it felt, it's what my wife would've wanted. She wouldn't want me to be alone, letting only her fill my heart. Not ever having kids. She always said I'd be a good father and then I was. A good husband for her, too.

I miss them so much...

I wiped away the tears running down my cheeks.

"What are you doing?" I said aloud to myself. "Why are you thinking about this now?"

I needed to think about the Garden of Eden. I should pray for Eric and Lacy and pray for Sarah and my students. Work was piling up on my desk as this project and the V-7 mission had taken a lot of my time. I was in danger of retreating back into my shell. My impulse was to block the pain before it became too intense. What I always did as soon as I felt something.

A noise in the hallway startled me and became a welcomed interruption to my thoughts. Who was it? I didn't think anyone else was still in the building. Probably maintenance. Before I could consider any other possibility, Hope Gala-gher walked in.

I quickly wiped away the remaining tears. She may have noticed them.

"Hope, what are you doing here so late?" I asked as I cleared my throat from the frog that had formed.

"I had a few papers to grade," she said with a warm, comforting smile.

Hope, the professor for Old Testament Studies, had been my first hire. Probably the easiest decision in my whole tenure. Immensely qualified, an expert on the Old Testament, Hope was well liked by her students and faculty alike. Homely in appearance, she always dressed in a long black skirt, well below her knees, usually with a white blouse that covered her arms and went all the way over her shoulders and halfway up her neck. Her hair was always in a bun. A pair of wire-rimmed glasses rested on her nose and she peered over them when teaching. Never wore jewelry.

No wedding ring.

"I heard about your project," Hope said. "The search for the Garden of Eden. Very ambitious. How's it going?"

She stood at the door with her arms crossed, glasses in hand, leaning against the doorway jamb. Like me, she was always careful to maintain the appropriate appearances. Her being a single woman who'd never been married, alone at night in the office of a widower in a Bible college and seminary, we both seemed as tense as a flagpole.

I looked away almost embarrassed and then looked back. Like a double take. I noticed something I'd never seen before. Behind the modest façade was a beautiful woman. Slim figure. High cheekbones. Dimples. Shy smile. Warm and friendly eyes. Very little if any makeup. None needed. Quiet and gentle spirit. Like the Bible described as a virtuous woman. Not adorned in a lot of jewelry and makeup and concern with outward appearances. But an inner beauty that made her beautiful on the outside as well.

"Do you have a few minutes?" I blurted out without stopping to think about it. I suddenly felt nervous and stumbled over my words. Unsure of myself.

"I mean, maybe I could run some things by you. Pick your brain. You're the expert in the Old Testament... I'm sorry. You probably have plans."

I wasn't making sense. It felt like a schoolboy asking a girl on a date. That's not what it was. She might be able to help me with the Garden of Eden search. No one knew more about the Old Testament than Hope.

"Sure," she said. "I don't have anywhere I have to be."

I breathed a sigh of relief. "Great, have a seat," I said, pointing to the chair across from me at the conference table. "Are you hungry? I could call in some food."

"That sounds great." She settled into the chair.

"What do you like to eat?" I asked.

"Surprise me," she said with a grin.

I pulled out my air-line and looked up the number to my favorite takeout restaurant.

You have already surprised me.

I felt something I hadn't felt in years. Something very unexpected.

* * *

Near the Push-On valley

As much as Eric would like to see Lacy's hand-to-hand combat skills in action, he didn't want to see them now. The plan was for them to get in and out of the Push-On Valley without being noticed by anyone. They weren't to the valley, and the plan was already out the window as the Naryan patrolman exited his vehicle, straightened the gun on his hip, and walked toward them.

Eric looked at Lacy and was reassured by her manner. She didn't seem the least bit concerned or afraid. Not that Eric was afraid. He and Lacy could disarm and disable the man before he knew what hit him. It complicated things though. A confrontation would make it even more complicated. Eric would do anything he could to avoid one. He hoped Lacy would show similar restraint.

"How are you, officer?" he said in a friendly voice.

Lacy remained silent. Women in the east spoke only when spoken to.

"Better than you, apparently," he replied with a smile on his face, nodding toward the flat tire but obviously looking us over carefully.

Eric didn't know how to take his manner. He'd encountered many Naryan soldiers, guards, and patrolmen over the years, and none were ever this friendly.

"Yeah. We had a flat tire," Eric said. "But thankfully we have a spare. We should be on our way shortly."

The patrolman stood at the back of the vehicle where the trunk was still open. The hidden compartment with the stash of guns was in his line of sight, although it would be nearly impossible to detect it without a search which Eric knew was imminent.

"Could you help me with this for a second?" Eric asked, doing anything he could think of to get the man away from the trunk. Lacy moved to stand behind Eric. There, she was in closer proximity so she could react more quickly if necessary. Eric almost smiled at the fact she was playing the part of the obedient wife perfectly. Lacy kept her head and face mostly dutifully covered.

The patrolman knelt down next to the tire as Eric struggled to get the blown-out tire off. He didn't need his help but pretended. Together, they were able to finally get it off and the other one on.

"Are you headed to the Push-On Valley?" the officer asked.

"No. Just north of that," Eric said. "Our friends have a cabin. We're staying there. It's our anniversary."

"Congratulations. You should go to the valley. A lot of good hiking there."

"I don't think we'll do a lot of hiking. We're mostly just going to hang out at the cabin and relax for a few days. Get some time alone."

Eric picked up the spare and threw it into the trunk with a thud and quickly closed the back, not bothering to put the tools in. Also, hoping the gesture was not obvious to the patrolman. Lacy picked up the tools and put them in the back seat. She grabbed a soda and gave Eric one so he'd have something cold to drink.

Lacy didn't offer the patrolman one. It would have been inappropriate for her to do so. Eric didn't offer him one either. He just stuck out his hand and thanked the patrolman for his help as the man took Eric's hand and shook it. Eric went around to the driver's side and got in the car. Lacy waited until he was in and then got in herself in case the patrolman intended to spring a surprise attack on them.

They both waved as they drove off. Eric kept looking in his rearview mirror until they were out of the sight of the patrolman's car.

"Definitely a trap," Eric finally said.

"Yeah. He was too friendly. Just checking us out. A real patrolman would have asked for our papers. Searched the car. He didn't do any of that."

"Also, he told us to go hiking in the Push-On Valley. That was too obvious. He wanted us to go there. To let us know it was safe."

"What do we do now?" Lacy asked.

"We walk into their trap," Eric said with a sly grin.

"That's fine, as long as we set one of our own."

"That's exactly what I intend to do." Eric said. "First, we need to find a place to call Ted."

* * *

Qary was growing impatient. The pag-anites should've already sent Church-Well and other operatives to the Valley. They'd had enough time. He wondered if his plan was actually going to work. Did they get the intercepts? Did Church-Well figure it out?

He'd taken down all the checkpoints to make it easy for them to get to him. A few of his men patrolled the roads to the valley, but he hadn't heard anything as of yet. He had more than fifty men out of the field, hiding in the valley, waiting on his instructions. The big operation was taking a lot of time and manpower.

Even though Qary had doubts about his plan, he knew it would work. It just needed a little more time.

As if reading his thoughts, his air-line rang. A temporary tower had been constructed to allow for communications within a ten-mil-ead radius. The connections weren't good but good enough to where they could understand each other.

"Al-Tay is great," Qary answered. The standard greeting for Naryans. Al-Tay was the name of god. The name god used when he spoke to Sal-Am for the first time.

"Two people—a man and woman—were stopped along the road. They had a flat tire," a man on the other end of the line said.

"What did they look like?" Qary asked.

"I don't know. She was covered. He was just a man."

"You idiot! What did they look like? How tall was he? What was the color of his hair? How old was he?"

"He was tall. Brown hair. Muscular. I don't know how old he is. I didn't ask."

Qary raised his fist to slam it into the table but stopped himself. "Were there only two of them?"

"Yes. They said they were going to a friend's cabin for their anniversary. I told them they should go hiking, just like you said for me to." He paused as if waiting for some praise. With none forthcoming, he said, "They said they wanted to be alone. If you know what I mean..." the man laughed on the other end.

"I don't think it was the pag-anites," he added.

"It was them," Qary said under his breath.

Definitely Church-Well. My plan is working. They are on their way here.

"Keep a look out for anyone else," Qary said, hanging up his air-line.

Qary walked out of his tent and found his second in command. "Prepare the men. Two of the pag-anites have been spotted on the road to the valley. A man and a woman. This is going to be easier than I thought. Get everyone in place tomorrow morning. They won't be here before then. Is everyone ready?"

"Yes, commander. The men are anxious for the battle. We are ready to kill the pag-anites."

"Remember. I want the man alive. Give strict orders not to kill the man. I don't care what you do to the girl. The men can have her. It will be a reward for the victory. Bring the man to me."

"Al-Tay is great. Al-Tay is great," Qary kept saying to himself, over and over again as his commander rushed off.

11

Hope and I were laughing so hard my side hurt. I don't even remember what I said that she thought was so funny, but I felt a lot of my tension release as I became more and more comfortable with her. I'd just finished my last bite of food and washed it down with a gulp of a new drink called K-OK that was all the rage on Ven-Us. She preferred a glass of water which was still half full and her plate of food was half-eaten.

Before the food came, I explained to her my theory about the Garden of Eden actually being in the west based on Ven-Us's backward rotation. She found it fascinating and a strong possibility she'd never heard before. I started to tell her about the discovery of gold at the Great Wall when our food arrived. We hadn't returned to the topic and spent the time talking about students and some of the crazy things they said and asked. The reason we were cracking each other up.

The conversation continued without losing momentum until we finished eating. A pause finally afforded a perfect time to go back to the discussion on the garden.

"Years ago," I said, "they discovered gold when they built the Great Wall. They found it near where the House of the Rock stands."

"I didn't know that," Hope said, brushing aside a strand of bangs that had released itself from the tight bun on her head. Cute. I wondered what she looked like with her hair completely down. The thought caused me to momentarily forget what I was saying.

"They discovered gold at the Great Wall," Hope reminded me.

I hoped she hadn't caught the reason why I paused. My staring at her might be too obvious.

"Right. Genesis obviously mentions gold. The river flowed to where there was gold. Also, as you know, the word *rock* has significant importance in the Bible. Upon this rock, I will build my church," I said, quoting a familiar Scripture.

Hope nodded. "Hamm sacrificed Casik at the rock. Jesus was killed at the rock."

"Christ is the solid rock," I added. "Those two significant events in the Bible all happened right at the House of the Rock," I said. Hope was engrossed in the conversation as much as me. "That can't be a coincidence. It had to be something God planned. What if the rock is also associated with the fall? What if Jesus was killed at the same spot where Adam and Eve ate the fruit?"

"Interesting," Hope said. "Almost like God was bringing redemption to the exact spot where sin entered into the world. Sounds like something God would do. Redeem something that was lost right where it was lost."

"Right," I said nodding. "I have no proof, yet, but it's an interesting theory."

"You know there is an Eden rock," Hope said.

My heart suddenly thumped hard in my chest and I forgot to breathe for a moment. "I didn't know that. I've never heard of the Eden Rock. I don't remember it in the Bible."

"It's not in the Bible," Hope explained. "You're familiar with the writings of Flav-Ious?" she asked.

"I've obviously heard about him and read some of his writings. I'm not that familiar though."

"Flav-Ious was a historian," Hope explained. "He recorded ancient lore. He spent his life trying to learn stories about the descendants of Hamm and the folklore that's been passed down from generation to generation. I've read most of his writings. I wrote a paper on his writings for my doctorate."

"There's a lot of controversy as to whether his writings were accurate or not," I said, vaguely remembering her mentioning Flav-Ious and her paper in her job interview.

"We have no way of knowing for sure," she continued. "Some things are obviously verified by the biblical text, and some archeological discoveries have confirmed parts of his writings. I don't know of anything that has been disproven."

"Anyway. You said he wrote about an Eden rock." My anticipation was growing to the point of impatience.

"Right," Hope said, obviously realizing she'd gotten distracted off the main point. "He only mentions it once." She stood. "Wait a minute."

Hope walked out of my office. A couple minutes later, she returned with a large book in hand. She flipped through the pages, but I barely noticed. Her hair was down, no longer in a bun. Long and flowing now garnering my full attention.

She stopped and ran her hands through her hair, shaking it out.

The action sent an indescribable feeling down my neck and into my arms. I could tell I had a childish grin on my face which I tried to remove but without much luck.

"What?" she said, noticing me staring at her with my mouth open.

"You look so beautiful with your hair down. I like it."

"Thank you," she said, blushing a little. That made her quickly go back to concentrating on leafing through the book.

I wondered if what I said was appropriate. Hope was a subordinate in many ways. I wasn't her direct boss, but she did answer to me in some ways. Did that complicate things?

Complicate what? Nothing has happened. We just ate a meal and are now having a professional conversation.

Relax. You're doing nothing wrong. Enjoy it.

"Here's what I'm looking for," she said, thankfully interrupting the war raging inside me.

"What is this book?" I asked.

"These are from the writings of Flav-Ious. Here's what it says."

My air-line vibrated. I wanted to ignore it.

Ted Cole-Man.

I couldn't ignore it. Might be about Eric and Lacy. "I need to take this. Sorry," I said as I stood and walked out of the room. My thoughts were in disarray. Hope and her hair. The Eden Rock. What she was saying could be very important information. On the other hand, why was Ted calling? Is everything okay?

"Hello, Ted," I said anxiously.

"I heard from Eric and Lacy." No acknowledgement or greeting. Must be serious, I concluded before he said another word.

"Are they okay?" I asked. "They couldn't be finished with the mission yet."

"They're fine. They are just outside of Ida-Mon."

"What did they want?"

"They think they might be walking into a trap."

"I've thought of that myself. The intercept seemed staged to me. I've also been thinking about how I ran into Qary. It's almost like he wanted me to see him. I can see why they're worried. What did you tell them?"

"I said I should've sent you. You were never afraid of a trap. You just went in and killed everybody and then told me about it later."

I laughed. "I don't think they're afraid. Just being cautious. What are they going to do?"

"What can they do? I told them to not waste time calling me. Just be careful. Either it's a trap or it's not. Nothing anyone can do about it until we know. It's not like they're going to take any more precautions than they would have."

"Do you want me to go there now? I might be able to catch up to them." I hoped he said no. Before, I wanted to go on the mission. Hope was giving me a reason to be here.

"Not yet. Let's see what happens. They have to find those missiles."

"Why do they think it's a trap?"

"They had a flat tire and a patrolman stopped and helped them."

"He helped them?" I said incredulously. "That is strange. Never known a Naryan policeman to be helpful."

"They also said there are no checkpoints leading to the valley. They've all been removed."

"If they were building missiles in the valley, there would be checkpoints everywhere. I agree with them. It must be a trap. Since they know about it, they'll have an advantage. Keep me posted. Let me know if you hear from them again."

"I will."

I started to hang up.

"Row," he said.

"What?" I replied.

"Go out and do something. The night's young. I hate to think of you all alone."

I hung up the line but not before making sure he could hear me laughing.

I'm not alone my friend. Definitely not alone.

* * *

I walked back into the room and smiled broadly when I saw Hope. "Sorry about that," I said. "An important call that I had to take."

"Everything's okay, I hope."

I dismissed her comment with a wave. "Where were we? Oh, yeah. You were about to read the writing about the Eden rock. I'm fascinated by this."

She still had the book open and began reading the passage from Flav-Ious's writings. "You were at the Eden Rock. Where the Garden of God once stood. Where there was sacrifice made."

"Why have I never heard of that? Do you have any idea what it means?" I asked.

"It's a fairly obscure writing. Scholars aren't really sure what it means. Who was there? Adam and Eve? Satan? Jesus? It's all confusing. Flav-Ious didn't clarify who he meant was there."

"Obviously, it's not Scripture, so we can't assume it's even right," I said what I was sure she already believed. "Still... I'm glad you showed me that writing," I said emphatically. "It doesn't prove my theory, but it does add weight to it. What if the rock at the wall is the actual rock in the Garden of Eden? I've touched that rock. How amazing would that be?"

We discussed it for a few more minutes. The time seemed to pass in a blur.

Hope finally said, "I should go. I've had a good time, though."

"Me too," I said enthusiastically though disappointed she had to leave.

She hesitated for a moment and then said, "How would you like to have a good time at the end of the week. Come over to my house. I'll cook dinner to repay you for the one tonight."

"I'm sorry," I said. "I have a strict rule to only have a good time no more than once a week."

She laughed as I grinned mischievously.

"Well, I can't guarantee it'll be a good time. I'm not the best cook in the world. You'll have to eat the meal first and then tell me if it was a good time."

"I'm sure it'll be great. I would love to. Let's do it." Now I was *really* glad Ted hadn't taken me up on the offer to go to the east.

I walked her over to the door. Hope turned to face me and stuck out her hand for me to shake.

"It's been fun," she said as I shook her hand.

Rather than releasing it, I pulled her toward me and into a hug. "We're friends," I said as I hugged her warmly. A chill ran down my spine. I could smell her hair and could feel her warm body next to mine. It'd been years since I'd been that close to another woman. Amazing to me that I didn't feel any guilt. It felt good.

I let her go and sheepishly backed away. She didn't immediately leave.

"I just thought of something," Hope said, pausing. "Jesus said Hamm and Adam saw his day and rejoiced in it. What does that mean?"

I started to answer but then stopped myself. I wanted to answer thoughtfully. "I don't know in the context of what we've talked about tonight. However, I have studied that question. When Hamm sacrificed Casik on the rock, I've always thought it was a picture of Christ. I think it means Hamm saw into the future by faith what would happen to Jesus."

"What if he actually saw Jesus that day?" she asked.

"I hadn't thought of it literally. It's always seemed figurative to me. There are many similarities between Casik and Jesus that are what I call shadows. A reflection of something in the future. Casik was sacrificed on the rock. So was Jesus. Casik was resurrected from the dead, three days later. Jesus was in the grave for three nights and rose again on the third day."

"Adam was there too," she said. "Maybe God let Adam and Eve live beyond the one hundred twenty years because God wanted Adam to see the sacrifice and know that God made a provision for his sin. You know what I mean? Maybe even let him see or meet Jesus. Am I making sense?" she asked hesitantly.

"I do understand. You are making sense," I replied. "I never thought of it quite that way either."

"What if... Follow this reasoning," she continued. "Adam sinned and was thrown out of the garden. God put a rock at the spot sort of as a memorial. Maybe that's the Eden rock Flav-Ious wrote about. Adam saw the sacrifice of Casik on the rock. God's way of telling him everything was going to be okay."

My thoughts bounced back and forth in my mind like a ball caroming off a wall. Excitement built with each word she spoke. She was on a roll. I didn't want to slow her down.

"It says an angel of the Lord was the one who spoke to him. That might be Jesus," she stated.

"Right. Many scholars believe the angel of the Lord was actually Jesus," I added. "That makes so much sense."

"Casik was placed on wood as a sacrifice," she said her words more slowly, with emphasis. "Jesus was placed on a wooden cross and then crucified there at the rock." She ran both hands through her hair again and moved closer to me. Obviously not ready to leave yet.

"Casik willingly got on the rock to be sacrificed," I continued. "Imagine that. Would you climb on that rock? I wouldn't. Especially right after his father told him he was going to kill him and make him the sacrifice.As far as he knew, he'd be burned like the lamb. Casik was a grown man. Yet, he crawled onto the rock. He let his father tie him down. He watched as he plunged the knife into his heart. Killing him. Jesus did the same thing. He crawled onto the cross. It even says that he laid down his life willingly for us. Both stories are such a powerful example of sacrifice."

"God told Hamm to sacrifice his only son even though Nary was also his son," Hope added. "That's one of the reasons the Naryans crucified Jesus. The Quan-di denies that Hamm ever sacrificed Casik. Jesus made them mad when he said that Hamm saw his day when he put Casik on the altar. They thought it was blasphemous."

I rubbed my temples. So many things to think about.

"Anyway," she said, sensing that I was getting tired.

I jumped in and said, "You may be right. You've been a big help. Thank you."

"You're so welcome."

Hope kissed me on the cheek, turned and left. A feeling pulsing through me I never thought I'd feel again. I walked slowly back to the conference table and tried to sort out the range of emotions.

Do I like her?

More importantly, does she like me?

Are we right about the rock?

The thoughts were wrestling for my undivided attention.

Neither one was winning.

12

Before (Ven-te 225)

Hamm untied his son from the wood that bound him to the rock. Casik was dead. The wound fatal. Adam looked away. Probably as much from the pain on Hamm's face as horrors of the scene of Casik with a knife protruding from his heart.

Hamm knelt before the rock and prayed, "Lord, my son, my only son, is now in your hands. The Lord giveth and the Lord taketh away. I believe my son will live. Casik is the son of promise. I ask you now to raise him from the dead."

Adam and Hamm worshipped God at the rock. Hamm continued to believe God would raise his son from the dead. Hamm would look up from praying, look at Casik to see if he'd come back to life. When he hadn't, he would bow his head and pray some more. After several hours of prayer and worship, Casik had not moved, and darkness was about to fall on Ven-Us. If they didn't leave soon, they'd have to spend the night there.

"We have to leave now before it gets dark," Adam said.

"I will not leave my son here alone," Hamm said. "Wild animals will come and tear his body apart."

"You can't stay out here with him," Adam said. "The animals will get you as well."

"Let's take him back to the camp," Hamm said as he took his son off of the altar and lifted him into his arms. He carried Casik all the way back to the camp. Once there, he laid him on the bed in his tent. Clearly distraught.

Adam had followed him all the way, continually trying to console him.

Hamm knelt beside the bed that held the cold, lifeless body of his son and prayed again.

God, I thank you that you have heard my prayer. For this child I prayed, and the Lord has granted me my petition which I asked of him.

Terah burst into the tent, saw her son lying on the bed and let out a loud scream. His bloody shirt revealed where the wound had pierced his heart. Thankfully, Adam had removed the knife and left it at the rock.

"What have you done?" she cried out.

Hamm stood and reached for his wife, but she pushed him away and rushed to the side of the bed laying her head on her son's chest. Sobbing uncontrollably.

"Our son lives," Hamm said. "He's not dead; he only sleeps."

Eve entered about that time. Adam took her in her arms as she turned her head away from the awful sight.

Terah was on the floor next to her son's bed, curled in a ball, obviously in unbearable agony. Casik lay peacefully on the bed, his arms folded. Their worst fears had come true.

Eve told Adam she kept telling Terah not to worry. That Hamm would never hurt their son. He obviously had.

"Have you gone mad?" Terah shouted at Hamm. "You killed our son." She stood and grabbed Hamm and pushed his head down toward their son.

Hamm didn't resist. He knew Terah wouldn't understand at first.

"Look at him!" she screamed. "He's dead. It's all your fault."

Hamm broke her grip, grabbed her by the shoulders, and turned her toward him. He shook her gently but firmly.

"Casik is the son of promise," he said. "God would not tell me to sacrifice him if he wasn't going to raise him from the dead."

"God wouldn't tell you to kill our son," she said as she beat Hamm's chest with both of her fists as hard as she could.

Hamm didn't know what to say so he didn't say anything, which apparently only made her more enraged. Finally, he said, "God did tell me. I only did what he told me to do."

"How can you be so sure? What if you're wrong. How could you take such a chance with your own son's life?" She started hitting him again.

Hamm grabbed both of her arms to stop her.

Terah was strong, but finally, she collapsed at his feet in mental, emotional, and physical exhaustion.

Eve rushed to her side.

Adam took Hamm by the arm and led him outside. They could hear Eve trying desperately to console Terah.

Hamm's heart was breaking. Not for his son but for his wife. His faith hadn't wavered. God would raise his son from the dead. Would Terah ever forgive him for putting her through this pain?

"Adam, the angel of the Lord told me to sacrifice my son," Hamm said. "I did as he requested. My son will live. I'm sure of it."

"What if the ram in the thicket was supposed to be the sacrifice? Maybe God was testing you to see if you would be willing to sacrifice your son. I tried to get you to stop. But I was too late."

"I didn't see the ram in the thicket," Hamm said as tears rolled down his cheeks. "I don't know. Maybe I was wrong."

Wails came from the tent.

Hamm started to go back in, but Adam stopped him. "You have to give her time. She's just lost her son."

"Don't say that," Hamm said angrily. "She hasn't lost her son. God is going to raise Casik from the dead. This was a test. A test to see if I would believe God. Maybe the ram was the sacrifice. I don't know..." His voice trailed off as the thought that he may have wrongly killed his son instead of using the ram became almost too much to bear.

When he regained his composure Hamm said, "Either way, God will save my son. I know it. I just have to convince Terah to trust God."

Adam didn't say anything but maintained his strong grip on Hamm's arm.

The wails turned to cries. The cries to moans. Eventually, all they could hear from the tent was quiet sobbing.

* * *

Three Days Later

Hamm lay on the floor of his tent, unable to sleep. Casik still laid on the bed above him. He'd refused to allow him to be moved, instead insisting his body not be prepared for burial. No one was allowed to grieve. Hamm was still convinced God would raise Casik from the dead, and he'd spent each night in the tent with his son, waiting to hear from the angel of the Lord. The body had started to decompose. A foul smell permeated the tent. He remained undeterred and refused to leave his son's side. He hadn't eaten in three days. Everyone became concerned about him.

Terah slept in Adam and Eve's tent even though she now believed as well. The faith of her husband had convinced her God had told him to sacrifice Casik. If he really did, then God would raise him from the dead. Three days had passed, and while maintaining their faith was hard, they drew strength from each other. She'd told Hamm she was sorry for doubting him and not having enough faith.

Hamm had been kind and gentle toward her and understanding. The whole circumstance had drawn them closer together. Hamm remembered the conversation that finally persuaded her.

He had said, "Remember when I told you God would give us a son?"

Terah nodded. "I didn't believe you," she said. "I thought I was too old."

"And what happened?" Hamm asked.

"I had a son. Just like you said I would."

"No. Just like God said you would. God didn't give us a son to take him from us. Remember, God said my descendants would be like the stars. I don't have any descendants to carry on our legacy. That's why I'm certain God is going to raise Casik from the dead."

"What about Nary?" Terah asked in barely a whisper. "He's your son." No anger could be detected in how she said it. Just quiet resignation of something they all wanted to forget.

"When God spoke to me, he said, 'Take your son—your only son—and sacrifice him on the altar.' That confused me at first. Why did God say take my *only* son? It's because Casik is the only son that God recognizes. The only one God gave to us. Nary was never supposed to be my son. I hear Nary is leading the people to worship other gods. Even sacrifice children on the altar. He was never supposed to be my son. I regret the day he was born. Casik is the son of promise. If God doesn't raise Casik from the dead, he'll give us another son."

"Oh no!" she said. "I'm not going through childbirth again." A large grin formed on her face. "God is just going to have to raise Casik from the dead. I'm not having any more kids."

Hamm was relieved that Terah believed him. It would've been too hard to maintain his faith without her. The whole camp thought they were crazy. Even Adam and Eve weren't convinced.

The morning of the third day had come and the sun had started to rise. Hamm said another prayer and thanked God for hearing his petition and raising Casik from the dead. He believed faith was thanking God for what he was going to do, not so much asking him to do it. If he believed God was going to raise Casik, then why ask? Just be thankful. So, he prayed another prayer of thanks. One of thousands he'd said over the last three days.

The truth was, he'd soon know. He looked at his son who was resting so peacefully. A slight grin was on his face. If Hamm didn't know better, he would think his son was only sleeping.

At that moment, an angel of the Lord appeared to Hamm and startled him. He said, "Rise up. Take your son, your only son, and go to the rock."

Just as quickly as he appeared, he left. Hamm scrambled to his feet, and threw on his clothes and sandals. He Took Casik in his arms and headed as fast as he could to Adam and Eve's tent where they were all likely still sleeping.

Hamm burst in without warning. "Wake up!" he shouted.

Adam bolted up from the bed. A sliver of light shone through the opening of the tent signifying the dawn of the day. Eve rubbed the sleep from her eyes. Terah was a deep sleeper. Hamm called out her name louder until she stirred.

"What's wrong?" Terah asked, groggy and not having gained her bearings yet.

"An angel of the Lord appeared to me this morning and told me to go to the rock," Hamm explained. "Quick! Everyone get dressed. We're going to see a miracle today."

Terah jumped up after hearing those words. They all scrambled to their feet. Hamm took Casik back outside.

"Just a few more minutes, son," he said to Casik. "I can't wait until you wake up."

* * *

Many in the camp stirred from the commotion and came out of their tents to see what was happening. Hamm told them to stay there. They'd all be back, including his son.

Hamm, Terah, Adam and Eve left and went to the Eden rock. Hamm carried Casik's body with renewed strength, even though he hadn't eaten in three days. Everyone's eyes were as wide as coins. Their mouths gaped wide open. Huge smiles were on their faces. Yet fear and anxiety was obviously pulsing through their veins competing with the excitement and anticipation. They admitted as much walking to the rock.

The rock still had the wood on it, from the offering, soaked in Casik's blood. Hamm laid Casik on the rock in the same position he was when he died. Adam, Eve, and Terah looked on with great anticipation.

Terah nervously wrung her hands. She rocked up and down on her feet. Intermittently clapping. Nervous energy with no outlet. Adam held Eve in his arms. He nodded to Hamm approvingly.

Hamm didn't know exactly what he was supposed to do. So, he stood there looking around, unsure if they should stand or kneel. Sing praises or pray. Casik was about to be raised from the dead. Hamm was sure of it. As certain as he'd ever been of anything in his life.

Am I supposed to do something?

Suddenly, the angel of the Lord called to Hamm from heaven a second time and said, "I swear by myself, declares the Lord, that because you have done this and have not withheld your son, your only son, I will surely bless you and make your descendants as numerous as the stars in the sky and as the sand on the seashore. Your descendants will take possession of the cities of their enemies, and through your offspring, all nations on earth will be blessed because you have obeyed me."

Hamm looked around to see if others heard what he heard. A glow came on all their faces confirming they each heard the voice of the Lord.

"Fear not!" the angel said. "For I bring you tidings of great joy. Your son will live." Immediately, all fear lifted from Hamm, and he was overwhelmed with joy.

Terah ran to him and threw her arms around his neck, obviously overjoyed, having heard the angel say her son would live.

"Adam and Eve," the angel of the Lord said.

"Yes, Lord. We're here."

"God is going to give his son, his only son, for the sins of the world. Casik is a sign. I've allowed you to live to see this day. Through one man's sin, your sin, death, and unrighteousness entered the world. Through one man's sacrifice, God's only son, man shall be made righteous on this very spot. I have let you live beyond one hundred twenty years so you would see this day."

Adam and Eve fell to their knees and worshipped God.

Hamm and Terah did as well.

Suddenly.

Movement.

On the rock. Casik stirred. He coughed. Then sat straight up.

Terah was the first to see him. The others had been distracted by the angel. Terah took her son in her arms and kissed him profusely.

Casik seemed stunned like he was not sure what was happening. His wound was completely healed. The only evidence it ever existed was the blood stain on his shirt.

"God has answered our prayers!" Hamm shouted. "Our son lives!" Everyone gathered around Casik, hugging him, kissing him, slapping him on the back. Alternating between thanking God and thanking him for coming back to them.

"Our son has returned. Kill the fatted calf," Hamm said. "There will be a great celebration throughout the camp tonight. Casik is alive!"

We should rejoice," Hamm said. "Not just in Casik. God has allowed us to see in the future. We have seen the coming of the Son of God."

13

Now (Ven-te 2200)

The rest of the trip to the Push-On Valley was uneventful. Too easy as far as Eric was concerned. He was becoming more convinced than ever that they were walking into a trap. Not walking into, per se. They intended to bring as much firepower necessary with their own element of surprise. A trap they would set for the trappers.

They'd found an area to hide the vehicle which gave them a good vantage point of the main road without being seen from the road. Several patrol cars, like the one that stopped earlier when they had the flat tire, were seen patrolling back and forth, obviously looking for someone or something. Only one person was in the vehicle each time. Definitely doing reconnaissance. Each one was conspicuously trying to seem inconspicuous.

Eric could see right through the guise. Not that he expected a firefight by this point, but they anticipated something different. Missions have a certain feel. In the field, one can sense when something's not right. There weren't enough patrols to make them think they were protecting something as important as missiles yet enough patrols to give away the fact the Naryans were looking for some kind of trouble. Trouble was exactly what they were going to get.

They discussed their next move. Eric was the leader of the mission, but Lacy appreciated him including her in the decision making and said so. They agreed on the need to get to the observation point as soon as possible. Already dark, the nighttime would provide perfect cover. No soldiers would be out at night.

However, the main concern was hiking through rugged terrain in complete darkness. Night glasses let them see almost as if it were daylight, but the technology wasn't perfect. The last thing they wanted was for one of them to sprain an ankle or wrench a knee hiking on an unfamiliar trail.

The more prudent thing was to stay in the car, hunker down for the night, eat a good meal, and get a good night's sleep. Row had a saying taught to them in training. *Eat when you can and sleep when you can. You never know when you'll get your next chance.* They considered it good advice ingrained in them by their instructors.

Row was famous among operatives and had a number of sayings, some of which hung on the wall of the training facility. That one made perfect sense at the moment, and after eating a good meal, they rotated in three-hour shifts. One slept while the other kept watch. By the next morning, well rested and well fed, they were ready for whatever lay ahead.

Eric spent his time on watch pouring over the map, plotting their path to the observation point. They'd stay off the main hiking trails and forge their own path through the woods which weren't that dense this time of year. He told Lacy the plan to head straight up the hill to the top of the ridge and walk across it to the observation point.

He wanted to get to the high ground quickly. There, they'd have a tactical advantage and the ability to see what was going on below them. Another one of Row's tactical sayings, "Everything travels faster downhill than uphill. Including bullets."

The next morning, they set off and Eric set a quick pace which Lacy easily matched. Hardly out of breath, they reached the top of the hill in less than thirty minutes, made easier because they were carrying a minimal number of supplies. Traveling light was the best option. Agility and flexibility seemed more important to them than the supplies. The explosives were left behind. The likelihood of finding missiles in the valley was low, in their estimation, and the munitions were heavy and would only slow them down. They could always go back and get them if they needed to.

Each brought four packets of FRTEs—food ready to eat. Small and light packets of a high calorie liquid which provided energy for up to twelve hours. Each carried one container of water strapped to their belt. Eric carried a water filter. The valley had many streams for water. No reason to be loaded down and carry more than they needed for a day.

Ammunition for their weapons was the one thing they didn't go light on. Eric had a GK-47F on his belt. A light automatic handgun but deadly accurate at close range. Both carried a KH 614 standard issue high-performance assault rifle bigger than a pistol but smaller than a large submachine gun. It could fire a beastly rate of 950rpm— rounds per minute. Inaccurate at a range longer than a hundred yards for most people, Eric and Lacy could hit a leaf off of a tree at a hundred yards if they had time to aim the weapon. Each had more than 200 rounds of ammo on them. Enough to kill a small army if necessary.

Both wore hiking boots, lightweight for running, but heavy enough for rugged terrain and almost impossible to wear out. Waterproof, comfortable. They wore the usual military operative fatigues, a hat to shield their heads and faces from the sun, and several personal items. Eric carried a K-Bar knife with serrated edges. He wasn't sure what Lacy was carrying, but he figured she had more than one weapon hidden in her camouflaged outfit. Maybe not. Her hands were as lethal as any knife. Or at least that's what he'd heard. A fact, he hoped he didn't have to find out today. The nagging ominous feeling about the mission still cried out from inside of him. The only thing easing the feeling was having Lacy next to him.

Neither spoke for the first few minutes as they were on full alert. Finally, Eric broke the silence. "What did you study in school?"

"Prison Justice."

"Really?" he said with surprise.

"Growing up, I wanted to be the warden of a jail."

"Are you serious?" Eric laughed, looking back at her with surprise.

"Why are you laughing?" she said, frowning at him.

"You don't look like any wardens I've ever met. Most of them weigh three hundred pounds and sit around smoking cigars."

Lacy ignored the comment or at least didn't respond to it. Instead she said, "When we were young, I used to chase my older brother around the house, tackle him, arrest him, and lock him in the closet. I was the jailer. He was the prisoner." They both laughed. "My mom used to get so mad at me. My brother didn't seem to mind. He liked it. At least until he got older. Then, I had to *make* him get in the closet."

"How much older was he?"

"Four years."

Eric stopped walking. "He was four years older, and you could make him get in the closet?"

"I've always been stronger than I look."

Eric liked her attitude about things. She didn't come across as bragging, just confident. She wasn't defending herself or trying to read him her resume of abilities. Row had another saying, *If you've done it, it's not bragging.* His even more famous quote was, *If you can back it up, no reason to brag.* Lacy seemed to embrace that philosophy.

"What did you want to be growing up?" Lacy asked.

"This," he said emphatically. "My dad was in special operations. I grew up hearing his stories. This is all I've ever wanted to do."

"He must be proud of you."

"My dad died a few years ago. Heart attack. He was injured on a mission and never fully recovered."

"I'm sorry."

"He lived long enough to see me graduate, though. I miss being able to tell him my stories. I guess I can tell them to my kids, if I ever have any."

"What about your parents? Were they in the services?" Eric asked, diverting the subject away from him.

"Not hardly." Lacy said with a chuckle. "My dad's a banker. My mom works as a salesperson at a women's clothing store. The worst injury my dad ever got on the job was a cut on his finger from a piece of paper."

Eric laughed. "And here you are. What do they think about having a daughter who can kill a man a hundred different ways with her bare hands?"

Lacy shrugged. "We don't talk about it much. My mom thinks I'm crazy. I think my dad is proud of me, though. He doesn't really say. They were at my graduation."

Eric noticed that the conversation was slowing them down, so he picked up the pace. They walked along the ridge, staying mostly in the tree line so as not to be seen in the valley.

He suddenly stopped when he spied a group of Naryan soldiers walking on the trail below them. He held his fist in the air signifying for Lacy to stop.

Lacy immediately bent down in a crouched position.

He pointed to his right.

She looked where he pointed and then held up ten fingers to indicate how many of them there were.

The soldiers were armed with older model M93 submachine guns. Some looked to be in disrepair; the men appeared to be not very well trained. The guns were around their shoulders, rather than in front of them. Some even carried them on their backs with the barrel and trigger behind them, facing down. The men were laughing and obviously joking around when they should have their guns in front of them, on alert. They also should've been quiet, careful not to alert an enemy of their location which they unknowingly had done.

Eric and Lacy could take them all out before they even got a shot off if they wanted to. But they weren't there to start a war or kill anyone they didn't have to kill. The mission was to find and locate missiles. If they weren't there, the rules of engagement were to get out without being seen if at all possible. The only caveat—take Qary out if they spotted him and the opportunity presented itself.

Besides, shooting the patrol would give away their location. They needed more information. How many patrols were there? Why were they patrolling? What were they protecting? He thought he knew, but so far, everything he thought was only speculation. The presence of a ten-man patrol, did confirm activity in the area. They weren't there for no reason. Why would soldiers even be in the Push-On Valley? He needed to find out the answers to these questions, hopefully without them knowing he was there.

He didn't like the fact the patrol would be behind them now. Nothing he could do about it, other than get to the observation point. Row said it was well hidden, and they'd be safe there.

Once the patrol passed, Eric quickened the pace even more—so fast they arrived at the observation point ahead of schedule.

Lacy was still not out of breath, though, obviously in peak physical condition. As was he.

The observation point gave them a perfect view of the valley. They wouldn't have found it had Row not given them good directions.

"When we get home, remind me to thank Row for telling us about this observation area," Lacy said.

If not for the reason they were there, the view from the spot was magnificent. The lush hills to the south and east made a beautiful backdrop for the river that ran between them.

"We can see everything from here," Lacy pointed out. "Look. There's the main camp. Down by the river. Right at the mouth where Row said it would be. Probably a spring right there."

Eric pointed in another direction to another patrol. Ten men to the east of them in the valley. They spotted five more patrols.

"Patrols are everywhere," Eric said. "I wonder why?"

"I've spotted three snipers. All in the hills above the camp." Lacy pointed them out to Eric.

He hadn't seen them. "You have good eyes."

"The sun is reflecting off of their scopes. They're amateurs. Any good sniper would conceal his weapon so it couldn't be seen," Lacy explained something Eric already knew but listened attentively to her anyway.

He didn't pay as much attention to detail as Lacy obviously did. That made for a good team. He might not have spotted the snipers. As every moment passed, he was more and more thankful to have her with him.

"Well… I don't see any missiles," Eric said. "But this place is heavily fortified. There's a whole army down there. But why? All for one man. I can't believe they set this big a trap just for Row."

"He's not just one man," Lacy replied. "He's a force by himself. They know they can't take him down with just a few men. This does seem like overkill though."

"I say we get out of here," Eric said. "There aren't any missiles. We completed our mission as far as I'm concerned."

"Wait!" Lacy said in a way that startled Eric. "Look down there. The man that just came out of the tent. Smoking a tobacco stick. That looks like Qary."

"How can you be sure?" Eric asked.

"He's older than the pictures we've seen of him, but I'm sure it's him. Same height. Similar build. Has a beard."

"They all have a beard."

"He has a scar on his left cheek."

"How can you see that far?"

Lacy was looking through glasses that magnified objects at a distance.

Eric was in front of her and hadn't noticed. "Where did you get those?" Eric asked. They were new prototypes for training purposes only and weren't approved yet for the field. He didn't have them when he went through training.

"I may have borrowed them," she said sheepishly.

"Stole them you mean."

"You know what Row always said."

"Easier to ask forgiveness than permission," they said in unison, laughing quietly. Careful to not be so loud they gave away their position.

Lacy looked through the glasses again to confirm the scar was on the left side of the man's face.

"The scar is on his cheekbone," she said, handing Eric the glasses. "I don't know if you know the story, but Row gave Qary that scar during one of the torture sessions. Row made a makeshift knife from a spring in his bed. He hid it in his hand. When they came for him, he somehow loosened one of the ropes that bound his hands enough to slash Qary in the face. Row didn't say, but I think he paid a heavy price for it that day."

"That's definitely Qary. You know what that means?" he said. "We're going to have to go down there and kill him."

"Before we kill him, we need to find out if there are any missiles. If there are any, Qary knows where they are."

"He'll never tell us," Eric said.

"He might. I'm very persuasive," Lacy said smugly. "Maybe we'll give him the same treatment he gave Row. I bet Qary breaks in no time. Row never did. Qary will talk. All we have to do is capture him."

"That's all," Eric said sarcastically.

"It won't be that hard."

"Where are you going to question him? I don't think the soldiers are going to stand around and watch you do it."

"Back at the car."

"So, you're just going to walk into camp and kidnap him. We have to assume he won't go quietly. You'll have to disable him. Then we have to carry a two-hundred-pound man through the hills to the car. Without alerting the other soldiers. Get him to tell us where the missiles are. Then kill him. Not to mention, escape the country without detection with the whole nation of Naryans looking for us. Have I left anything out?"

"Except the part about killing him. We're going to take him as a prisoner back to the states."

"Are you serious?"

"Yes. He has a lot of information that would be very helpful to our side. Plus, I bet Row would like to have a word with him. Alone."

"Do you have a plan for this?"

"I do."

"I can't wait to hear what it is," Eric said, as they huddled together.

14

Eric agreed with every aspect of Lacy's plan except for one thing—he wanted to be the only one shot at. That hadn't gone over very well with Lacy. They'd gone back to the vehicle from the observation point and a heated argument had ensued.

"I'm not leaving you behind," she insisted, while organizing the supplies for her part of the plan.

"I'll be fine," he said dismissively while working on his supplies as well.

"Why can't we stay together?" she asked.

Eric zipped up a large backpack, having finished loading the explosives which he would carry into the hills by himself. Lacy would go south along the ridge to Qary's camp. He'd go north back the way they'd just come to the observation point. From there, he'd go due east to the far side of the valley, hopefully arriving before Lacy got into position.

"We've been over this," he explained sharply. "Qary is the primary focus of the mission now. You have to capture him and get him back to the states. We have to find out if there are missiles and if he knows where they are. When they discover he's gone, all hell is going to break loose around here."

"The reason we need to stay together," Lacy interrupted.

"When they figure out Qary is gone, every soldier in this valley is going to be looking for you," he retorted. "You have to get to the border and into the states before anyone finds you. I have to put myself between you and the soldiers. I can hold them off long enough for you to get away from here."

"You can't hold off a hundred men."

"Row held them off for more than a month. He killed six hundred men in that month until he was captured. When he ran out of bullets, he used their own guns to kill them."

"Is that it? Are you trying to be a hero, like Row?" Lacy seemed to regret the harsh words as her shoulders sagged and her head drooped, showing her young age and inexperience for the first time.

Even then, Eric admired her determination. The fact she wouldn't give in easily was a quality that would serve her well in the upcoming battle which was now inevitable.

"No, I'm not..." Eric stopped himself, trying to regain his composure so he didn't say something he regretted. He took a deep breath to get control of his anger. Lacy meant well. He didn't look forward to getting shot at. He placed his odds of getting out alive at fifty-fifty. Not odds he shared with her. But he'd thought about the plan and tried to figure out a better way. Nothing came to mind. This was the best plan. He knew she wouldn't like it for obvious reasons, but he hadn't expected her to push back as hard as she did.

"I'm not trying to be a hero," he said. "Do you think I look forward to getting shot at by a hundred soldiers?"

"I know. I'm sorry. That's not what I meant," she said in a softer tone.

"Look, everything's going to be okay." He stopped what he was doing to put his hand on her shoulder. "Just get Qary. That's the most important thing. Get him back to the states. I know you can do it."

"This should be our decision. What happened to, 'we are a team?' Row always said there's no I in team. You aren't the only one affected by this decision. If anything happens to you—"

"Nothing's going to happen to me. But I'm the leader. I have to make the decision. And it's final. If we go together, we'll both get caught and die. The whole mission will be a failure." He shook his head. "Not going to happen on my watch."

"We can get Qary together and get away before anyone knows about it."

"You need me to distract them," he said, raising his voice, becoming more annoyed. It was time for Lacy to drop it. If he needed to use a stronger tone with her, he would. "Hopefully, when the soldiers hear the explosions, they'll all run toward it. That's when you nab Qary."

"We can set the explosives together on a timer," she exhorted.

"We have to keep them off the radio. If we do it together, the other soldiers will call it in, and we won't get ten mil-ead down the road before they catch up to us. Trust me. This is the best plan. Your idea was brilliant. Everything about it is great. You just need me to distract them long enough for you to get away. I know what I'm doing. They won't catch me. Hopefully, you can disable the radio when you capture Qary."

Lacy sorted the rest of her gear in silence, obviously not convinced and still steaming.

"Once you have Qary, get back to the car as soon as you can. Don't wait for me. Head straight for the wall," Eric exhorted. "Don't even go back to Ida-Mon. Take the back roads. You're a good driver. I read your file. Don't let them catch you. No matter what."

"You should take all the food supplies," Lacy finally said.

"I have enough to carry as it is. The explosives are going to weigh more than two hundred pounds."

"I'll at least leave the food bin here," she said. "And the extra ammunition. I'll hide them over in the woods. Just in case you need them."

"That's fine." Eric knew he wouldn't be coming back this way. This was too close to the road. He'd stay between the soldiers and the road and hold them off as long as possible. There wouldn't be time to pick up the supplies. When they got close to the road, he'd circle back around behind them and pick off as many as he could and try to get them to chase him in the other direction. Eventually, he'd have to figure out how to get back to the tunnel himself. He had no idea how, but it was something he'd worry about later.

Right now, he needed to focus on what he needed to take with him. No reason to argue with Lacy about something unimportant. Food and water would be the least of his worries. Row had a saying he suddenly remembered. *Pick your battles.* Meaning don't argue about things that weren't important. At least letting her hide the supplies for him would make her feel like she had a voice. A small consolation, and she'd never know the difference anyway.

When everything was packed and they were ready to leave, Eric could tell from the look on her face that she needed a pep talk.

"Look at me," he said strongly, holding her shoulders and forcing her to look him in the eye. "No fear. You can't worry about me. You'll get distracted. Focus on your job. Let me do mine. We are a team. A good team. You're the best I've ever worked with. Make me proud. We're doing something really important today."

"I know," she said, looking away. "Promise me you'll be safe."

"I can't. You know that. That's a promise we can't make. What we do has risks. We do everything we can to minimize them, but they're there. No promises will take them away. Rely on your training and you'll be okay. Two of us are better than a thousand of them. Okay?"

"Okay," she said as she threw her arms around his neck. "I'll be praying for you. The Bible says two can put a thousand to flight. That's what we're going to do today."

"God will be with us," Eric said with determination. He put the backpack over his shoulder and headed up the hill, looking back one last time.

Lacy gave him a slight smile.

"I'll be praying for you too. We're both going to need it." Eric muttered to himself as he disappeared in the woods.

* * *

The terrain on the south side of the hills was much more rugged and rocky than the north had been. Some of the bushes had thistles which Lacy was careful to avoid so as not to break the skin. Though rougher hiking, she didn't spot any patrols. The Naryans seen earlier appeared to be lazy and undisciplined. They'd stay on the other side of the hills, rationalizing that no one would be foolish enough to try to traverse the south side to get to the camp. Or at least that was what she hoped they were thinking.

Underestimating her would be a deadly mistake on their part.

She felt bad about the exchange with Eric. More so because he was right. If she successfully captured Qary, she'd need a head start. Qary was the head of the Naryan armed forces. Getting him to the states was more important than anything else. More important than even their lives. That's what they signed up for. Lived for. They risked their lives so others could remain free. What came with that was a monumental responsibility. One she'd thought about often in training. This wasn't training. This was real life. Real bullets. Real consequences.

Lacy suddenly felt anxiety. Her shoulders tightened. The muscles in her neck, arms, thighs, all tensed in anticipation. She made a conscious effort to relax. The first phase of her mission was about to begin. She had to take out the three snipers. The first was straight ahead of her, hiding behind a rock. Facing out. Looking for a target. Looking for her.

She quietly slipped off her pack and snuck up on him. There was no weapon in her hand. None needed. She'd snap his neck with one move. Before he even knew what had happened.

There was a hesitation. Hers.

Do I have to kill him? He wouldn't hesitate to kill me if he had the chance. What if he has a wife and children? Thoughts she was supposed to put out of her mind in combat.

She was near him now. The point where a decision had to be made. So close she could smell him. His sweat. Days without showering. Tobacco smoke mixed with some type of fish he had for lunch. Probably caught in the stream and then cooked on an open fire.

The moment before killing a man was different than she'd imagined it to be. She'd thought it would be thrilling. Exhilarating. It wasn't. It was cold. Calculating. Emotionless. She felt like a robot.

If she moved both her hands simultaneously, he'd be dead in an instant. One would grab his forehead, the other his chin. A violent jerk in either direction would snap his spinal cord and kill him instantly. In practice, she preferred left hand on right side of head, right hand on chin. Snapping his head to the left. A maneuver Lacy had practiced hundreds of times on a test dummy. This was a real person. His life would be in her hands.

If she only used one hand, a blow just slightly above his right ear, with the palm of her hand, would knock him unconscious for several hours—a blow harder to administer, but highly effective. He'd never know what hit him. Either way. Lights were going out. His fate was sealed. She didn't know which she'd do.

Her senses heightened. Every muscle tensed. Her heart raced. She could feel the beat of her heart in her ears. She was on him in a second. Springing like a cat on a prey. He turned his head slightly toward her from the slight noise of her foot scraping a rock on the ground. Their eyes never met. Thankfully. She'd rather not see his face.

Walking away, she wondered between breaths. Why only one hand? She had let him live. Why? Didn't matter. It was done. She'd figure out the why later.

Two more to go...

The second one was just as easy as the first. Both were in the wrong position.They should have set up against the rocks so no one could sneak up on them. A mistake she took full advantage of. She was relieved she'd shown mercy to both of them. Their deaths were unnecessary. What was the point? They were no threat to her now. A new doctrine was forming in her.

Lacy's rules of engagement.

Always use the least amount of force necessary to achieve your end result. An eye for an eye if necessary. Grace and mercy when possible.

She suddenly remembered some words Row had spoken to them in training. He had said the rules of warfare were complicated. The moral dilemmas were real. She understood it better now. Millions of lives would be saved if she captured Qary. Killing whoever had to be killed was necessary in order to save lives. It suddenly all made sense.

The third sniper heard her when a squirrel made a sound. He turned her way and saw her before she could strike a blow to knock him unconscious. She had no choice. Kill or be killed. She was at peace with it.

He drew his handgun off his hip. Hers was out before he ever had a chance to fire. She'd found a muzzle in the supplies which suppressed the sound.

Her first kill.

He had a radio. She could hear the chatter of the patrols. A hostile had been spotted in the woods, and everyone was scrambling to the northern hills. That was part of the plan. Eric wanted them to see him and then chase him. To the east. Away from her. Into his trap.

A smile came over her face as both of them had executed the first part of their plans perfectly. Now, she had to wait for the second part of the plan.

It wouldn't be long.

Lacy made her way to the base camp where Qary was last seen. She hid in the bushes behind his tent. Ten soldiers, on high alert, paced in front of the tent. Their guns were dutifully raised, and they were looking around with purpose. Qary was obviously inside.

Probably, these were the better soldiers guarding their leader. That made sense. Still a mistake. Some of them should have been guarding the back.

From Lacy's vantage point, she had a good view of the valley and the base camp. Only ten feet away from the back of the tent, she could hear muffled words from inside. Qary was speaking to someone on the radio. A sense of urgency was in his voice. She could hear him ordering soldiers to the northern hills. That's exactly what Eric wanted.

Speak louder so I can hear you.

At that moment, the ground shook. An explosion. On the eastern side of the northern hills. A large plume of smoke billowed into the sky. Lacy hadn't anticipated such a large explosion. The ten soldiers fell to the ground. Qary bolted out of the tent.

This was the perfect opportunity.

Lacy raced from hiding to the back of the tent and slipped under it, suddenly in Qary's headquarters.

She rushed to his desk and hurriedly flipped through the papers where she found plans, and the location of the missiles right in her sight. She quickly memorized them.

There were more explosions.

Qary was barking orders. He sent all but four of the men away toward the explosions. Just like Eric had predicted.

She moved to the front of the tent. Qary walked back that way. She tensed again. *I have to take him alive. Without the soldiers hearing me.*

Qary walked back inside and Lacy bounced from behind. She had to move fast to get her arms in place. It took most trained combatants two seconds to respond to a surprise attack. Her right arm moved around him to his chest. Her left arm slid behind his neck. She pulled him backward toward her. Leaning him back slightly. He was taller. She was on the tip of her toes. Leaning back allowed her right arm to slide under his chin, against his neck. She started squeezing with all her might, cutting off the flow of air to his lungs and blood to his head. She clasped her left hand behind his neck like a vise.

Get him to the ground.

With her left foot, she kicked his left leg out from under him. They fell backward to the ground. Him on top of her. She let out a slight grunt as the ground temporarily knocked the air from her lungs with the weight of him on top of her. Something she was used to. She'd done this many times with bigger, stronger men.

Qary reached his hand toward his neck to her arms. An instinctive reaction. Also a waste of time. His hands should be striking her. Use his elbows or the top of his head to strike blows to get her to loosen her grip. Anything to save his life. Lacy knew from experience that it was too hard to resist moving your hands to the force of contact though and to what was cutting off the supply of air. He'd be weakened by the time he realized he needed to use his hands to try and hit her. If he even knew it was a her. Her grip was stronger than most men's.

More explosions.

Plan two was working. Eric was wreaking havoc with the soldiers. There would be confusion all around. They were ordered to run toward the explosion by Qary. She'd heard him say it on the radio. Still, they didn't know what they were running into.

Then gunfire erupted. Automatic weapons were blasting throughout the valley. She didn't know if any of the gunfire was Eric's or not.

God, keep him safe.

Knowing Eric was facing gunfire emboldened her further. She tightened the grip harder as Qary kicked his feet back and forth. He rolled them over trying to free himself from the grip. She was now on top of him. Still from behind. The grip secure. She wrapped her legs around his to keep him from standing. The grip around his neck was like a boa constrictor. Lacy was careful not to apply it too hard as to do permanent damage to his throat and trachea. If they collapsed, he'd die in a few minutes with no possibility for air. She applied just the right amount of pressure.

She could sense strength fading from him. Her only concern would be if any of the soldiers came back in the tent. All she knew to do was keep him between her and them. Thankfully, they were still outside guarding the tent, unaware of the danger to their leader within. She kept him on the ground, with her behind him. Just in case any soldiers came in. She could bolt to her feet and use her weapon, if necessary.

Finally, Qary quit fighting. His body let out only slight convulsions. He didn't put up enough of a fight to alert the soldiers who were obviously focused on the explosions and gunfire in the hills.

Lacy released her grip and allowed herself a moment to catch her breath. Her heart pounded in her chest. She had to move quickly and secure Qary's hands behind him. She tethered a rope around his neck that would act as a leash. She dragged him across the ground to the back of the tent. Before she left, she grabbed the missile plans off of his desk and disabled the radio.

She slid him under the back of the tent and dragged him into the cover of the bushes behind them. A gag around his mouth prevented him from making any noise. Not that he'd be able to speak for a few minutes. The pressure to his neck certainly bruised his vocal cords.

She went back into the tent and rigged two explosives at the entrance. The flap still hid a view from the soldiers outside. She attached a rope between the two. As soon as the rope moved, it would detonate the two explosives and hopefully take out all soldiers within a hundred-foot radius of the tent.

Lacy then slipped out the back of the tent and paused to look at the northern hills which were now on fire from explosions and gunfire. She went back to where she hid Qary, just as he started to regain consciousness.

"Hi, Qary," she said. "I'm a good friend of Row's. Remember him? It's nice to meet you."

15

Eric was out of bullets. The Naryans weren't, witnessed by the whizzing sound that kept zinging by his ears. The dirt and rocks flew up from the ground around his feet. The classic pop, then a loud whack as bullets hit the trees around him. The explosives set a few hundred feet apart, were the only thing keeping them from overrunning his position. He had one explosive left. The biggest one. He had saved it for last.

This would be his last-ditch effort to save himself.

As he sprinted away from the bomb getting as far away as he could before it detonated, he noticed a familiar bend in the trail. The road was just down the hill, and the vehicle. He hadn't realized he was so far west, so fast. In the fog of battle, losing perspective of time and distance was to be expected. Still... Not part of the plan. He wanted to keep the Naryans as far away from the road as possible.

Panic rose inside of him. Had he waited long enough? Was the vehicle still there? Was he leading them right to Lacy? Or was she already gone? He prayed she was.

He had to look. The bomb would buy him some time. He ran full speed down the hill and came out of the clearing just as Lacy sped away. He waved his arms wildly, but she was already well down the road. Going up and over a hill. Out of sight. Eric stood in the road, his hands flailing around in disbelief. Mixed emotions flooded his soul.

She made it. Thank God.

I almost made it too.

A huge sense of relief came upon him, followed by the realization of how close he came to be driving away with her. If he'd just arrived a minute sooner...

At that moment, the last explosion rocked the mountain, sending boulders cascading down the hill as trees erupted in fire. Eric could hear the screams of Naryans caught in the blast. A crescendo of cries for help echoed through the valley, then silence, then more intense cries and moans from the injured.

His opportunity to escape was before him. The Naryans would be held up for several minutes trying to get through the debris. Probably hesitant to rush forward in case another bomb awaited them. A plan formed in his mind. He should head south. Steal a car. Go to the safe house. Regroup. Let things die down. Then leave for the wall. He'd get there in a couple of days. A week tops.

Lacy...

She must have Qary. *She wouldn't have left me behind unless she had him.* He looked around for evidence. The blown out spare tire was laying on the ground.

Qary's in the trunk!

He has to be. Lacy took the tire out of the trunk to make room for him.

Eric jumped up and down with excitement.

"She did it!" he shouted. "She's amazing."

He quickly calculated in his mind how long it would take her to get to the tunnel. It wasn't enough time. The Naryans would come off of the mountain and flag down one of the patrols. Then use their radio. They'd remember the blue-colored truck. It wouldn't be long before they discovered Qary was gone. They'd close roads to the border. Set up checkpoints.

She needed more time.

Eric looked back up the hill. He needed to keep them away from the road. Lacy had obviously dismantled the radio system. He'd taken a radio off of a dead Naryan. There had been no communications for a long time.

How can I buy her more time?

He was exhausted. His ears rang from the concussion blasts. Small cuts oozed blood, probably from rolling around on the ground dodging gunfire. Maybe the thickets. His ankle throbbed. His back hurt. He wasn't sure why. He didn't remember what had happened to them.

His head was pounding. His heartbeat had only just started to slow.

What can I do?

He remembered Lacy's voice. *I'll leave you the food and the extra ammunition. I'll hide it in the woods.* He vaguely remembered her walking that way. He pointed in the direction he remembered her walking, carrying the supplies.

He ran to the spot, and ignored his body crying out to him to lie down and rest. The ammunition was in the trees right where she said they'd be. Suddenly, he was glad she insisted on leaving it for him.

Thank you, Lacy.

As he reloaded his weapon and put the remaining ammunition in his pockets and belt, he immediately regretted how hard he'd been on her. Her only concern had been for himself and the mission. The vehicle being gone was confirmation that he'd made the right call. Still, he would apologize the next time he saw her.

If I ever see her again.

He took out a FRTE and quickly downed one of the liquid energy packs. Drank two waters, and the cold drink soothed his dry, parched mouth and throat.

Rejuvenated, Eric ran back up the hill toward the enemy with new resolve. At the fork, he continued down the trail toward the smoke and debris from the explosion. As the smoke began to clear, he saw Naryans trying to make their way through the debris. They were throwing rocks, moving logs, climbing over dead bodies, advancing toward him.

He opened fire, killing several. At first, they retreated and ran the other way. Then they started coming in waves. Eric kept firing with purpose. Adrenaline pulsed through his veins. Escape was probably no longer an option. The picture of Lacy crossing the border with Qary, drove him to keep firing. He would stand between the Naryans and Lacy until his last bullet was shot, or he died. Whichever came first.

He held his ground as the Naryans advanced, running back to safety no longer an option for him. He only fired when he had a clear target, saving ammunition. His position wasn't ideal, but the Naryans seemed cautious. Unsure what to do. Leaderless. Seemingly, afraid to move toward him. If they all attacked him at once, they'd overrun him in no time. The first in line would all die. He'd pick them off. They didn't know he couldn't get all of them. He was almost out of ammunition again. He had just reloaded for the last time.

Some of the Naryans regrouped and tried to flank him from below. Stupid mistake. They should have gone to the high ground. That's where he would go now, but he wanted to block the trail and keep them from making it to the road.

He easily cut down the ones below him. A spray of bullets taught them a lesson of warfare they'd never have the chance to learn. Finally, several went to the high ground. Some even managed to get behind him. Instead of going to the road, thankfully, they were still engaged with him. He fired a volley of bullets their way until he ran out. He threw the gun away in exhaustion and laid down.

Until everything went dark.

* * *

Lacy pounded her fist against the steering wheel. The V-7 special forces training motto echoed in her head, *No Man Left Behind.*

"I left him! I left a man behind!" she said. The voice in her head accused her, sending waves of guilt through her mind as the feelings overwhelmed her.

I had no choice. She pushed back against the guilt.

Lacy had waited at the hill as long as she thought she could. Somehow, she managed to get Qary to the truck. She threw the blown-out tire on the ground, bound Qary's legs and then lifted him up and threw him in the trunk.

At first, she was resolved to go find Eric. Help him. Join the fight. They could escape together. She could hear the sound of gunfire just up the hill. They were close and Eric was alive. He had to be. They wouldn't be firing unless he was. She recognized the sound of his gun.

A debate had raged inside of her.

I can't go help him. I have to get Qary to the border. That's more important.

No Man Left Behind.

She remembered a story Row had told them in training. Some Naryans were suspected of making a chemical they were smuggling into the west. A drug that altered a person's mind, caused hallucinations, and a temporary high. Demand had increased as young people were getting hooked on the drug.

Row was tasked with finding the people who were making it. He went undercover with another operative. They went east and found the warehouse. He'd described it as a makeshift temporary building in a bad part of town. They set explosives and destroyed what had become a small factory. A gunfight ensued, and his partner was shot as they tried to run away. His leg was shattered from a bullet that ripped through his flesh. Row was running ahead of him and didn't notice his partner had been shot until he reached the cover of safety.

Row didn't know if he was dead or alive. He just lay there in the middle of the road. Row had a perfect opportunity to escape. He had to make a split-second decision. Fight or flight was how he'd described it.

Instead of fleeing, he rushed back to his partner's side. Bullets were flying. He picked him up, put him over his shoulder, and carried him to safety, saving his life.

When asked why he did it, Row said what was going through his mind were the words, "No Man Left Behind." It became the motto for special forces. Don't leave anyone on the battlefield, something ingrained in them by their trainers.

She left a man behind.

Tears rolled down her face. She wiped them away, angrily. The thought of Eric, alone on the mountain, sent a sharp pain piercing through her soul. One man against an army. Protecting her. He would've never left her. He'd have come back to the fight, if the roles were reversed.

Remember Qary. The missiles. The thoughts became stronger as he tried to overcome the regret.

Row had said there were exceptions to the *No Man Left Behind*. It wasn't black and white. Sometimes the right thing was to save yourself. If there was a more important reason.

She had raised her hand and asked Row the question, "How will you know when it's the right thing?"

"No one can answer that for you," he said. "Not in a classroom. You'll have to trust yourself when you're in the battle. Trust God. Do what you think is right at the moment."

The words resonated. She did what she thought was right at the moment. Getting Qary and the location of the missiles was the most important thing. Row's last words on the topic resonating, *Don't second guess yourself. No regrets.*

She had followed orders. Eric commanded her to leave with Qary if she had the chance. That's what she did. No question, Ted would think she did the right thing. So would Eric. What she did will save lives. If she had died on the hill, the location of the missiles would die with her. The entire planet was at risk. That was more important than one man. More important than Eric.

Time to focus. I'm not safe yet.

Two Naryan patrol cars coming down the road toward her shook her back into reality. She let off of the accelerator to slow down, not wanting to draw attention to herself. She was too far away from the wall to let them call in something suspicious. The two cars didn't seem to be headed anywhere with a purpose. They passed her as she let out a sigh of relief.

One suddenly stopped and then turned around. The other kept going down the road. The one started following her, or at least, it seemed like he was.

Stay cool.

His intentions became clear when he flashed his lights, signaling for her to pull over. Her first instinct was to outrun him, which she could easily do. That wasn't prudent. She couldn't outrun them all to the border. If she ran, he'd get on the radio and call for help.

She pulled to the side of the road—a back road like Eric had told her to stay on. No cars were coming or going. He started walking up to the door. She rolled down the window, moving the gun from the passenger seat into her right hand, hidden under her right thigh. Out of sight of the officer.

She decided not to say anything. The proper response to an officer by a Naryan woman was to speak only when spoken to.

"Your head isn't covered," he said.

Lacy touched her head with her left hand. She forgot. Not even sure she remembered where her scarf was. The backseat, she suddenly remembered. On the floor. She let go of the gun in her right hand and let it fall to the floor. She reached back and felt around on the floor of the backseat until she found it. She quickly wrapped it around her head.

"I'm sorry. I forgot. My husband's not here with me, so I didn't think—"

"Always wear it," he said angrily. "Even if he's not with you."

Lacy knew more and more women in the east were defying the law set by the religious leaders for women to have their heads covered at all times in public. The hardliners were cracking down on all women who dared to go against the authorities. Most officers were hardliners. Lacy wanted to wrap the scarf around his head and make him wear it. The thought almost made her laugh out loud as she pictured it in her mind.

A bang. Pounding. Loud sound. Coming from the trunk.

Qary was banging something against the inside wall. Probably using his bound feet. Maybe his head. His hands were bound behind him.

"What's that noise coming from the trunk?" the patrolman asked.

'I don't know," Lacy said as she opened the door to step out of the car, improving her ability to disarm the patrolman, if necessary. Something that was becoming likely. He wasn't going to let the sound go without a search.

"That's strange," Lacy said, still trying to pretend she didn't know. That guise wouldn't last long.

"Open the trunk," he ordered.

"Let me get the keys," she said and went back to the front seat and retrieved the gun from the floor. When she came back, the officer was focused on the noise coming from the trunk. Lacy pointed the gun at him.

Startled he said, "Wait! Don't shoot." He held his hands in the air.

"Make a wrong move, and I'll shoot you. Step around to the back of your car," she said as she removed his gun from his belt.

"Get your keys," she said. The officer fumbled in his pockets, found them, and held them out toward her.

Lacy kept both hands on the gun which was still pointed steadily at his head. "Go around to the back of your car and open the trunk," she said firmly.

He followed her instructions, nervously looking at the gun, then nervously looking at the trunk. Probably realizing what the sound coming from the trunk was. A horrible situation he was about to find himself in.

"Now, get in there."

He started to protest.

"Now!" she shouted.

She closed the trunk lid and threw the keys into a field off the road. She shot a hole in the tire. The sound of gunfire caused a loud squeal from the trunk. She opened the door and ripped the radio off the dash and threw it into the field as well.

Out of the corner of her eye, she caught a glimpse of the other patrol car coming back toward them. Lacy rushed back to her car, threw the scarf off of her head and started the car. The tires squealed as she sped away.

In her rearview mirror, she could see the other patrol car stop by the other car. She hoped he would get out of the car to find out what had happened. Instead, he turned on his overhead lights and started driving her way.

"Hold on, Qary," Lacy shouted. "The ride is about to get very interesting!"

16

Back in the West

I've been shot at, tortured, and beaten to within an inch of my life. I've gone days without food, water, and sleep. Been sweltering hot and bone-chilling cold. Endured some of the worst conditions humanly imaginable.

This is worse.

I sat in my car waiting for my six o'clock dinner date with Hope, my hand was shaking, my mouth was dry, and I was fidgeting because I was fifteen minutes early. I thought it rude to arrive at her house early, so I parked down the street away from her house. She could still be getting ready, straightening the house, preparing the meal. I was always early for business meetings. This was different. Everything had to be timed perfectly. I would knock on the door of her trove at exactly six.

Why am I so nervous?

The neighborhood was modest but cozy. A dead-end street that ended in a large circle with probably thirty troves lining the road. The sun was setting. Children were playing in the yards and in the street. A typical Ven-Us setting in every way. At least in the west. Several cars were parked in front of a house. Probably a church Bible study or possibly a fellowship. Maybe a birthday party or anniversary. A couple of cars passed. Likely fathers coming home from work, I deduced as I saw a kid run into her father's arms when she saw him. It brought a smile to my face until I thought of my daughter, causing unwanted feelings I quickly tamped down.

I looked at the timepiece on my wrist. It was one minute later than the last time I looked. The seconds seemed to be ticking slower than normal. The closer the clock came to six, the more anxiety built up in me. I took a deep breath and let it out slowly. Then I closed my eyes for a moment and tried to clear my mind.

It didn't help.

I thought of Mia. I think she would approve of my date. And approve of Hope. I could see them being best friends if Mia was still alive. I was determined not to bring Mia up tonight in conversation. Women don't want to hear about a wife on a first date. Not my wife... my ex-wife. Not ex... dead. The problem was how I would describe Mia to someone. I'd never called Mia anything but my wife, even after all these years. How could I explain that? Especially, how much I still loved her and missed her.

Could my heart love two people at the same time? Was it fair to Hope? I think she'd understand, but how could I be sure? I was glad dinner was at her trove. I still had pictures of Mia prominently displayed in my trove. Should I take them down? Did Hope even know I was married before? Did she know I had a daughter?

I tried to dismiss the thoughts. They were making me more nervous.

Think about something else.

Eric and Lacy... We hadn't heard from them. Definitely, not a topic to calm my nerves. I suddenly realized how Ted felt all those years back when I was out in the field. Not knowing was the hardest thing. I'd much rather be in the middle of it, knowing in real time what was happening, rather than sitting here waiting.

It never seemed to bother Ted. To some he was the most uncaring person they'd ever met. That wasn't fair. He wasn't uncaring. He cared about the mission as much as anyone. And the people in it. He just always had control of his emotions and never let anyone see them. I used to be good at that too.

That's what I needed to do now as I squinted and forced my eyebrows down and closer together. I pursed my lips into a serious frown. I needed to get control of my emotions. Presenting a calm demeanor to Hope was a priority.

I wanted to be warm, but distant, trying to create a calculus like I did on missions. Careful. Emotionless. Aloof.

Are you crazy? That's not what Hope wants in a guy.

"This date is going to be a disaster," I told myself. "Maybe I should call and cancel. Tell her something came up. I'm sick." My thoughts swirled around in my head.

I picked up my air-line and seriously considered calling her. I started dialing the number then stopped. That would be inconsiderate. She'd gone to all the trouble to prepare a meal. She'd think I was a flake. That's not fair to her. I decided that I could endure a couple hours together with her.

Pull yourself together.

I'm sick. Something is seriously wrong with me.

A counselor had said as much. Every year in the field, we were required to come home for a month and endure four counseling sessions. I thought they were a waste of time. I was fine. The counselor always wanted to know how I felt. How did it feel to get shot at? To kill another man. Such stupid questions. *How do you think it felt?* Part of the problem... It felt good to me. I liked it. Felt no remorse at all. I was afraid to tell her.

I finally told her as much in the last session, when I opened up a little. "In the field, most people don't let themselves feel anything," I had explained. "They become numb. A robot. A killing machine. I feel just the opposite. I become alive. Energized. The more people I kill, the better I feel. Not better. That's the wrong word. Satisfied. I rationalize it. I'm doing something good for my country. But it's more than that. I think something's wrong with me, but I don't want to admit it."

The counselor, a woman, diagnosed me as having a sotomoform disorder. The ability to compartmentalize my feelings into action.

She called it *backlash*. When stress became overwhelming or too intense, I organized the stress into energy. It then propelled me into action. Some people break down from the stress. Become immobilized. Paralyzed with fear. Afraid to make a decision. I become more efficient. More competent. More fearless. Which was why I was the best at what I did.

"That's not really who you are," she said. She was concerned that I was losing my heart and my ability to care for others. She felt like I might lose myself completely if I stayed in the field much longer. She recommended to my supervisors that they take me out of the field.

I stayed five more years because I was too effective an operative. The counseling was not to get me out of the field but to make sure I was effective *in* the field. They liked what they heard from her. All she did was confirm what they already knew. I was a focused and determined operative. They were encouraged. I dismissed it as psychobabble. Now, I wasn't so sure.

Five minutes to six.

I started the car. I'd wait until one minute and thirty seconds to six before I'd drive to her trove. I'd brought wine. I checked and double checked the bag to make sure it was still there, like I used to check and double check my ammunition. My knife. My supplies. As if they would suddenly disappear.

The wine was still there.

I put a mint in my mouth. Two more in my pocket. I'd written out notes for topics of discussion. I pulled them out of the center console and refreshed my memory. Do you like pets? Where did you grow up? Favorite movie? Favorite air-box show? Do you like the old songs or new? I hoped she liked old songs. Favorite foods? Any brothers or sisters?

Three minutes to six.

I'm being ridiculous.

I should go ahead and go. Maybe her clock is fast. I don't want to be late.

One minute early isn't going to hurt anything if I was wrong. I pulled forward, slowly accelerating. Stopped in front of her trove —white on the outside, a metal roof like all troves on Ven-Us. The white paint and the metal reflect the sun's rays away from the trove and is easier to cool. Her house faced west. With beautiful views of the mountain. The house looked like Hope. Warm and friendly. Flowerpots on the porch. Carefully manicured lawn but not over-done with too much landscaping. A welcome sign over the door. Nothing fancy. Everything understated. Just like her. Dinner would probably be very basic. I liked basic.

I opened the car door, picked up the bag with the wine and started walking with purpose, suddenly feeling better.

The nervousness and stress organized into energy, into resolve. I knocked on the door. I'd planned how I would knock. Two knocks and then a pause, then a synchronized two beats. A friendly, comedic, knock, executed perfectly.

The nervousness returned, only stronger than before. So much for that counselor. "What does she know?" I mused. She obviously had never been on a first date, at least the first in twenty years.

The door opened. Hope smiled. She seemed happy to see me. Then she gave me a warm hug and a soft kiss on the cheek. She took my hand and led me inside.

I suddenly felt much better.

* * *

Dinner was nothing like what I expected.

Hope had a tray of appetizers ready for me. Brie cheese tarts, lightly breaded and fried then dipped in a special sauce. A meal all by itself. Delicious. One of the best things I'd ever put in my mouth.

Next was light conversation. I went through my list.

"Do you have any pets?"

"No, but I love dogs."

"Little or big?"

"Little. Inside dogs. That don't shed. I'm allergic."

"Where did you grow up?"

"Lived here all my life."

"Favorite movie?"

"The Winds of Change."

That figures. Most women love that movie.

"Favorite air-box show?"

"I don't have an air-box." I looked around the open room. There was no air-box. I hadn't noticed.

How do you get your news? Weather? Sports? Questions I wanted to ask but didn't. A little strange to me that she didn't have an air-box.

"I prefer to read," she said.

"Favorite book?"

"The Bible."

"Besides the Bible?"

"Smith's Bible Commentary."

I laughed. She wasn't offended. She knows she's different. *So am I.*

"I prefer the Abridged Bible Commentary," I said.

"I like that one too," she said warmly.

I suddenly drew a blank. I've only been here ten minutes, and I'm out of questions to ask. *Did I forget any?* It seemed like I had more prepared.

Favorite songs, I suddenly remembered.

It didn't matter. She started asking her questions. I wondered if she'd also made a list. The conversation never hit an awkward pause. My fears were unnecessary. We talked non-stop until time to eat.

As was tradition, the meal began with a communion. Jesus said, "as often as you eat and drink, do this in remembrance of me." On Ven-Us we took that to mean, every meal.

We broke bread, took a drink of wine, and prayed blessings upon the meal. It felt comfortable, normal.

Then came a salad of mixed greens with chestnuts, tomatoes, diced carrots, candied pecans, and homemade dressing. Her grandmother's recipe.

She told me she'd worked her way through college as a chef at a famous restaurant. She was joking when she had said she didn't know how to cook.

I was so glad I hadn't cancelled. She never would've forgiven me if I had stood her up. She had spent hours preparing the meal. I felt guilty that I'd even thought about cancelling.

She described the main course as beef tenderloins baked in a tarragon butter sauce, with sweet peppers, zucchini, and onions, cheese mashed potatoes with chives, and crème fraize, on the side. The most common dish on Ven-Us. Her own recipe. The best I'd ever had.

I kept complimenting her profusely throughout the meal. I could tell she was shy, embarrassed even, though clearly appreciative. She gave a slight smile, confirming she was glad the meal had gone well as I helped her move the dishes off the table to the sink.

She suggested we step away from the table and turned out the light in the kitchen then lit a candle. It flickered on the counter, casting a calm and peaceful shadow over the room that was now mostly dark as the sun had finally set to the west.

We moved over to the couch. Waddled might be a better description. I was stuffed.

"What's for dessert?" I asked.

"Nothing!" she said with a laugh. "I have some iced cream in the freezer if you're still hungry."

"I'm glad. To be honest. I don't think I could eat another thing."

She moved closer to me.

I put my right arm around her.

She laid her head on my shoulder, which seemed natural. We both let out a sigh at the same time. It occurred to me that she'd been nervous too. She wanted the night to be perfect. Clearly. She'd gone to so much effort for me. It turned out perfect.

"I'm so glad we did this," I said.

"Me too," she said sweetly. "I like you."

She lifted her head off my shoulder and turned toward me. Slowly. Deliberately. Cautious, but with confidence.

I placed my hand on her outer left thigh.

She brushed her hair aside as she looked into my eyes, tenderly and affectionately.

My right hand moved to behind her head and gently directed it toward me.

Our lips came together, purposefully. Softly at first. I closed my eyes, savoring the moment. A feeling flowed through me like electricity. I could feel her energy as she increased the intensity of her kisses.

Passion. Desire. Romance. Feelings... Release.

For me. Twenty years of pent up love unable to be expressed was suddenly released from its prison where it had been locked in.

I lost control of the feelings and began kissing her more passionately. She changed her position, so her body was closer to mine. So, I could hold her tighter.

I had no idea how long it lasted, but suddenly our lips parted. We both let out a huge breath.

She looked down as if she couldn't believe how good it felt. Unable to look me in the eye. I wondered if it could ever be that good between us again. A first kiss. We'd never have another. I wanted to remember every second.

I took her hand and said, "That felt good."

She turned toward me. "It did," she said emphatically. "It's been a long time for me."

"Twenty years for me," I confessed.

"Really?" she asked, surprised.

It all came out like a flood. Mia. My daughter. The loss. The subject I had wanted to avoid. I'd never dated. Mia was the only person I'd ever kissed. Until tonight. The only person I'd ever loved.

Until tonight.

She was understanding and hadn't known about the bomber. Only knew I was married once before and she had died. Hope was tender. Gentle. Asked what Mia was like. How long we were married. She asked about my sweet little Meg. I showed her a picture of both of them, together.

"She looks like her mother," she said.

I nodded.

It was okay that we talked about it. It seemed right.

We kissed again. She started it—like she wanted to make me feel better. Take the hurt from me. Let me know that someone could love me again. If I'd let them. Let her...

She stroked my arm.

I ran my fingers through her hair.

She settled back down on my shoulder. Closer. More relaxed. Let herself completely go so all her weight was resting on me.

The evening was perfect.

Until my air-line vibrated.

I kept it in my pocket. A call at the worst possible time. I didn't answer it. I was supposed to always look. I had to be available at all times. Technically, I was even supposed to have my gun on me right now. But how could I explain that to Hope? Why would a seminary dean be carrying a gun?

A few seconds later, a ding signified a voicemail. Then an air-message. A special ding warned me it was urgent.

I pulled the air-line out of my pocket. My heart jumped. Ted.

Call me! Urgent. Now!

"Who's that?" Hope asked, obviously seeing the message.

How could I lie to her after the moment we'd just shared? I couldn't. That's not how I wanted to start our relationship.

"It's my boss," I said.

"At the seminary?" she asked. "What could be so urgent so late at night?"

"Not that boss. I have another one. Can I explain later? I need to call him back," I said.

I stayed on the couch, next to her. She wasn't supposed to hear the call, but it didn't feel right leaving her. She wouldn't understand.

"Lacy's back," Ted said with no emotion evident in his voice.

My heart sank. He didn't say, *Lacy and Eric*.

"She has Qary!" he continued with more emphasis.

I stood straight up from the couch.

"What? I don't know what you mean."

"Lacy kidnapped Qary and brought him back here."

"Kidnapped," I said loudly.

Hope jumped. A concerned look of fear flashed across her face. I wondered how the one side of the conversation sounded to her.

"She brought him back through the tunnel. He's in a holding room."

"At headquarters?" I asked. Still not believing what I was hearing.

"He's here. Lacy got the plans for the missiles. We know where they are. They're not in Push-On. That was all a ruse to get you to go there. A trap set for you."

Suddenly, the anger returned, overwhelming the joy I'd felt only moments before.

"I need you to go with Lacy and take out the missiles," he said.

"What about Eric?" I asked hesitantly.

"We don't know where he is."

"Is he dead?" I asked.

Hope's eyes were as big as coins. Her mouth agape. I stood from the sofa.

"We don't know. There was a big gunfight. Lacy had to leave him behind. To get Qary back here."

"She did the right thing."

"How soon can you get here?"

"I'll leave right now," I said, as I looked at Hope and shrugged my shoulders.

"Is Qary talking?" I couldn't help but ask. The words blurted out before I thought of the consequences of Hope hearing them.

"No. As you can imagine, he won't say a word."

"Give me five minutes with him. I'll make him talk. I'll beat the hell out of him, like he beat me. I'll kill the son-of-a-bitch," I said with such vitriol.

It startled Hope.

I knew my eyes were full of fire. My fist balled. My shoulders tensed. I'd suddenly transformed into a madman.

Hope stood from the couch as well and walked to the other side of the room—away from me. Seemingly afraid. Probably totally confused. Wondering who this person was she'd just kissed and was starting to fall for.

A rush of regret flooded through me. This was why I didn't get close to anyone. If they really knew me, they wouldn't like who I'd become. Better for Hope anyway. I had a mission bigger than her. I had to get to the missiles and take them out before they killed everyone. She'd just have to understand. She deserved better. I had too many demons. I was too messed up inside.

I hung up my air-line. Immediately apologetic, but cold. Aloof. Trying to put distance between us. I could see her shaking. That caused me to soften my tone.

"I'm sorry," I said.

"I don't understand," she retorted. "Who were you talking to? Who are you? Why are you going to beat that man up? Who are you going to kill? Who was kidnapped? Are you some kind of criminal? You need to leave." The questions came as rapid fire as a machine gun. The candle now threw an eerie, frightening shadow over the room.

"I can explain," I said as I took two steps toward her.

"No!" she shouted as she moved further back against the wall. She put her left hand up and out in front of her to stop me. "Just leave," she said, as tears formed in her eyes, her lips quivered, her body shook and her voice cracked.

I hesitated too long, wanting to explain.

"Get out! Now!" she finally shouted angrily.

I grabbed my things and rushed to the door. I didn't know what to say. Thanks for the dinner seemed so inappropriate.

"It's not what you think," I said. "But I have to go."

Tears were streaming down her face.

I ignored them.

Her words were harsh. I felt a new loss. I blamed Qary. Anger rose in me like a volcano ready to erupt. Eric was missing. There were missiles after all. The destruction of the planet became front and center in my mind. Suddenly I felt unbelievable stress. I instinctively knew what to do with it. All of it was now channeled into focus, energy, resolve, revenge.

Fire and brimstone.

Backlash.

PART TWO

17

Thirty years later (Ven-te 2230)

"Can u talk?" the V message that lit up on my air-line said.

"I'm walking into a meeting," I responded.

"It's important," my son Seth replied. He was a student at the seminary where I was dean for almost thirty-five years.

"My meeting is with the President. Is it more important than the national security of the United Ven-us States?" I was Minister of Defense in charge of all the armed forces of the UVS. I met weekly with the President to discuss national security issues. The agenda for today's meeting was particularly important.

"LGN"

I recently learned it's the young people's way of saying, "I'm laughing."

"Talk to your mom."

"WD"

I've known for a while WD means, "will do."

We had three kids. Our oldest son, Rowan, Jr., was a SOS, special operations officer, primarily assigned to the east. Relations had thawed considerably with the Naryans, so his operations were mostly intelligence gathering. He had never been shot at. Thankfully. Our daughter, a stay-at-trove mom with two young kids, jokes that she gets shot at every day. Her husband was the pastor of a local church.

In one month, I would turn seventy years old. I suspected my wife was planning a big surprise birthday party even though I insisted I didn't want one. While I appreciated the sentiment, my mind was on bigger matters. This meeting being the most prominent matter concerning me.

I struggled to get out of the chair of the waiting area, which had plush cushions that I sank into. After pausing to gain my balance, sticking my hands out like a blind person to steady myself, I slowly walked through two double doors into the office of the President each step getting easier as my body gained momentum. Sarah Hatch-Ard Rob-inson stood from behind her large, red oak desk and walked around it to greet me warmly.

When Sarah was elected the first woman president of the UVS, three years before with sixty-three percent of the vote, she called me out of the blue and asked if I would consider serving as her Minister of Defense. I had a saying that went way back, "If your country asks you to do something, then you do it, if it is within your power to do so." I agreed even though I felt there were many others far more qualified which I expressed to her, but she insisted.

Until the call, it had been many years since I'd heard from her. Twenty something years since she graduated from seminary. The one where I was dean and Seth now attended.

The office was newly constructed in a pie shape. A unique design that others were skeptical of. Her idea, I think, and it turned out great from my perspective. A definite improvement from the past president's offices, which I had been in many times. When Sarah became president, she added a woman's touch to what were the administrative offices of the president and vice president and also her personal residence. An ambitious remodel which had produced amazing results. The "people's trove," as it was commonly known, had not been renovated in years. Sarah thought the country deserved a trove they could be proud of. She had certainly made it so, from where I was sitting.

She'd started tours of the building. When I arrived that day, I saw hundreds of tourists lined up to get free tickets to the tour. Her personal residence and the pie shaped office were not part of the tour.

Only private parties were allowed in those areas. My wife and I had spent several nights in the Red-Ford Bedroom. The most famous bedroom in the house where President Red-Ford passed away after a lengthy illness. Probably the most beloved of all presidents of our past, although Sarah was matching his popularity at least in the first three years of her six-year term.

After a few pleasantries, Sarah got right down to business.

"What is your assessment of Qary?" she asked.

"Surprisingly positive," I replied.

"My thoughts as well. He seems to be implementing some of the reforms he promised."

"I was extremely skeptical when he rose to power," I said. "It's been almost twenty years. and my worst fears have not materialized."

More than twenty years ago, Qary led a coup to overthrow the leaders of the Naryan Nation. With the strong loyalty he had developed over the years as the leader of the military, the coup was fairly easy to attain as all of the officers in the military sided with him and supported the coup. He took the title of Supreme Commander and began waging war with the west. A war that only succeeded in costing his country much of their riches while resources were diverted from the good of the people to the expansion of his military.

"I think he's losing some grip on his power," Sarah said. "I don't know if that's good or bad."

"Sometimes the devil you know is better than the devil you don't know," I added.

"Recently, he seems to have softened his stance and had made peaceful overtures to the west," I continued. "Perhaps a last-ditch effort to retain power. We're trying to assess whether the suggestions were sincere or simply a scheme to get us to let our guard down."

"He's tried to set traps before, as you are fully aware," she said.

"Do you have the border wall numbers I asked for?" she asked, changing the direction of the conversation.

"Of course." I opened my notebook and began reading some statistics.

"Over the last year, 5,123 Naryans have defected to the west. There have been 143 deaths in the east from people trying to scale the wall. That's down from 575 the previous year."

"That's a positive improvement. I knew the numbers were down. I just didn't realize they were down that much."

"I think it's because Qary has loosened the restrictions at the border wall. He's changed the policy to allow more people to move freely through the wall."

I paused to see if Sarah had any questions. I didn't figure she would. I wasn't telling her anything she didn't already know. These meetings were often repetitive. The weekly assessment didn't change much unless something major happened. With no questions forthcoming, I continued.

"The diplomatic trove we set up in Ida-Mon is now fully functioning, and they are leaving our diplomats alone. There have been no major incidents over the past year. We've been monitoring their trove in the UVS, and we're seeing no illegal activities. We monitor all their communications to the east, and we've seen nothing nefarious."

"I'm sure they know we're listening," she said.

I only nodded. My thoughts were ahead of the conversation.

"Here's the thing," I said, getting right to the reason for the meeting and something that would be a brand-new idea. "This battle between the east and the west has been going for more than two thousand years. If there's any opportunity for peace, I think we should pursue it."

"How would you suggest we do that?" the President asked.

"I think we should invite Qary here for a peace summit."

"To the west?" she said, her eyes widening in surprise.

"Why not? The worst he could say is no. Maybe he says yes. Let's look him in the eyes. See what his true intentions are."

Sarah paused, evidently thinking about all the ramifications.

Before she could speak, I added, "I was reading about Casik and Nary in the Bible. Do you remember the story of how they met after their father Hamm died?"

"I do remember, but it's been awhile since I read it," she said.

"Let me remind you of the story." I began telling it, not waiting for her approval.

* * *

Ancient times (Ven-te 227) At the time of Casik and Nary

Casik sent word to his brother, Nary, that their father, Hamm, had died. Nary traveled to the west and helped his brother bury their father. After the funeral, Nary said, "Out of respect for my father, I will let you live. For seven days. We will grieve the death of our father. After that, I will return to the west, and I will kill you."

Casik didn't respond, not wanting to provoke confrontation sooner. He needed time to prepare a defensive plan.

Nary left without another word. Casik relayed the conversation to his mother, Terah, who responded in fear.

"You must leave at once. Pack all your possessions and get as far away as possible," she said strongly.

"You know Nary," Casik retorted. "He'll chase me to the ends of Ven-Us. There is no place where I would be safe. I have a different plan."

"What plan?" his mother asked.

"I'm going to give him half of the possessions my father gave me when he spoke the blessing over us. That way, he will have gotten what he thinks is his rightful birthright."

"Those rightfully belong to you," she said.

"I know. But God has blessed our possessions. We now have double what father gave me. Nary will be stealing what is not his. God told Hamm to give them to me. I am exchanging them for my life. That really means they have been stolen. The Lord God will replace what is stolen from us seven-fold as the Word of the Lord says. If we give, it will be given back to us."

"Nary doesn't care about possessions," Terah replied. "He just wants revenge. What makes you think he won't kill you and then take all your possessions?"

"The Lord God will protect me. He will change Nary's heart. I am the child of promise. I know who I am. God raised me from the dead. He did not raise me to die at the hand of an unbeliever. I think this plan will work."

Terah seemed unconvinced, but Casik was determined to carry out his plan.

After seven days, Casik sent his servants with the possessions to meet Nary who was walking toward the west, likely to kill Casik. He followed behind his servants by a quarter of a mil-ead. Far enough away to still see and hear what was happening but disguised so Nary wouldn't know it was him.

Nary came toward the servants with about four hundred armed men. It seemed like he was about to order his men to attack the servants but stopped, perhaps because he saw the flocks and herds with them because the first thing he said was, "What is the meaning of all these flocks and herds?"

"For Casik, to find favor in your eyes," the servant who Casik designated to speak for him said. "He wants to give you the rest of the firstborn inheritance."

At that moment, Casik removed his disguise and started walking toward Nary confidently, his shoulders back, his head held high. Unafraid.

Nary saw Casik and ran past the servants with the four hundred men trailing behind him. Their swords were drawn, ready for battle, but Nary's sword wasn't drawn.

Casik felt no fear, even though Nary and his men were running toward him. He didn't move. He trusted in God. As Nary neared, Casik set his feet and braced himself for the attack that never came.

Instead of hitting him, Nary threw his arms around Casik's neck and kissed him. He kept saying "I'm sorry" over and over again.

They both wept.

"I'm sorry, too!" Casik said between sobs the years of anger and hatred suddenly released by the gift. By God miraculously softening Nary's heart.

Casik said, "I want you to have the flocks and herds and possessions, so that you have the possessions of the first born."

"I already have plenty, my brother. Keep what you have for yourself," Nary said.

"No please!" Casik insisted. "If I have found favor in your eyes, accept this gift from me. For to see your face is like seeing the face of God, now that you have received me favorably. Please accept the present that was brought to you, for God has been gracious to me, and I have all I need."

Because Casik insisted, Nary accepted it. They ate a meal together that night in Casik's camp.

The next day, they met at the rock. They agreed to a covenant between them. No more wars. They carved on the rock the words, *So Were Casik and Nary*, right under the words *Adam and Eve were here*.

There was peace... Between the west and the east. For the first time.

They only wished their father had lived long enough to see it.

* * *

Now (2230)

"Qary said yes," Sarah said enthusiastically.

We were back in her office, for the weekly briefing. She'd send a messenger to Nary, inviting him to a peace summit in the west

"Really?" I couldn't believe what I was hearing. I never expected Qary to agree to a meeting in the west. "He's willing to meet here?"

"He is," Sarah said. "Maybe he really is serious about peace."

"Remember the story I told you about Casik and Nary. The peace they forged. That was so unexpected to Casik. That was the last time the two sides have ever come together. We've been at war ever since. You'll make history with this peace summit. Maybe God can change Qary's heart the same way he changed Nary's. This is exciting. Historic. I can hardly believe it."

Sarah said, "I want you to be there. In the meetings. They're going to be in three months. We are calling them the Ven-Us Great Wall Peace Summit. The meeting will be in Freed-Om Square. We will erect a makeshift building. This will be the biggest event on Ven-Us in centuries. Maybe a lasting peace can come from it."

"Let's pray that happens."

"How do you feel being in the same room with Qary? Remember what happened last time?" Sarah asked hesitantly.

"I remember," I said as my mind wandered into the deep recesses of a time, I'd tried so hard to forget.

18

(Ven-te 2200)

I sped away from Hope's trove, enraged. My emotions fishtailed sideways like my car when I almost sideswiped a four-door sedan coming into the neighborhood as I sped out.

I blamed Qary.

Hope was the best thing that had happened to me in twenty years, and now I'd lost her. I could see it on her face. She was afraid of me. She saw who I was and what I had become. In the same way I'd lost Mia and Meg before, I've lost her forever. Hope and I would've had a future. I was certain of it. Now that future was gone. Ripped away from me, just like Mia and Meg were suddenly ripped away from me twenty years ago.

By Qary. Everything bad that had happened in my life was because of him.

Rage wasn't building inside of me. I was already a raging furnace, like the flames licking outside of the fireplace threatening to destroy the whole structure. I didn't know if I could hold it in for the thirty-minute drive. The powerful emotion wanted revenge. My shoulders were tense, both of my hands gripped the steering wheel like a vise. I only had to contain myself and hold in the rage for a few more minutes. I would get the release. When I killed him.

The counselor had warned me. "If you don't leave the field, the pressure will get so great, you will eventually lose yourself, your moral compass, and your sanity."

I was on the edge of doing just that.

Unlike most people, when this level of stress happens, my mind grows more alert. Most people break down, are hospitalized, and put on medication. For me, everything slows down. It's like I see the world in slow motion. Every detail becomes enhanced, like the zoom lens on a camera that can focus on an object, making it closer than it actually is. This is very helpful on the battlefield. I can see everything. Who's getting ready to fire, the enemies' next move. I know when to move forward, when to retreat. When to fire, when to wait.

"What's wrong with that?" I had asked the counselor. "It makes me good at what I do."

"Your brain processes information under stress so fast, it risks overheating, like a computer not getting enough ventilation. Like a malfunctioning pressure cooker that will eventually explode. It's physically impossible for you to maintain that level of stress for that length of time."

That's what was happening now. I felt like a pressure cooker.

What was wrong with that? I already had my plan developed. That fast. I'd take three guns into headquarters. Qary would still be in a holding room near Ted's office, waiting for questioning. I'd see Ted first and find out where the missiles were being constructed. He'd already have a vehicle ready for us in the basement, full of explosives, guns, ammunition, and supplies. He'd want me to meet with Lacy to make sure she was in the right frame of mind to go on another stressful mission right away.

It wouldn't matter. She wasn't going. I was going alone. I wouldn't tell him or Lacy that. It was the only way.

I would play along and make them believe everything was normal with me. I'll make Ted think I'm in the right frame of mind to go on the mission.

I knew I wasn't, but I'd get the job done. At what cost, I wasn't sure.

I focused back on the plan. I'd insist on seeing Qary. Ted would say it wasn't a good idea. I'd protest. Eventually, he'd give in. I can hear him say I deserved to see him, considering the hell he'd put me through. Ted would want my gun. After I gave it to him, he'd ask for the other one, knowing I would have more than one on me. He wouldn't think I'd have three.

I'd walk into the room where there would be one table and two chairs. Nothing else. I'd sit across from Qary, look him in the eye, wait for him to open his mouth, and then shoot him between the eyes. Without saying a word. I wouldn't give him the satisfaction of hearing my voice.

I could see the whole thing clearly in my mind. Like a movie playing in a theatre or on an air-box. I smiled at the thought of seeing Qary lying dead on the floor.

Blue and red lights alternating in my rearview mirror caused me to mentally push pause on the movie. I was traveling well over a hundred mil-ead per hour. Somehow, the police officer had managed to catch up to me. No problem. I'd pull over, flash my credentials. It's a national security emergency. He would let me go on my way, maybe even offer to escort me.

Right now, the counselor had said, *you're good at what you do, even great. Eventually, the stress will become so intense, you'll start acting irrationally.*

I wanted to make the trip alone. The officer would cost me some time. Rather than pulling over, I turned my vehicle sharply to the left, fishtailing, struggling to hold the road. I accelerated quickly, not realizing I had turned onto a one-way street, going the wrong way. Headlights were coming toward me. I dodged the first car, and then sharply turned right on the first street, nearly hitting the lamppost. I accelerated faster, ignoring the street signs. The buildings were a blur as my car flew past them at unbelievable and unsafe speeds.

I took the next curve, barely slowing down. I gripped the wheel hard, trying to maintain control. Afraid I was going to catapult off the road where I would probably roll a dozen times in the field. Something I caught a glimpse of out of the corner of my eye. Somehow, the car that was not built for such abuse, managed to make the curve as the tires re-established their grip.

The officer was nowhere in sight. I'd lost him. I let out a huge breath.

The long stretch of road I found myself on allowed me to play another movie in my mind. They were stored there, like old home movies stored in a cabinet or an attic. Pulled out on special occasions, like reunions and such to reminisce and remember the good times in the past. My movies would never want to be played at a reunion. They were too horrid to watch.

Mia and Meg were walking on Freed-Om Square, hand-in-hand. They were laughing. Meg was skipping around, pulling her mommy from one site to another. I can see the bomber. His eyes are darting to and fro. Unsure. Afraid. Then resolve comes on his face. He moves his hand to the vest and pulls a chord. An explosion erupts. Shards of brads, nails, pieces of metal, coated with acid, accelerate at an unbelievable pace into unsuspecting men, women, and children.

The movie ends. I don't allow myself to see the carnage.

Eventually, the memories will become so overwhelming, you won't be able to differentiate between what's real and what's not real. It's like people who watch horror movies. They become numb to reality. Unfortunately, you have seen the horror in real life.

The counselor had warned me, but I didn't listen.

The movies in my mind were vivid, full color, as if they were happening at that moment. Qary was always in my movies. I saw him in Freed-Om square, standing on the side, watching the bomber, laughing.

I see him in the prison movie. In real life and in my movie, he never actually touched me. He ordered everyone else to do horrible, unspeakable things, and then watched as they did them. Laughing diabolically. He was a madman. Inhuman. No rational person could ever do such a thing to another human being. Qary kept coming up with more sadistic ways to hurt me. He ordered my hands tied behind my back for days at a time. So tight, my shoulder dislocated. I banged it against the wall, hard enough and at just the right angle to push it back into place. The pain was excruciating. I had refused to cry.

"Why was that?" I asked the counselor.

"It's your defense mechanism," she said. "Row, you have a strong will to live. You feel that if you express emotion, then you will have given in. Eventually, you will become incapable of feeling emotions, good or bad."

In my movies, I can't actually feel the pain. The counselor said that would happen. I'd bury the hurt so deep, I wouldn't remember the pain. I'd only remember what caused it. Disassociation was her term for it. A disorder that would eventually lead to pathological and obsessive behaviors. It might even lead to memory loss.

I haven't been that lucky. I remember everything, vividly.

You will lose your heart, she said soberly.

The words echoed as I pulled into the parking space at the building, banging the car against the curve but barely noticing. I took my gun from the storage area inside my car and placed it on my hip. I went to my trunk and pulled out a second gun and placed it in my pocket. The third and smallest gun would be placed in my sock. Not yet. I had to go through security first.

I took a deep breath, pushed the movies out of my mind, and walked into the building, through the four levels of security, and into Ted's office. Perfectly composed and calm, resolved, and ready to go on the mission.

"When do we leave?" I said.

"Tonight," Ted said. "A truck is down in the basement. It has everything you need. Go talk to Lacy. She's in the conference room. Make sure she's in the right frame of mind to go. She's been through a lot."

"Still no word from Eric?" I asked.

"Nothing. I wouldn't expect to hear from him yet. He was in a big gunfight in the valley. She could hear it as she was driving away. I don't know what to think. Just hoping for the best."

I left Ted's office and took the short walk to the conference room.

Lacy wasn't sitting down. She was pacing back and forth, wringing her hands. A look of relief came over her face when she saw me and then guilt, as her shoulders sagged, and her head turned down. Maybe she was afraid I'd judge her for leaving Eric behind.

"How are you holding up?" I asked matter-of-factly. I didn't feel any emotions. I wanted her to learn how to do the same. If she was looking for comfort from me, she wouldn't get it.

"I'm okay, Row," she said as she straightened her shoulders and stiffened her upper lip. Resolve returned to her face and her eyes were suddenly steeled, her jaw locked in place, her hands were no longer wringing. No longer shaking. The exact result I was looking for.

I knew immediately she was fine. Not fine in the normal sense of the word. Fine in the same way I'd been fine when I'd been in her position. Fine to go on another mission.

I didn't say anything. I just gave her a reassuring look.

"I'm okay! Don't take me off the mission. I want to go with you. I can handle it," she blurted out, talking fast.

She was doing her best to convince me she was okay. I felt guilty for knowing she couldn't go. That was not part of my plan. Not because she wasn't ready or capable of handling it. This was a one-way trip. I wouldn't be coming back. She was too good an operative to take on a suicide mission.

After I shot Qary, my plan was that I'd walk right down to the basement, into the vehicle, and drive off, leaving her behind. I'd race to the tunnel and drive the vehicle through it to the other side. I'd drive to the missiles and destroy them. Then I'd drive to the prison where I was sure Eric was being held. I'd free him, burn down the prison, and take him back to the tunnel. Once I made sure he was safe, then I'd drive to Ida-Mon, to Qary's headquarters. Destroy them. Set fire to the surrounding buildings.

Then it got sketchy. If I survived all that, I planned to go to their main place of worship. It's where their so-called spiritual leaders preached hate, war and the mandate to kill the pag-anites. That's where the suicide bombers worshiped. I'd burn them all down and kill anyone who tried to stop me, until eventually someone would.

You will eventually lose your soul. The counselor's words resonated in my mind.

I ignored them.

"You'll be fine," I said to Lacy and walked out of the room and back to Ted's office.

"Lacy will be fine," I reassured Ted. He nodded as if he agreed and nothing more needed to be said.

"Tell me everything you know about the location of the missiles," I said, sitting down across from him.

Lacy had followed me out of the room and entered behind me. Ted spent the next half hour briefing us on the mission. When he finished, I told Lacy to get some rest and something to eat and then meet me back in the conference room in an hour.

She left reluctantly, but from my tone, she obviously knew not to question.

"I want to see Qary," I said strongly.

"I knew you would say that," Ted replied. "I understand why. You should have that right, after all he put you through."

"Thank you."

"I need your gun," Ted said.

"Why? Do you think I'm going to shoot him? We need intel. I just want to talk to him."

Ted held out his hand. I reluctantly pulled the gun out of the holster and handed it to him.

I started to leave the room.

"Row, I need your other gun," Ted said emphatically.

I shrugged my shoulders in disbelief. But I pulled the gun out of my pocket and handed it to him with much protest.

"He's in the interrogation room," Ted said, not asking about a third gun. "Be careful what you say and do, it's being video-taped."

"Can I rough him up, even a little bit?" I said jokingly.

Ted glared at me. I backed out of the room, bowing slightly. A grin came on my face. He didn't search me for any other guns. If Ted had taken my third gun, I would've killed Qary with my bare hands if I had to. The gun was better. I didn't want to touch him. I wanted it to be quick.

The movies started up again. This time in fast motion. My mind scrolled through them frame by frame. Freed-Om Square. Meg, Mia, and Qary. The prison guards and Qary. The ten years of battles and Qary. Hope... and Qary.

The rage returned with a vengeance. I noticed a tic. My head involuntarily moved to the right. My hand shook as I turned off the camera to the room. I struggled to open the door, unable to do so. My coordination was suddenly impaired. I stopped for a moment, as my vision blurred. I suddenly saw double. I put my hand out against the wall to keep from falling down.

The stress may eventually overwhelm your senses, the counselor had said.

I shook my head from side to side. Then slapped myself in the face as I tried to regain control. I touched my gun to make sure it was there. Not once, not twice, but three times.

I gripped my left wrist with my right hand and managed to secure my left hand on the knob of the door and was able to turn the knob. I walked into the room. The bright lights blinded me for a moment.

The interrogation room was a ten by ten space, with white walls, no pictures, one table and two chairs. Qary sat in one of the chairs, his legs and hands bound. The chains on his legs were attached to the floor. He was older than I remembered. Roughly six-foot, medium build, muscular, sinewy, but not brawny. He wore a full beard. His hair was matted, dirt and grime were caked onto his fingers and under his nails. The scar was clearly visible on the side of his face.

I'd never actually seen the scar where I sliced him open in prison with the shiv. I smiled as I realized it looked like a question mark. A half circle at the top and then a straight line down toward his jaw. I removed the smile before he looked up. I wanted him to see my resolve. I walked over to the chair, pulled it out, and sat down.

He slowly raised his head until our eyes met. Recognition flashed across his face. Then fear. Only for a moment, as he quickly regained the smug demeanor. His mouth slightly pulled to the side. His eyes were squinty. A sudden look of disgust came over his face. The defiant look he must have prepared for what he likely thought was another interrogator, turned to hate when he saw it was me.

Neither of us spoke for what seemed like two minutes. Maybe longer.

I pulled the gun out of my left sock and changed it to my right hand. I gripped the handle and put my finger on the trigger. He saw my actions and likely knew what I was doing. He showed no fear.

"Hello, Row. I'm surprised to see you. I should've killed you when I had the chance," Qary said.

I didn't say anything. Only maintained my stare.

"I remember the last time I saw you," he continued. "In the prison. I remember you crying out like a little baby. Squealing like a little pig."

On the outside, I was calm. On the inside, the pressure was building. I wanted to wait until it exploded like a volcano. It wouldn't take long.

"You are a pathetic little man," Qary said. "Weak. Don't get me wrong. I admire you. I could never break you. Didn't matter what I did, you wouldn't talk. That's why you're weak. Stupid. You will endure what I put you through for a lie. For a false god."

I shifted in my chair. My weight moved to the left side so I could easily raise the gun on my right. I still didn't say a word. I couldn't see my own face, but I imagined it was expressionless. I wanted it to be cold, calculating, intimidating to him.

"You'll never find the missiles in time," he said. "You're too late. They will go off and the pag-anites will be destroyed. Nothing you can do about it."

You won't live to see it.

"So, you don't want to say anything," Qary said the words slowly, mockingly. "Let's talk about your wife and daughter. I bet that will get you talking. Did you know I was there? I saw the whole thing. At a distance. Where I could get away fast. I watched them die."

Suddenly, I saw two of him. Two chairs. Two faces. I blinked my eyes several times. Then shook my head from side to side. I gripped the gun harder. The mention of my wife and daughter triggered more stress. The stress overwhelmed my senses.

He kept talking. I couldn't hear him or understand the words.

This is not who you are... The counselor's words were speaking softly to me in my ears.

Thoughts flooded my mind. "Is this who I am? Can I murder a man in cold blood? Was it murder? I could rationalize things in the field. The enemy was trying to kill me. This was revenge. Was this who I had become? What kind of man would do what I was about to do? Did it make me no better than him?"

You will lose yourself, the counselor said. *You will lose your heart. You will become someone you don't want to be.*

Qary was talking louder. Spitting words. I couldn't process what he was saying. All I could really hear were the words of the counselor.

Suddenly I heard another voice. Still and small.

Blessed are you when they revile and persecute you and say all kinds of evil against you falsely for My sake.

The word *Jesus* formed on my lips. I eased back in my chair.

But I tell you not to resist an evil person. But whoever slaps you on your right cheek, turn the other to him also.

"Qary is an evil person," I said under my breath.

Don't resist him.

But I say to you, love your enemies, bless those who curse you, do good to those who hate you, and pray for those who spitefully use you and persecute you.

"How can I love him, Lord?"

Forgive as the Lord has forgiven you.

"How can I forgive him, Lord?"

Qary spit in my face. "Say something," he shouted. "Don't just sit there. Say something."

Then they spat in Jesus's face and beat Him; and others struck Him with the palms of their hands. But he said not a word.

I released the grip on my gun. Placed it back in my pocket.

"I forgive you," I said.

Then I stood, turned, and walked out of the room.

19

Without looking back, I walked out of the interrogation room where Qary was held. He yelled and screamed for me not to leave. He hurled expletives at me and rattled his chains. His voice was hoarse from yelling and probably from Lacy's chokehold. The bruises on his neck seemed consistent with a very powerful rear naked choke. I hadn't heard how Lacy kidnapped him and made him come back here, but it made sense now.

I suddenly felt very proud of her. I remembered her as one of my trainees a few years before. She was exceptional then. Now, she was a legend in the making. I tracked Qary for ten years, unable to capture him. She did it in one mission, her first no less.

I knew immediately what I had to do. The weight of the planet had lifted off my shoulders. Technically, the weight of unforgiveness, bitterness, resentment, hatred, and revenge lifted off of my heart. As if God had reached down from heaven and supernaturally removed all the pain and hurt from my soul as only he can do.

Most people don't believe that's possible. I don't know if I even believed it could happen to me. Can it happen that fast? It just did. The remedy, cure-all if you will, had been there all along. The thing the Bible says God designed for everyone's emotional trauma and pain—forgiveness. That was the antidote. Qary was the source of all of my emotional pain; forgiving him the cure for all of it as well. I would never completely forget the past, but it just meant it no longer had a hold on me. God did in one minute of spiritual healing what a counselor would take years to accomplish, if she ever actually could.

The movies were gone. The pain was gone. So was the stress. Lifted off me like an elephant who suddenly stood up from sitting on my chest. I could breathe normally again. The double vision, tics, urges, obsessions, were all gone. Vanished, disappeared like a puff of smoke in the wind.

I found Lacy and told her to follow me to Ted's office, but I pulled her aside into an empty hallway first. I took both her hands and looked her straight in the eye.

She seemed surprised by my actions. Like she wasn't sure if she was in trouble or not.

"Good job, Lacy," I said strongly. "What you did is remarkable. Bringing in Qary. I tried for ten years to capture him. You did good. You saved a lot of lives. I'm proud of you. You're going to be a great operative. Just always remember one thing."

"What?" she said, her eyes focused totally on me, hanging on my every word.

"Know who you are and never lose that," I said.

She nodded but didn't speak at first. I'm sure she didn't understand. It had taken me all these years to understand it. How could she from a few short words? I hoped it wouldn't take her as long as it took me.

A tear formed in her eyes, and her voice cracked as she said, "Thank you. I was taught by the best."

I smiled and said, "Let's go talk to Ted."

My pace was slow and deliberate. Normally I walked as fast as I could everywhere I went when I was on or about to go on a mission. Lacy was used to a fast pace as well, and she struggled to hold herself back, to keep pace with me.

My sense of urgency was gone.

Ted looked up from what he was doing as we both walked into the room and sat down in the two chairs in front of his desk.

"What?" he asked.

"There are no missiles," I said.

"What do you mean, there are no missiles? Is that what Qary told you?" Ted asked.

"Not in so many words."

"You're not making sense. Qary is a liar. You can't believe a word he says."

"Exactly. That's how I know there are no missiles. Qary said to me, 'You'll never find the missiles. You're too late.'"

"We're not too late," Ted said. "We know where they are."

"There are no missiles," I said again with emphasis. "He never would have said it like that if there were. The missiles were a ruse to get me to go there so he could kill me. Nothing more. The only reason he told me we were too late was because he wanted to dare me to go and find them, knowing I couldn't resist the challenge."

I looked over at Lacy. Her eyes were steady, but her mouth was slightly distorted in obvious skepticism.

"He wants me to walk into another trap. Unless the missiles are being shot off in the next few minutes, he knows I have enough time. I can get to the missiles in less than four hours. He knows that. He wants me to go there. These plans are fake. He figured if he didn't succeed in the Push-On Valley, then I would find the plans and walk into another trap. His backup plan in case his first one failed."

I paused to let that sink in. Ted didn't push right back with any rebuttal of his own.

"Let me see the plans Lacy brought back," I said.

They were large blueprints. The paper was approximately sixty inches wide, and thirty inches long. Each page contained engineer sketches of a launch pad and missiles. Four of them. Each identical.

"Have you had an engineer look at these?" I asked.

"Not yet," he said, "We just got them."

"These aren't even real plans," I said. "Look at the configurations. They don't even make sense. These were created to make them look like real plans."

Ted turned them back toward him and studied them closely. He'd studied engineering in school.

"You're right," he acknowledged. "No missile would even get off the ground with these configurations."

"What does this mean?" Lacy asked. "Are we not going to the east?"

"Not to look for missiles," Ted said.

"Then we have to go back there and look for Eric," she said.

"Not yet. We just got an intercept. I haven't had a chance to tell you. The message was about Eric.

"Is he alive?" she asked hesitantly, almost dreading the answer.

"Yes, he's alive. He's injured. We don't know to what extent yet. They're taking him to a prison." Ted continued. "We don't know where. When we know, we'll develop a plan to go get him. You and Row can go to the east and help him escape."

"It won't be me," I said. I took the third gun out of my pocket, along with my credentials and set them on Ted's desk.

"What are you doing?" he asked.

"It's time for me to leave the field for good," I said. "I won't be any good to you anymore."

"That's nonsense," Ted said.

"No. I'm sure of it. There are younger, faster, smarter, more talented people than me." I looked at Lacy when I said it. "I've lost a step. I've lost something."

What I lost—the backlash. It was gone forever. I knew it. I wouldn't last five minutes on a battlefield. Stress turning to action turning to supernatural ability was all true, but the mechanism to turn it on was gone forever. It would never return.

Ted nodded as a look of resignation came on his face and his lips drew down into a frown. He knew when an agent passed the point of no return. Everyone eventually did. I'd passed it once before, ten years ago, and again tonight, for the last time.

Ted knew the signs. He wouldn't argue. He stood and held out his hand.

I shook it without saying another word, pulling him toward me into a hug which he strongly reciprocated. A rare show of affection for Ted.

Lacy stayed seated, probably not sure what to do. Leaning over her, I whispered in her ear, "I'll be praying for you. Remember what I said. Don't lose who you are."

She nodded in understanding. In no less than five minutes, I was out the front door to my car, and drove away. For the last time as an operative.

For the *first* time in twenty years, my soul was at peace.

Now... *Hope*

I have to talk to Hope.

* * *

Now (Ven-te 2230)

I walked down the stairs from Sarah's office, through the one security portal, and out the back door to the circular driveway where a large, black, standard-issued government all-terrain vehicle waited for me along with my driver, Joe Bar-Ton. He'd been assigned to me since my appointment as Minister of Defense. More than a driver, Joe was a former special operations officer, now in the Stealth Service, the detail that protected government officials.

"Where to?" Joe asked.

"My trove, please. I'm tired."

The sun was setting on Ven-Us and we had spent a long day planning the peace summit having learned earlier in the day that

Qary had accepted the invitation. Joe started the vehicle and pulled out of the secured grounds, looking every direction to make sure we were safe.

The drive to my trove took ten minutes longer than usual because of the heavy traffic, now commonplace around the government offices. The central government had grown to more than one-hundred-thousand employees, five thousand of which worked for me in defense. The areas around the government facilities were growing faster than anywhere else on the planet. Commercial and residential construction everywhere. The traffic was the proof of the boom that had come to our area.

My trove was in a secure gated neighborhood with about forty higher-end troves. The name of the neighborhood was *Treasure Troves*. It had a lake, tennis courts, swimming pool, and a flog course. The course, while beautiful, seemed to me a total waste of real estate and a total waste of time for the participants. Twenty holes of flogging a small, white ball around a lengthy straight and narrow path with various obstacles between the start and to what they called a "plain" in the fewest number of flogs. A flog being each time someone struck the ball.

The plain was a small green surface, perfectly manicured, with a small hole in the ground in varying locations on each plain. Different iron sticks were used to flog the ball depending on the distance to the hole.

I tried to play several times but never got into it. Flog was like torture to me. Which was saying something, considering my past. Not really torture, extreme frustration. A few floggers were finishing up their rounds as we drove through the neighborhood passing several majestic-looking holes and a number of spectacular houses built around the flog course.

Joe turned onto my street and around to the back of our driveway where our vehicles were housed inside of the car troves. They were conveniently hidden from the road, which my wife insisted on. She thought the car troves looked tacky on the front of the trove facing the street.

After thanking him for the ride, I walked to the door where lights were on throughout the two-story trove suggesting my wife was home.

The kids had moved out several years before. Only the two of us lived in this massive trove. We'd considered downsizing, but the thought of moving didn't appeal to either of us, and as Minister of Defense, I had to be in a gated and secured building. Our trove was wired with all kinds of security systems, alarms, secured air-lines, and secured computer lines, and we didn't want to go through the time and inconvenience again. The first time took six weeks for the construction workers to install bullet-proof windows, a safe room, impenetrable doors, and a whole lot of other things I thought were a waste of money.

"Honey, I'm home," I called out as I walked through the door.

"Good timing," Hope said. "I have dinner ready for you."

She walked out of the kitchen and greeted me with a warm and very welcoming kiss. Which I held longer than she probably liked as she was cooking and wanted for that to be her main focus. She pulled away when a timer went off in the kitchen, signifying something delightful was about finished cooking. The smell permeated throughout the house. Some type of beef dish.

"How are you doing?" I said a little louder so she would hear me in the other room. No response. Not unusual for Hope. When she was cooking, every distraction was ignored. She made sure I felt welcomed every time I came home, but her attention was on making the perfect meal. That was more important at the moment than kissing me or answering any of my questions.

"We're eating in the dining room tonight," she finally shouted from the cooking area.

"What's the occasion?"

"No occasion. I just wanted to cook you your favorite meal tonight. You've been working so hard."

My heart warmed at the thoughtfulness. She made me feel special every night when I came home. Somehow, she must have sensed I had something important to tell her. Two things actually. The peace summit and what the doctor told me a couple weeks ago.

She didn't know it, but the doctors had diagnosed me with a heart ailment. They didn't know how long I had to live. Could be five years or I could go tomorrow. They gave me some medicine but only to control the symptoms. Wouldn't make any difference to the length of my life, so I didn't take it after the doctor mentioned the side effects. I preferred to live with my own side effects rather than the artificial ones the medicine would create. The side effect being death.

I was determined to make the best of it. I hadn't gotten up the courage to tell Hope. Maybe she already sensed it. That could be the reason she was making the day even more special than it always had been. We all knew each day was a gift, and we often casually said how we never know when today might be our last day. That fact was becoming more real with each passing day. The doctors said it would be quick. Everything would be fine, and then all of a sudden, I'd be gone. In an instant. At the blink of an eye.

I've lived a full life. Regrets for sure but marrying Hope was not one of them. She had made the last thirty years the best of my life.

In the dining room, candles, an appetizer, and a glass of wine awaited me.

"How did you know I would need this tonight?" I said back over my shoulder loudly enough to where she could hear me in the other room. The Brie Cheese Tart melted in my mouth. The same appetizer she made me on our first date. I wondered if the rest of the meal was the same as well. She said it was my favorite meal.

"You always need it," she replied with a chuckle. "You just don't always get it." She smiled brightly as she walked in from the kitchen carrying two plates of a no-doubt perfectly conceived and prepared meal.

After setting the plates down, rather than sitting down, she stood behind me and loosened my neck cloth which was tied around my neck and went down the front of my shirt to my belt buckle. She removed my jacket and rubbed my shoulders for a few seconds. She moved my hair back into place, where it had mussed from removing the jacket.

"Sit down, honey," I said. "I don't want your food to grow cold."

We began with communion and a blessing over the food which was our common practice at each meal.

For the next ten minutes, she talked nonstop about her day. The food store to get all the ingredients for dinner. The hair salon, where she got her nails and hair done.

I complimented her, although I wished I had noticed sooner.

Seth needed something at school, so she ran it over there to him. He's doing well.

The church was preparing meals for some needy families, so she dropped some perishables by that she got at the food store. She picked up my shirts and suit jackets at the air cleaners. Came home, dropped off the food. Then had lunch with her friend. Came home and spent the afternoon cleaning the trove and cooking dinner.

"Did you have a busy day?" she finally asked.

"Not as busy as yours," I said with a laugh. "Mostly, I just spent my time saving the planet from bad guys."

Hope didn't seem offended. I didn't mean to say what she did wasn't important. I meant it as a joke, and by her reaction she took it as such.

She could tell me her day first. I loved looking at her as she talked. Hearing her voice. Amazed at how much she could get done in one day. She wasn't being self-centered, she just loved to tell me about her day. That was her way of connecting with me. Someone had written a book a few years back called, *Men are From Mars, Women are from Earth.* I never read it, but she raved about it for weeks. One of the things I remembered was that she was fascinated by the fact that women spoke sixteen-thousand words a day, while men only spoke seven thousand— the difference in our nature which we had accepted in each other a long time ago.

Hope took another bite of food as I looked at her lovingly.

"Did you do anything else important other than saving the planet?" she asked in her typical dry sense of humor.

"I also solved the problem of planetary peace today. Just a typical day. Like yours."

We both laughed heartily. She knew I wasn't making fun of her. I said it light-heartedly. Jokingly. My mind was elsewhere. Should I tell her what had happened today or if I should wait for a more serious moment? What the doctor said would have to wait. It would ruin the moment.

Sensing something, she said, "What is it? You have a serious look on your face, like you want to say something."

"Qary accepted the invitation to the peace summit." I chose the ironically easier topic.

"Oh..." she said, knowing the gravity and all the personal feelings that would come with me seeing Qary again after all these years. She knew about the invitation but dismissed it by saying he would never accept, so she shouldn't worry. I had obviously been wrong.

"You really were working on planetary peace. Well, that's a good thing, right?" she said supportively. "I mean... if he's serious about peace."

"It seems like he's serious or he wouldn't have accepted."

Hope's eyes suddenly widened. "You don't have to go to the east, do you?"

"No. He's coming to the west. The peace summit is going to be at Freed-Om Square."

Hope didn't say anything as she let the new development sink in. Neither of us had eaten a bite since we started this line of discussion. We both apparently realized it as we took a bite at the same time, putting a halt to the discussion for a moment while we chewed our food.

"I'm sure everything will be fine," Hope said.

Not knowing how to respond, I just took another bite.

"You remember the last time I saw him," I finally said.

"Our first date," she replied.

"You almost didn't open the door."

"It was three o'clock in the morning!"

"You weren't asleep."

She glared at me, although in a loving way.

"I wasn't going to open the door," she said. "But you were banging on the door so hard, I was afraid you were going to wake the neighbors."

"That's not why you opened it," I retorted.

"No. It was when you said those five words," she said. "Do you remember them?"

"I do remember them," I said, as my voice trailed off and the memory of that night rushed back into my mind.

20

Before (Ven-te 2200)

The drive back to Hope's house took much longer than the drive from her house a few hours earlier since I was driving the speed limit and not acting like a maniac. I wondered if I would see the policeman who I had a vague recollection of illegally dashing away from. One-way streets, flashing lights, high speeds, extremely erratic behavior were a blur as I was already trying to decompartmentalize and forget my past, including even my most recent past.

I'm a different person than just a few hours ago. Hope had to see that. Would she understand?

She has to.

How do I explain my behavior? How much did she need to know about my past? I didn't know exactly what I would say.

The truth. I need to tell her the truth.

My only chance of convincing her was to be completely honest with her. Something hard to do when trained as an operative to hide that part of my life. When I was in the field, I had to lie to keep from being outed as a spy. It became second nature to me. The lies were sort of a convenient truth. A necessary discretion for the greater good. I'm not sure how much I was even allowed to tell her. So much of it was classified.

Doesn't matter. I'm telling her everything.

A police car was sitting on the side of the road looking for speeders. I laughed out loud. Was it the same one? If it was and he somehow recognized my vehicle, I'd flash my credentials and explain that it had been a national emergency. Classified.

That wouldn't work. My credentials were on Ted's desk. The first time in as long as I could remember being without them. Not that I was worried. One call to Ted, or even the President, for that matter, and I'd be set free with apologies. But it would take several hours to straighten things out. I didn't have several hours. I had to get to Hope's trove tonight.

Fortunately, the police car didn't move. My reaction to him was different. Normally in that situation, my mind would have started racing. Thinking through every possible scenario and how I could get out of it. Instead, peace was my first response. My life was changed, transformed. It felt good.

Even the thought of talking to Hope was not making me nervous. Going back there at three in the morning was certainly irrational. Maybe I hadn't changed completely. But for some reason I had to go tonight. My instincts had always served me well over the years. Now, they were telling me to go see her and explain things because tomorrow she might not understand after having a night to think about it.

Maybe my still-obsessive personality was guiding me; maybe it was the Holy Spirit leading me to go there; maybe I was making a mistake. We'd soon find out.

I passed the spot where I had sat for fifteen minutes waiting to go to her house for our date. I'd been so nervous. Almost cancelled the entire date. Maybe that would have been the best thing. None of this would have happened if I had cancelled.

That wasn't completely true. *No!* Ted would have called me anyway. I would've still met with Qary. Who knows? There might have been a different outcome. I might've killed him. Gone to the east and died in my rampage. My time with Hope was what stopped me and led me to forgive him. She was the catalyst that gave me a hope for the future and a reason to keep living. Perhaps it was all part of God's plan.

Everything would work out according to God's plan, I told my-self as I parked the car and walked to the door. The neighborhood was calm and peaceful. A street light illuminated the walkway to her trove. A flicker of light came through the curtain of Hope's trove. The candle was still burning.

She's awake!

Without hesitation I knocked on the door.

Nothing. No response. Listening intently, I couldn't hear a sound coming from the other side of the door.

The knock was louder this time. If she wasn't awake, she was now.

"Hope, it's me," I said, a little above a whisper, not wanting to wake the neighbors but loudly enough so she could hear me.

"Please open the door. We need to talk."

No response.

My air-line was in my pocket so I pulled it out and dialed her number. It went straight to her voicemail. I knocked louder, becoming less concerned about the neighbors.

"Go away," I heard a voice say from the other side of the door.

"Hope, I'm sorry. I have to talk to you. Please let me in. I need to explain."

"It's three o'clock in the morning."

"I know. I'm sorry. I have to tell you what happened tonight. You'll forgive me. You have to."

"I forgive you, but I don't want to talk to you. Leave me alone."

"Something happened tonight. Something really big. I need to tell you about it. Please open the door."

"Tell me tomorrow at work."

"No. It has to be tonight. Please open the door."

"Why should I?"

"Because... I want to marry you."

Dead silence.

From both of us. Five words I hadn't planned on saying. They just flew out of my mouth like an uncontrollable hick-up. I told Mia I wanted to marry her on our first date as well. I wouldn't tell Hope that, but it worked out well for Mia and me. It would work out well for us too. I was sure of it.

It doesn't take long for me to know what I want, and I wanted to marry Hope. I wouldn't have said it unless I meant it. Even if it was spontaneous and without much thought, the sentiment was real.

The door cracked slightly ajar. I could barely see Hope's face peeking out from behind it. "You want to marry me?" she said more as a question than a statement.

"Yes. We're supposed to be together. If you let me in, I can explain. You'll know I'm serious."

The door opened further. I could see her now. She was still wearing the same clothes from dinner. Her eyes were red. She'd been crying.

I wanted to take her in my arms and comfort her, but she'd already walked away from the door, leaving me at the entrance. The door was still open, giving me permission to come in. I stepped inside and closed the door behind me. The candle on the counter still flickered. Most of the wax was gone. But it was holding on, still burning, unwilling to finally give up its purpose. Sort of like how I felt in that moment.

"Will you marry me?" I asked gently.

"Don't be ridiculous," she said strongly.

"I'm serious."

"You don't even know me."

My laugh pierced the darkness. "I've known you for seven years. I hired you. More importantly," I said, pausing. "You know me. We've been working together all these years. You know my heart. You know my character."

"The man I saw tonight..." her voice cracked as tears started to form again. "I don't know that man."

"I know. I've led a secret life very few people know about. I used to work for the V-7. I was a spy in the east for ten years. After my wife died."

"You said you *used* to work for them. Sounded to me like you still do."

"I don't. I mean... I act as a consultant sometimes. I train recruits. They call me when they need information on the Naryans. You know... their religious beliefs. That kind of thing. I try to help them with their missions. As an expert, you know."

The words weren't coming as smoothly as I would've liked. Explaining honestly without giving away too much information was a difficult road to navigate through.

"What about tonight?" she said with disdain. "What happened that made you so angry? You frightened me."

"We captured a high-value terrorist tonight. Someone we've been tracking for years. That was why they called me."

"I heard you say you wanted to beat him up," Hope said more angrily. "You wanted to kill him. Who was he?"

"The man who killed my wife and daughter."

"Oh... I didn't know." Her words were hesitant, more understanding and her tone softened.

"I tracked him for ten years in the east but never caught him. He's a very bad man. He's responsible for the deaths of tens of thousands of Christians. We have him in custody. He wouldn't talk. That's why I was so angry. It just brought everything back up. All the feelings."

Hope had been standing behind the chair as if keeping something between us as protection. She walked around the chair and sat in it. A little more of her guard going down, physically and emotionally.

"There's more," I said.

The couch seemed a safe distance from her. So and I sat down there, across from her, not wanting to do anything to upset her further. The thought occurred to me that I was sitting right where we had been so comfortable just a few hours before. Where we touched, kissed, where I had stroked her hair. The memories flooded back into my mind. I quickly suppressed them.

Focus.

Hope needed to know everything. Her heart was softening and maybe even turning back toward me. While I longed for her touch again, it might happen, but we weren't there yet.

"I spent three months in a Naryan prison camp," I said as tears formed in my eyes. I don't know if she could see them in the dark, the candle was growing close to extinguishing. Even if she couldn't, she could hear it in my voice. "The man they captured tonight tortured me for three months," I continued. "That's how I got the injuries to my arms and legs. I was so angry tonight when they told me he was at the headquarters. All I could think about was revenge. He hurt me so much. Took my wife and daughter from me. Took three months of my life away from me. Put me through hell. I've been living with it all these years."

"I'm sorry," she said sweetly, "I can't imagine how you must have felt."

"I'm sorry, Hope. I couldn't tell you before. It's all classified and confidential. It was our first date. I didn't think I could tell you everything."

"I know. I can't be mad at you for not telling me. We didn't know each other that well. I'm glad you told me now. I promise I won't tell anyone else."

"I know you won't. But I had to tell you."

"Why?"

"Even though I'm not supposed to."

"Why are you telling me all this?"

"Because I love you. I know that if we're going to have a future, you have to know."

"What happened when you saw him?" She didn't respond to me saying I loved her. Somehow, I understood. It sounded weird to me, saying it so soon. She obviously needed more information and more time to process things.

"I wanted to kill him..." my voice trailed off. "I actually was going to. I had a gun. I wanted revenge."

"Did you kill him?" she asked hesitantly. Her jaw tensed and her shoulders were raised. Fear suddenly became obvious in her voice again. She's going to think I'm a fugitive. A murderer. Hope's eyes flitted around the room as if she was looking for a way of escape.

"No. I didn't kill him," I said quickly and emphatically.

"What did you do?"

"I told him I forgive him."

"Really? That must've been hard to do." Her shoulders retreated back down to their normal position, and the tension left her face as she seemed reassured by that response.

"Hardest thing I've ever done in my life," I explained. "But I had to do it. Forgive him. I thought I already had. I've said the words, but my heart wasn't really changed. Until tonight. I kept hearing the words of Jesus in my head, words of forgiveness. Turn the other cheek. Love your enemies. Don't fight evil with evil. Fight it with good."

"You do seem different. Even different than before you got the phone call. I always thought you were a little uptight. Like something was always bothering you. I never could put my finger on it. I sort of understand now."

"I'm a different person. I know what I want now. I want to be with you. I want to marry you."

"I can't marry a spy. I don't want that lifestyle."

"I quit tonight."

"What? You quit?"

"I did. I'm through being a spy. I already turned in my credentials."

"I hope you didn't do it for me."

"Maybe. But mostly I did it for myself. It's like I said, that person I had become was not who I really am."

I wanted to get up and go to her, but I resisted the urge. She would come to me when she was ready.

"Hope?" I said her name sweetly with an inflection so she would know I was about to say something important.

"What?" she asked quietly.

"I don't want to lose you."

"You won't," she said as she stood from the chair and walked over and sat next to me.

She wrapped her arms around my neck and squeezed tightly. I could feel her tears wetting my shirt. I was certain she could feel mine on her cheek. Neither of us said anything for what seemed like several minutes.

"Does this mean you'll marry me?" I asked, still holding the embrace, not wanting to see the reaction on her face in case it wasn't what I wanted to see or hear.

Hope didn't answer immediately. She pulled back a short distance and stared into my eyes, her hands were still on my shoulders. Thinking. Maybe looking to see what she could tell from my eyes. Someone once said the eyes were the gateway to the soul. If they were, I hoped she could see how much I loved her and wanted to be with her. That I couldn't live without her. Or at least I didn't want to.

Finally, after several moments she said, "Yes. I will marry you."

Joy flooded inside of me as I wrapped my arms around her again, squeezing her even more tightly.

"You've made me so happy," I said.

Our lips met. At the same spot they had a few hours earlier. Although this time with no secrets. No past hurts were standing in the way. There was a promise of a future. I thought it couldn't get any better than our first kiss.

It did.

At that exact moment, the candle flickered out as if it had stayed lit just long enough to give us the needed light to get to this point.

Its job completed. The light in the room went out. The light in our hearts for each other turned on forever.

* * *

(Ven-te 2202)

Our wedding was held at the seminary, and was the biggest event ever held there, particularly after President Redford accepted our invitation to attend. Something we never expected when we sent it out to him. No one at the seminary knew of my secret life and my students were very impressed to learn that I knew the President enough that he would attend my wedding.

His presence complicated things in that security was tighter, the press attended, and it was televised throughout all of Ven-Us. I'd been concerned at the time about the publicity and had expressed this concern to Ted. Would this make Hope a target to Qary and the Naryans? He assured me not to worry. Qary was safely locked up in a prison cell.

Ten months later, I sat in my office in our new trove, taking care of a few minor personal matters. Hope was in the kitchen cooking dinner, two months pregnant.

My air-line vibrated. A V-message. From Ted.

Turn on your air-box!

One of the compromises we made after we were married was to get an air-box. We agreed to get one as long as I promised it would stay in my office and wouldn't be on much.

I quickly turned it on. Ted hadn't contacted me in several months and wouldn't if it wasn't something important.

My mouth flew open as Qary's picture appeared on the screen. The headline under his picture sent waves of fear through my body.

Naryan Terrorist to be Released.

I let out a yell, "No!"

Hope came hurrying into the room to see what had caused the reaction. Her eyes widened in surprise as she saw the picture and headline. The commentator from the VNN news channel said:

Our sources have just confirmed Qary Raabe Mal-am, a Naryan terrorist responsible for several suicide bombings in the west, is scheduled to be released later today in a prisoner swap. We don't have any of the details, but we understand the Naryans are going to release four western prisoners in exchange for Mal-Am. The swap is scheduled to happen in one hour at the Bur-gess Gate. Our reporters are headed to the scene now with their cameras. We will have a live shot from Freed-Om Square shortly.

I turned down the sound. "I'm going to call Ted."

She sat down in the chair across from my desk with a stunned look on her face.

The call was on speaker so Hope could hear the conversation.

"Did you see the news?" Ted asked in his usual manner without greeting me.

"The reports must be true, or you wouldn't have messaged me," I retorted just as matter-of-factly.

"They are true. He's going to be released in about an hour."

"Why are we doing this?"

"We're going to get Eric back. He's one of the prisoners we're getting in return. We're actually getting four prisoners in exchange for Qary."

"When did all this happen?"

"It actually has been in the works for several months. We had a deal worked out—Eric for Qary—but Eric refused to leave the prison. They had other prisoners we didn't know about. We thought they were dead. They tried to make Eric leave but word was that he killed a couple of their guards. He refused to budge, and no one was brave enough to go in and get him. Sounds like Eric."

So many questions and thoughts ran through my mind. Can't you send some people to the prison and get him out without giving up Qary? Is it worth it? Qary is a very dangerous man. Eric wouldn't want us to do it. I wouldn't have. Too big a price. Is saving one man worth risking the lives of thousands of others?

These were questions and thoughts I didn't bother bringing up. Ted had already thought about them and probably others. Eric was a valuable operative. We were getting him back. I was happy for him.

"Do you think Hope and I are safe?" I asked, a question Hope had scribbled on my notepad to ask him.

"I think so. You're out of the field. No reason for him to come after you now. I wanted you to know, though. So you could take precautions. I can send some security for a while if you want me to."

"That's not necessary. I can protect us. Thanks for letting me know."

We hung up.

"I agree with Ted," Hope said. "There's no reason for us to worry about Qary. He'll leave us alone."

Hope left the room and finished cooking dinner. A few minutes later she brought our plates of food to my office. We watched the air-box intently and waited for the moment when the prisoners were exchanged. Two hours later, several large, black government cars drove up to the gate. More than a hundred reporters were off to the side in a roped-off area. Cameras were zoomed in on the entire scene.

Qary stepped out of the vehicle with his hands bound and a smug look of satisfaction on his face. Several hundred soldiers with machine guns were positioned in and around the gate and square. Out of sight of the Naryans, but close enough to react if necessary.

After a few minutes, the gate opened. The camera zoomed in to the other side of the gate where Eric and three other prisoners stood. The prisoners looked to be in bad shape, clearly having been abused. Eric struggled to walk under his own power.

Qary's hands were released, and he walked slowly toward the gate, escorted by soldiers on each side. Tensions were clearly running high as Qary and our men neared the gate and then passed each other, each party giving the other a long, hard stare.

Ted and others rushed to their side.

Qary was on the other side of the gate embracing several of the men there to greet him.

The gate was quickly closed, and ambulances rushed to where Eric and the other men were standing. Eric refused to be cared for until the other men were attended to. They were carefully loaded onto stretchers. The camera showed the ambulances leaving, transporting them almost certainly to the medical facility on the military base. Eric refused to get on the stretcher, and instead, walked to the ambulance. He stepped into it on his own power and then sat down. The last thing we saw before the doors of the ambulance closed were the paramedics surrounding him and attending to him.

I turned off the air-box, not caring to hear any more of the commentary, glad his suffering was over. The gravity of the situation hit me all at once.

It was done. Qary was free. God help us all.

21

Still Before (Ven-2202)

Eric had three broken ribs, a dislocated shoulder, a broken nose, two broken fingers, three broken toes, an enlarged spleen caused from a blow to the abdomen, and a broken tibia, snapped in two from a bullet from a Naryan gun in Push-On Valley. The leg was crudely reset in prison without anything to dull the pain. Maybe by a doctor, maybe not. He was dehydrated, had lost thirty pounds and had slight swelling on his brain. His left eye was almost swollen shut from where the doctors had rebroken and reset his nose. Other than that, he jokingly said to everyone who asked, he was doing okay.

It took the surgeons six hours to repair everything. The leg had to be rebroken and secured by a long rod and seven screws. He lay in the hos-pital bed, his leg suspended by a traction pulley from above. A thick cast extended from his ankle to just above his knee, render-ing the leg immovable and holding the rod securely in place. His shoulder was in a sling. The fingers on his right hand were in a splint. Wires and tubes attached to his body were connected to a machine monitoring his vital signs and providing a steady IV drip.

A button next to his left hand shot painkillers into his thigh as needed. At first, he didn't want them and even refused to take any pain medication. Finally, the night nurse convinced him to try it, and he was hooked. He pushed the button too frequently now. So much so that the pain medicine made him a little loopy, and some-times he slurred his words like a drunk in a bar. It helped him to sleep and was a welcome respite from the nonstop pain he had felt for eighteen months in the prison. The button automatically quit dispensing when he reached his limit, and he was moments away from being able to use it again.

He'd not been physically tortured as much as mentally. The guards seemed reluctant to touch him physically because of all his wounds. They were afraid he would die, and he was their bargaining chip to get Qary back. He'd heard the prison leaders warn the guards that they would die if anything happened to the prisoner. They made sure it didn't. Not that life wasn't horrible, it merely wasn't as bad as it could have been. Not as bad as things had been for Row.

The door of his room suddenly flew open, waking him from a light sleep. He blinked his blurry eye a couple times as he tried to focus, not believing who he was seeing.

Lacy?

She ran to his side and gently touched his cheek and kissed him on the forehead.

"I can't believe it's you," Eric said. "They said you were on a mission."

"I was," she said, "but I came back as soon as I heard you were free."

Eric could see out of his one good eye that tears had formed in hers.

"How are you?" Lacy asked hesitantly.

"I'm fine," Eric said. "Never been better. As you can see. I'll be back in the field with you before you know it."

The doctors had said that wasn't possible. He'd never be in the field again. After the cast was taken off, he would have to learn to walk all over again. Eric refused to accept that. He'd be back in the field. Ninety days was how long he gave himself to recover enough to go back to work. Ninety days from the time they took the cast off.

Eric winced slightly. Not from the physical pain. The medication took care of that, and he wasn't feeling anything at the moment, although he could tell the medication would be wearing off soon. The conversation he knew Lacy was going to bring up soon was the source of the pain. Emotional pain the medication couldn't take away. He tried to put it out of his mind, hoping she might not bring it up.

After a few minutes of casual talk, Eric decided to preempt what he knew was coming and asked, "How did you get Qary to come with you?"

Lacy explained how she put him in a chokehold and then walked him out on a leash.

"I wish I could have seen that!" Eric said, immediately realizing he said the wrong thing.

Lacy winced. "I should've waited for you," she said, her voice pained, her eyes apologetic.

Eric raised his hand slightly and dismissed her words with a wave.

"No. You did the right thing. You had to get Qary back to head-quarters."

"A lot of good that did though. It was all for nothing. Qary's free now anyway."

Eric balled his left hand into a fist. He felt the same way but was struggling to keep from Lacy knowing it.

He was furious at Ted. Why would they give up Qary for him? He wasn't as high a value target as Qary. It wasn't a fair deal in his estimation. They'd argued about it until the doctors made Ted leave the emergency room. A topic they would revisit the next time he saw him, although nothing could be done about it now. Maybe they should've left Qary there. Ted said it was worth it. Qary hadn't talked but they got him out of the field for eighteen months. Cap-turing him saved lives.

Eric wanted to change the subject, but Lacy wouldn't let him.

"I'm so sorry," she said. "No man left behind. I shouldn't have left you."

Ted had told him Lacy was crushed by it. Eric didn't know whether to be hard or understanding with her. Really not sure either would make her feel better.

"It's what I signed up for," he finally said strongly. "I knew the risks."

"I was your partner. You were counting on me. I let you down."

"That's ridiculous," Eric said, deciding to take a harsher tone. "You have to stop blaming yourself. I told you not to stay. I would've been mad if you had."

"I feel so bad. When I see you like this..." She glanced at him from head to toe. "It's my fault. You wouldn't have left me. Will you ever forgive me?"

Eric realized how deep the pain went in her, so he decided on a softer tone.

"Look at me," Eric said.

Her eyes were watering, the pain evident on her face.

"It's okay. If you need forgiveness, then I forgive you. I'm going to be okay. I'm here now. It all worked out. God is working it for our good."

"I guess."

"Can you sign my cast?" Eric asked, changing the subject.

Several nurses and doctors and other visitors had signed their names and left a message on the cast on his leg. Eric had a remote that lowered the leg to the bed, which he was supposed to do every thirty minutes. Alternate between raised and lowered. It was time to lower it anyway. He pointed to a pen on the table.

Lacy found it and signed her name, and wrote a few words then drew a heart. As she finished, she accidently brushed up against his broken toes with her elbow, toes that were reset but not in a cast. The doctors said they'd heal on their own. When Lacy touched them, it sent a jolt of pain shooting through his leg. He let out a yelp.

"I'm sorry," Lacy said. "Did I hurt you?"

Eric could feel his face contorted as the pain lingered.

"I'm okay," he said through short quick breaths.

"I'm so sorry."

"It's okay," he said, trying to make himself believe it. Strange, feeling pain nonstop for eighteen months, then having a respite from it. When it returned, it seemed stronger than before. Or he was getting weaker. Perhaps the survival instinct in prison blocked out some of the pain or at least gave him the strength to handle it.

"Here, let me kiss it and make it better." Lacy leaned down and kissed his leg through the blanket.

"I have a pain right here," Eric said pointing to his cheek. "Can you kiss it and make it better?"

Lacy slapped the top of his leg gently. "Stop it," she said as she moved to the top of the bed and kissed his cheek anyway. "If I kissed everything that hurt on you, I'd be here all day."

"I owe you a kiss," Eric said.

"Why?"

"You know that ammunition you left for me?" he asked.

Lacy had a faraway look in her eyes like she was thinking.

"Vaguely."

"Remember, you said you were going to hide the ammunition in the trees in case I needed it. Turns out I did."

Her face brightened. "I remember. You told me not to. But I insisted. You're so stubborn."

"You are too. I'm glad, though. You saved my life."

"Really?"

"Really. I ran out of ammunition. I remembered you saying you would hide the extra ammunition by the road. So, I ran back and got it. It was a lifesaver."

"You came back to the road?" she asked as her eyes drooped, and she frowned.

"I did, but you were already gone." Eric didn't want to tell her he saw her drive away. It would only make her feel worse.

"Why do you owe me a kiss?" she blurted as if suddenly remembering what he'd said moments before.

"I said to myself that if I get out of this alive, I'm going to give Lacy a big kiss for leaving the ammunition for me."

He raised his good arm, extended his hand, and swept it from one side of the bed to the other.

"As you can see, I am clearly alive, and I'm a man of my word."

"Sounds to me like you're making that story up so you can get a kiss," Lacy said playfully.

"Maybe. Since you weren't there, you'll just have to take my word for it."

She leaned over and offered her cheek to him.

He didn't immediately kiss it.

"What?" she said as their eyes met.

"I said I owed you a big kiss."

He straightened and pushed himself up slightly on the bed and winced.

She moved closer to him, turning her head to fully facing him. He couldn't move his head any closer, so she leaned in until their lips met. Barely touched. Nothing like any kiss he'd ever had before. Better. Technically, probably the worst first kiss ever in the history of kisses on Ven-Us. Not big at all. To him... Spectacular. Electric. The best kiss he'd ever had.

The perfect painkiller for his emotional pain.

* * *

A guard was posted outside of Eric's hos-pital room. He knocked on the door and then leaned his head in and said, "There's a man and woman out here to see you. He said his name is Row. Can I let him in?"

"I've never heard of him," Eric said, giving Lacy a mischievous look as he said it.

"Okay," the guard said, and closed the door, evidently not knowing he was kidding.

"I'm on it," Lacy said, jumping up from the side of his bed and rushing to the door, sending another jolt of pain through him from the movement of the bed.

A few seconds later, Row entered the room with a woman Eric had never met.

"I can see you still don't have a sense of humor," Row said.

Eric smiled.

"How you doing buddy?" Eric said, happy to see him.

"Better than you, apparently. Although, I have to say I think your face looks better than I remember it." Row grinned widely as he said it.

The woman slapped his hand.

"Don't listen to him," she said. "My name is Hope. I'm Row's wife."

"You're married?" Eric said. "I can't believe you found someone to marry you. Especially a woman so pretty. It's nice to meet you, Hope." His ribs hurt when he laughed.

Lacy's turn to slap Eric playfully, although carefully, on the wrist.

"Nice to meet you, too," Hope said with a pleasant and friendly smile.

Row put his hands on Hope's shoulders and turned her so she was facing sideways.

"Look at this," Row said pointing to her stomach which was starting to show the pregnancy. "We're going to have a baby."

Hope smiled as Lacy came and gave her a hug.

"Congratulations!" Lacy said. "I'm so happy for you."

"That's just what we need," Eric said. "Another little boy Row running around Ven-Us."

"Might be a girl," Hope said.

"Let's hope so," Eric said. "And let's hope she looks like you."

"That's one thing we can agree on," Row said, putting his arm around Hope's waist and pulling her toward him while kissing her on the cheek.

"Will you sign my cast?" Eric asked.

"I've never seen that before," Row said, taking the pen off of the table. "That's a neat idea. Let's see, what do I want to say?" Row put his hand on his chin and rubbed it, thinking.

"You be nice, Rowan Church-Well," Hope said as she grabbed the pen from his hand, and wrote on the top of the cast. *Get well soon. Thank you so much for your sacrifice. Love Hope.*

She handed the pen back to Row. He started writing and then suddenly stopped. He looked up at the wall, not them.

"What?" Hope asked.

"Nothing," Row said as he continued writing. "I just thought of something. I'll tell you later."

Row sat the pen down and then circled the bed to the front near Eric but on the other side of Lacy and Hope.

"You're going to need someone to talk to," Row said, his tone turning more sober. "I want you to know that I'm here for you. You can call me anytime. I know what you're going through. Things seem okay now when everyone's around. But later, things might get harder. I want to help you. You don't have to go through this alone. I didn't really have anyone to talk to, and I wish I had."

"Thanks," Eric said. "It means a lot to me. But I'm doing okay."

"I know. But don't hesitate to call me if you need me."

They had a bond. Eric knew it. A club of two. No one else in the world could know what Eric had been through except Row. He decided that he would call him.

"Ted said you never broke. I'm proud of you," Row said.

The words meant more to Eric than anything anyone had ever said to him. Row was a legend in V-7 circles. His approval was like a shot of adrenaline that produced an immediate feeling of pride in him. Somehow made it all seem worth it.

Row patted him on his arm. Hope smiled at Row and then at Eric. They both hugged Lacy and then left.

No one said anything for a couple minutes as the solemnity of the moment sunk in.

"I'm proud of you too," Lacy said gently.

"You know what got me through it?" Eric asked.

"What?"

"You."

"Me? How did I get you through it?"

"I thought about you constantly. Almost every second of every day. You kept me going. I kept thinking about the next time I saw you. I could hear you talking to me. Encouraging me." A tear rolled down his cheek.

Lacy moved closer and wiped it off with the back of her hand. Eric continued. "I knew you'd blame yourself. I had to get back to tell you everything was okay. The pain was unbelievable. The days were the worst because I had to deal with the guards. At night, I could just curl up on the floor and think of you. I dreamed of you. You were there every night with me until I fell asleep. Then you were there with me when I woke up in the morning."

Lacy started to cry as tears formed and rolled down her cheeks. Eric raised his hand and wiped them away.

"The guards could never take that away from me. I prayed a lot too. That was something else they couldn't take away. God was with me. But so were you. I could feel your touch. I could smell your hair. I knew I had to get back to you."

"That's so sweet," she said.

Suddenly, they were kissing.

The big kiss.

The one he owed her.

He didn't feel anything else but her. The pain was gone if only for a moment.

Replaced with pure ecstasy. The best feeling ever.

22

Hope and I left the hos-pital in a somewhat somber mood, realizing the long road of recovery Eric had before him, both emotionally and physically. Neither of us said anything for the first few minutes as we drove back to the seminary.

"I think Eric is smitten with Lacy," Hope said out of the blue.

"Really? I didn't notice," I replied.

She rolled her eyes at me. "Typical man. We women notice these things."

"I hope you're right. A good woman could really help his recovery."

"Do you wish you'd had a pretty girl to help you recover when you first came back from the prison?" Hope asked jokingly.

"I wish I'd had you," I retorted with a wide smile.

"Good answer." She reached over and put her hand on my shoulder.

"Whew!" I said, as I brushed my hand across my forehead in an exaggerated motion. "You women have a way of putting your husbands in a bad situation. You ask us questions with a hundred wrong ways to answer and only one right way. Answer wrong, and you're in trouble. Fortunately, I've had eighteen months to learn the right answer. I feel sorry for guys like Eric who are just starting out and have no idea what to say."

Hope playfully slapped the back of my head with her hand.

"What was it you wanted to tell me?" Hope asked.

I shrugged my shoulders and looked at her, not sure what she meant.

"Remember. You were signing Eric's cast and then you got this far away look in your eyes. I asked you what you were thinking, and you said you'd tell me later."

I had been thinking about that very thing since we left the hospital. I just didn't connect it to Hope's question.

"I was thinking about the writings on the rock at Freed-Om Square," I said.

"What about them?"

"When I was signing Eric's cast, I noticed that several people had written things. They wrote on his cast because he means something to them. It made me think of the rock. Someone took the time to actually write something on it. And it wasn't as easy as just writing something. They had to take the time to carve it into the rock. What was it? I want to figure out who wrote on the rock, what they wrote, and why."

This was something that had baffled scholars and archeo-logists for centuries. There were what appeared to be three distinct carvings on the rock. Written at three different times in history. Over the years, they had faded to the point they weren't discernable. Archeo-logists wanted to examine them more closely, but they required the consent of the religious leaders which they wouldn't give. With the invention of carbon dating, archeo-logists were sure they could pinpoint the date of the carvings. However, it required samples to be taken from the rock, and the leaders refused to let anyone do anything to disturb what was the most sacred religious site in all of Ven-Us to both the Naryans and the west. The Naryans would've gone to war over it. So, no one had studied them in decades.

"I think it may be related to all that work we did on finding the garden of Eden. If we could figure it out, it would be the greatest discovery in the history of Ven-Us," I continued to explain.

We had developed a theory a couple of years before with the help of Sarah and Hope that the rock was at the actual site of the garden of Eden. The Eden rock, as described in Flav-Ious's writings. However, our work eventually hit a dead-end. Until more evidence surfaced to buttress our claims, we had kept them to ourselves. I always wondered if the carvings might shed some light on the subject.

"Why don't you ask Leo?" Hope said.

"That's a good idea."

Leo Ven-cent was a student at the seminary. Once a noted archeologist, Leo felt a call from God in a morning church service several years ago to surrender to full time ministry. He quit his job with the Natural Museum of Antiquities and moved all his possessions and his family to go to seminary full-time so he could start a new career in the field of religious education. Predictably, he had a certain fascination with old testament biblical stories and had taken several of Hope's classes she taught on the old testament.

He'd even led an expedition this past summer with several seminary students in search of some biblical sites on the far western side of Ven-Us. Leo took it a lot more seriously than the students, and he swore he'd never take them again. Several got in a dirt fight at the dig site, destroying some of their work, and the rest incessantly complained about the heat and the hard, meticulous work.

My air-line sat on the center console and was connected to my vehicle through a wire-less connection. I accessed my contacts and asked the air-line to dial his number.

Leo answered on the first ring.

"Leo, this is Dean Church-Well."

"Hello, Dean," he said in a monotone voice. Leo was a quirky guy. Short and as wiry as the glasses that always sat down on his nose. I could picture him on the other end of the phone peering over his glasses. Leo was the most perceptive and detailed man I'd ever met and an excellent student. I could see why he would choose archeology as a profession and why he would be good at it. How those skills translated into ministry, none of us were sure, but God's calling was irrevocable, and we were certain he would be used in a mighty way. Clearly dealing with inanimate objects more than with people.

"Leo, I'd like to pick your brain about archeo-logy. I have a project I want you to help me with. When could we meet?"

"I can meet anytime you want. I can even do it this afternoon. I'm at the lib-rary now, but I'm at a good stopping point."

"That would be great. We're headed back to school right now. How about thirty minutes?"

"That'll work. See you then," he said as he hung up and I did the same.

"Do you want to join us?" I asked Hope.

Without hesitation, she said, "Of course. I doubt the two of you could make the greatest discovery in Ven-Us history without my help," she said with a sly grin.

My turn to roll my eyes.

* * *

Not surprisingly, Leo was waiting at my office when we got there. The three of us went inside and gathered around the conference ta-ble.

He pulled out a notepad, two lead writing instruments and an adder. Although I wasn't sure what the adder was for. I guessed he just wanted to be prepared for anything.

"I'm sure you're familiar with the writings on the rock," I jumped right into the topic at hand, knowing Leo wouldn't be interested in pleasantries.

"I've actually studied them. I wouldn't call them writings," Leo said, which encouraged me that he had some knowledge of them, and I didn't even mind the correction.

"What do you think they are?"

Leo took a deep breath as if a long answer was coming. "Many scholars think they're pictures. I think they're words."

I didn't respond while waiting for him to continue. He didn't say anything else. A long answer was not coming. Leo was a man of few words, even in his chosen field of expertise.

"Is there any way we can determine what those words are?" Hope asked.

Leo picked a writing instrument off the table and tapped it on the notepad. "Obviously, if we could cut them out of the rock, we might be able to recreate the words by digging deeper into the rock. We could also determine whether they were cono-gryphs or lico-gryphs."

"What are those?" I asked, also adding, "Cutting them out is not an option."

Leo nodded, probably already knowing my last statement was true.

"Cono-gryphs are drawings. Lico-gryphs are carvings," he explained. "In ancient cultures, cono-gryphs were created by taking minerals from the ground to make a liquid they used for the drawings. They ground up metallic elements like manganese for black colors, iron oxide for red colors, rust for reddish brown, and then various mixed elements to produce the bright colors like yellow, orange, and the like. Then they created a crude tool to paint the figures on the rocks or cave walls. It's amazing how those have lasted throughout the years. Even the ones not in caves. Many of the drawings in the elements have still survived."

I looked over at Hope. She seemed as fascinated by this as I did.

"How come the rock writings, I mean, carvings have faded so much?" I asked.

"That's why I think they are carvings. The rain and the wind have eroded the rock over the years. That happens some with the drawings but more with the carvings."

"Is it possible to figure out the carvings with just the partial words?" Hope asked.

"If we could get close enough to them, we have instruments that would allow us to magnify the rock to several hundred times. I would look for small spots in the rock that aren't natural. In other words, it's unlikely erosion would erase the entire word. Since some of the word is plain to see, then we just have to look closely for markings of the rest of the word."

"Is that something you can do?" I asked.

"The rock is encased in glass," Hope said. "Will your instruments work through the glass?"

"There would be some distortion," Leo said. "But it's worth a try. We might be able to figure out some of the words. Or if they are words at all. Maybe they're drawings."

"Would you be willing to do it as a research project?" I asked. "I will give you extra credit for the effort."

Leo waived his hand dismissively. "I'd do it just for the fun of it. This would be an exciting project. Actually, it would be one of the great arche-ology discoveries of all time, if we could figure it out. I'm not optimistic, but I'm willing to try."

"That's all we can do," I said excitedly, unable to contain my excitement.

* * *

Two weeks later, Hope and I were in my office waiting for Leo to arrive. He'd called the day before and said he had some promising results to share with us. He asked if we could get a large screen to project images from his hand-held com-puter onto it so we could all see the images better.

I contacted the audio-visual department and had them bring it by earlier in the day and set it up, so it was all ready to go upon Leo's arrival. All he had to do was connect his com-puter to the cord already provided. Excitement built inside me as we anxiously awaited his arrival.

As expected, he was right on time. Leo meticulously went through his preparations. He connected the com-puter to the screen, then laid out in some orderly fashion known only to him, all of his notes and a couple reference books. He took out of a satchel, a notepad, two writing instruments, and an adder. Again, I wasn't sure what the adder was for since he hadn't used it the first time.

"What did you find?" I asked nervously.

Leo hit the keyboard and an image appeared on the screen.

"I studied three separate and distinct areas," he began. "All placed on the rock at different times in history. Likely, several hundred years apart. This is the oldest," he said, pointing to the screen.

"Is it a lico-gryph or a cono-gryph?" Hope asked.

I looked at Hope with amazement. How did she remember the two words? I didn't even remember which word was which until Leo answered her.

"They are all three definitely lico-gryphs. Carvings."

Hope appeared to be tracking right along with him.

Leo amplified the screen, zooming in on the letters. Several were clearly legible, but there were gaps between them.

"The following letters are easily discernible," Leo explained. "They are E E E E E DNA A A."

"You can't see all those letters with the naked eye," I pointed out.

"No," Leo said, "but I can tell with certainty that's what they are."

"How can you be sure?" I asked.

"I started by taking a photograph with a special camera and zoom lens. I then took it back to the lab and magnified the images. Parts of the words are clearly legible. I looked for areas where the stone had unusual indentations and traced the marks into the let-ters. It's not a precise science, but I am fairly certain these are the correct letters."

"What do they mean?" Hope asked.

"Not sure," Leo admitted. "There's a gap between each letter except for the DNA. These are areas where the marks have disappeared altogether. I think the DNA is one word. The rest are several different words with either missing letters or spaces between the words."

We all stared at the screen for a few minutes, trying to figure out what the letters meant. What was the message that someone thought was so important to write centuries ago? A mystery.

"Here's the second set of carvings," Leo said. "These aren't as old as the first carvings but are much older than the third. In my opinion, they're closer to the first in age than the third."

We looked at the screen as Leo read off the letters that were discernible.

"Y A N DNA ISAC E E OS"

"Is it a code?" Hope asked.

"I don't know," Leo said. "But the DNA is clearly the same word from the first writing. If it is a code, then that is a good starting place."

I didn't respond, because I didn't know what to say. I was more confused now than when we started.

"Where it really starts to get confusing is with the third carving. It's on the opposite side of the rock from the other two and is much younger than the others. Because it's newer, the letters are more legible," Leo said. "They aren't in any discernible order. However, I'm confident all the letters are there. If that's any consolation."

KFE GEST TH OWI ENHT appeared on the screen.

Something about the words were resonating in my mind, but I couldn't quite figure it out. They weren't written in code. I was certain of that. Why would anything that old be written in a code? That was a rather new phenomenon used to confuse an enemy. These weren't coded messages for their present day. These were messages for antiquity. What did they say?

Suddenly, I remembered the writings on Eric's cast. What was it? I couldn't quite pinpoint what my mind was trying to remember. I could picture the cast and the writings but didn't understand the connection to what I was seeing on the screen.

Then it came to me. I bolted from my chair and rushed to my desk and returned with a Bible.

"What?" Hope asked.

"When I was writing on Eric's cast," I said, "the writing on the top was backward. Not backward, but the person who wrote it, wrote the words standing on the other side of his bed. So, I was looking at the words upside down."

Hope and Leo exchanged puzzled looks, not sure where I was going with my reasoning.

Hope's eyes suddenly widened. "I know what you're thinking. In the ancient language, they wrote from right to left," Hope said. "Up until Christ. After Christ, everyone in the west started writing left to right."

"Exactly," I said, looking at my wife in admiration. "These words need to be read from right to left. The letters DNA is the word *and*."

Leo started writing furiously on his notepad. I just stared at the letters on the screen. The third set didn't make sense even when reading from right to left.

"Put the first one back up," I said to Leo. "Let's start there but look at the letters from right to left."

Leo pushed a button on his key-board and the letters switched direction.

A A AND E E E E E.

"Why is it that the A and E are so prominent?" Hope asked Leo.

"It's because they are harder to write than the other letters. So, whoever was writing pressed harder on the vowels than the consonants. Looking at it from this direction, the first word has four letters. The first and third letters of the first word are the letters A.

The second word is obviously *and.* The third word has three letters. The first and last are the letter *E.*"

"Adam and Eve!" Hope shouted, so loud I'm sure someone could hear it outside the office and down the hall.

The words suddenly became clear in my mind. Was I imagining it? Making myself believe it or was it really true? Is it possible I was looking at letters actually carved by Adam and Eve? Or was someone writing about them? We needed to know the rest of the words.

I rubbed my chin and face with my hands, thinking, trying to solve the puzzle. What were the other words?

As if on cue Leo said, "There are two more words. The third and fourth words are four letters long, and the E's are the second and fourth letters on both." If Leo was excited, he didn't show it from his voice.

"*Were here!*" Hope said in not as loud a voice, but just as excitedly.

A rush of adrenaline pulsed through my veins. "Adam and Eve Were Here!" I said aloud. "That's it! It has to be. The rock is the Eden Rock. It's where the garden of Eden once stood. This is the proof."

Leo's mouth formed a slight grin.

That's Leo's way of showing excitement.

"Put up the second set of letters," I said.

Leo pushed a button, and they suddenly appeared but in the reverse order from before.

SO E E CASI AND NA Y

"That's easy," Hope said. "So Were Casik And Nary."

Hope always excelled at games. Puzzles, crypto-grams, word games, board games. I was so glad she decided to join us for more than one reason.

She was not only smart; *she was cute too.*

"This is more confirmation," I said excitedly. "Scholars have always believed the rock was the spot where Hamm sacrificed Casik.

The same spot where Casik was raised from the dead and then where Casik and Nary made their covenant to no longer war with each other. This is proof they were at this rock."

"Too bad their descendants didn't keep the covenant," Leo added dryly.

Leo's words and mannerisms were emotionless. Maybe he didn't realize the magnitude of the discovery. Or maybe he did, and this was just his manner.

"What about the last set of writings?" I asked.

"Carvings," Hope corrected. I playfully shook my head from left to right, so she knew I'd noticed her correcting me.

Leo put them on the screen.

"These are different from the others," Leo explained. "They are in a different order."

I opened the Bible I had gotten earlier from my desk and flipped back to an old testament verse.

"Remember how the Naryans tried to build a tower to the heavens?" I asked.

Hope shook her head. Leo just sat there. Hope's eyes suddenly widened.

"God confused their language," Hope said. "So they wouldn't understand each other. The Naryans and the west."

"The third carving must have been carved by a Naryan. In a confused language. Same letters, just scrambled in a different order. How many years later do you estimate it was written," I asked Leo.

"My guess would be around nine-hundred-to-a-thousand years," Leo answered.

"Right around the time of Christ," Hope said, slowly emphasizing each word.

"I know exactly what the third writing says," I said emphatically.

Leo and Hope looked at me with blank stares.

I know what it says.
It was part of God's plan for the rock.

23

Before, continued

Hope sat at the conference table with an exasperated look, throwing her hands in the air for Leo and me to see, while I meticulously compared the biblical text to the letters on the rock.

"Patience, honey. Patience," I said. Not one of Hope's strongest points. I imagined patience was one of an archeo-logists biggest strengths, considering how long they had to toil for one small discovery. Leo looked like he would be fine waiting all day if necessary.

Admittedly, I left them hanging with the incredible claim saying I knew what the letters were. A puzzle, scholars had tried for several hundred years to solve. One I claimed to have the answer to and was taking longer to explain to them than they liked. Or Hope liked, anyway.

"Are you going to tell us," Hope said, "or is this a secret you're going to keep to yourself."

"Maybe he wants to keep the credit for himself," Leo said, laughing out loud.

Leo making a joke was so out of place I lost my place, which meant it would take even longer.

"I don't think he knows what the letters are," Hope said jokingly.

I held up my hand and said, "Brilliant minds take time to work."

"So do dumb minds," Hope said, making Leo laugh out loud a second time.

We were having fun. This was fun. Especially, as soon as I confirmed all the letters matched.

"Are you ready?" I asked, teasingly.

"Will you get on with it!" Hope said. "What are the letters? I'm dying to know."

"I'm reading from the gospel of Luco-Nius," I said slowly and deliberately.

Luco-Nius was the third of four gospels written by an apostle of Jesus. He documented much of Jesus's ministry. Of all the gospels, his had the most detail. The most educated of the apostles, Luco-Nius was determined to provide accurate descriptions of every event. Particularly the healings. Not surprising, since he was a physician by trade before becoming a beloved apostle.

"'The Naryan soldiers seized Jesus and led him away," I continued reading from the text. "'When they came to the place called the rock, they crucified him there. And they divided up his clothes by casting lots."

Hope's mouth suddenly flew open in amazement as she realized what I was about to read.

I continued. "'The Naryan soldiers mocked him. They offered him vinegar to drink but he refused. One soldier carved a written notice on the rock which read: This is the King of the West."

A somber mood swept over the room as the gravity of what we had discovered suddenly became apparent to all of us.

"Leo, put those letters back up on the screen," I said soberly.

NOHS TW ETG SFTI SE EKH HIIT

Leo wrote on his notepad to see if the letters matched the passage in the Bible.

Hope did it in her head as I saw her mouth out the letters.

The words matched perfectly, just scrambled, confused as the Bible had said about the Naryan language. Definitive proof that Jesus was crucified at the rock. Tradition had always said he was; now we knew for sure.

All three carvings on the rock were now verified. Three of the most significant events in human history occurred on that spot: the location of the garden of Eden and the fall; the sacrifice of Casik on the rock and his resurrection and the covenant of peace between Casik and Nary; and the crucifixion of Jesus.

"We need to confirm our findings again," I said, choking up. "Then we will write a paper for publication. The whole planet needs to know what we've discovered here today."

"It's huge," Hope said, "I'm so proud of you." Hope stood and walked over to my chair and wrapped her arms around my neck from behind. We held the embrace for several seconds.

"I'm proud of all of us," I said.

Leo, still wrote away on his notepad.

* * *

Nine months later

Our paper with the findings of the carvings on the rock was published in all the mainstream magazines. On the cover of most. Leo contacted the most reputable archeo-logy magazines who eagerly printed our story. I spoke to President Redford who encouraged me to contact the networks and set up interviews. He also lobbied behind the scenes to gain access to the rock for us so the findings could be confirmed.

Based on our publication, the religious leaders agreed to have the site of the rock examined more closely. Archeo-logists assured them they could do their research without damaging the rock or taking any samples from it. Leo oversaw a lot of the work. The glass case was removed, and the examination proved our work was a hundred percent accurate.

Two plaques were prepared, one on each side of the rock, with the words of the carvings on them. An exhibit was added, giving us credit for the discovery. I was asked to speak at the unveiling of the plaques.

Thousands gathered in Freed-Om square for my speech and several thousand Naryans gathered on the other side of the wall where they could hear the speech as well because of large speakers that amplified the sound.

All of the networks covered the event live, so the entire planet of Ven-Us could view the festivities. Schools were cancelled. Businesses closed. Commerce ground to a halt as most were glued to the airboxes in great anticipation of the unveiling.

An entire program was planned. A band played. A boys' choir sang. Several people made speeches about the significance of the event, mostly politicians and the like. The President didn't attend, citing security issues. He also didn't want to take away the spotlight from me. Not that I sought any notoriety. However, I realized the chance to speak to that many people, including Naryans, was a unique opportunity that few were ever afforded.

I walked to the podium, opened my notes, and looked out over the crowd, pausing a moment to take in the gravity of the words I was about to speak. I looked over at Hope who gave me a reassuring smile. I practiced my speech in front of her the night before. She was in awe of the content. Only made a couple minor suggestions. Hope said, almost prophetically, that my words might bring two nations together in peace. I wasn't sure about that, but I sensed it could be monumental.

I took a deep breath and began.

"Scores and scores ago, our forefathers envisioned a great nation. Conceived in liberty and dedicated to the proposition that all men are created in the image of God and that all men and women are equal in God's sight. We have gathered today to dedicate this ground... this hallowed place. We remember those who have gone before us. Adam and Eve stood at this very sight. Casik and Nary. Jesus. Sal-aam."

I knew mentioning Sal-aam would be controversial in the west. However, I didn't want to alienate the Naryans from the very first sentences. Sal-aam was at that sight. I didn't believe he ascended into heaven from the rock, but I didn't see anything wrong with ac-knowledging that he was there.

"Others have talked about peace at this very sight. And yet peace has been allusive all these years. The world may note and may long remember what we say here, but it will note more our actions in the coming days. For there is a great task remaining before us. Peace is more than words."

* * *

Qary stood in his office in the east, staring at the air-box in dis-gust. Every word spoken by Rowan Church-Well penetrated his soul and haunted his spirit. He could barely stand to hear the sound of his voice. Listening to Row was like listening to the incessant screeching of an owl, only worse. He'd heard it many times as he tried to go to sleep at night.

The last time he'd heard it was in the interrogation room years before when Church-Well calmly and succinctly said those chilling words, "I forgive you." Now he awoke many times in the middle of the night with those words echoing through his psyche, causing rage to rise inside of him like an inferno. Clever. Row said those words to hurt him, and they did.

He'd rather Row had thrust a dagger in his heart. When he first saw Row enter the room, he expected to be beaten. Tortured. Maybe choked to death. Mocked. Humiliated. Treated in the same way he had treated Row. Qary had accepted his fate. He saw Row reach for what was, certainly a gun in his sock. He deserved as much. The pag-anites had won. They had captured him. To the victor goes the spoils. The loser had no right to complain about the treatment of a superior enemy. The way he justified his treatment of Row. Then he had to be willing to take whatever he dished out.

Not that the west was superior. They had only won that moment in history. There'd be more battles. More victories for both sides. He couldn't believe he'd been humiliated by a woman from the west.

Taken captive. Led like a dog through the woods. Thrown into the trunk of a car. By a woman! He would've just as soon died than face the scorn back in the east from his fellow soldiers. He thought he'd never have their respect again, having been overtaken by a weak and feeble woman. Something they never learned as he emerged from prison as a hero. The ultimate warrior who had survived the treatment of the west.

The humiliation was his own to bear. Especially from Church-Well who made it worse by his false humility. His kindness. Qary didn't want his kindness; he wanted his wrath. He deserved his wrath. He didn't deserve forgiveness. He deserved to die for his actions. An eye for an eye was what the Quan-di commanded.

Forgiveness showed Row's weakness. A strong man took revenge. A weak man forgave. Church-Well would pay today for his weakness.

Qary had in his hand an air-line. The fate of Row and the thousands in the square were in his hand as well. He felt the satisfaction. His time for revenge had come. They should've killed him when they had the chance. Something they'd regret moments from now.

One of his fighters was in the crowd at Freed-Om Square. A warrior. A martyr who would lay down his life when the bomb attached to his vest exploded. Qary had a remote control on his air-line in case the warrior got cold feet and backed out. When Qary pushed the button, the vest would explode. The pag-anites and his man would never know what hit them until it was too late.

It had been a daring plan. One Qary had devised himself when he heard about the dedication of the plaques. That Church-Well would be there and would be speaking was a bonus. He spoke to his soldiers and asked for volunteers. More than a hundred of his most trusted men had begged to be chosen. He carefully selected one of his most loyal men for the mission.

Somehow, the bomber made his way across the border, through security, blended in with the crowd, and stood within thirty feet of the stage. He had taken a picture with his air-line and sent it to Qary, confirming his position. Qary could see him on the network feed on the air-box.

Perfect placement. Fool-proof plan.

The west called his man a "suicide bomber." That term infuriated Qary. The man was a hero. A freedom fighter. Waging battle against the pag-anites of the west. Beautiful young girls awaited him in heaven.

The bomb was ten times the power of the one that had killed Row's wife and daughter twenty years before. A tinge of regret pulsed through Qary at that moment. A few minutes before, he had seen Row's wife introduced on the stage. Clearly with child. Qary thought it cruel that he would kill two of Row's wives and two of his children. He only wanted to kill Row. He wished the wife wasn't there. He didn't care that he'd kill other men's wives, their women and children. The personal battle was with Row, not with his wife.

Though he regretted it, it couldn't be helped. Nothing he could do about it now.

The only question was the timing. When would he push the button? He turned his attention back to the air-box. Church-Well was standing on the stage, still speaking. The rage inside of Qary was building with each spoken word.

"God said that there is neither male nor female, Western or Naryan. God is not a respecter of persons. He shows no favoritism. God welcomes every nation who fears him. God told Casik and Nary that they would both build great nations. And they have."

Qary grabbed something off his desk and threw it at the air-box, causing a loud clang as it banged off the side.

"Al-Tay has chosen the Naryans," Qary shouted at the air-box. "God does show favoritism. Men are to rule over women. Nary was the first born. Naryans are the superior race."

Qary's heart was ablaze. His fists were in a ball. He reached for the air-line and started to push the button. For some reason he couldn't explain, he paused, wanting to hear more. The words were compelling. He had to give Row that much credit.

The networks panned across the other side of the gate at the Naryans. Thousands were at the gate, hanging on every word. Qary wondered for a moment if the blast would make it all the way to some of his people. That gave him pause as Row continued.

"But what makes a nation great? Is it the number of people in its ranks? Is it the strength of its weapons? Or is it the strength of the character of its people? Of its leaders? How is a nation great when it is filled with hate for another just because they are different? Just because they believe differently. I proclaim to you today that we are not great. We have not fulfilled God's plan for the two people. Not as long as a Great Wall divides us."

A roar went up in the crowd. They cheered for several minutes, not letting Row continue. The cheering could be heard on both sides of the wall.

Qary sat down in his chair. His hand slipped off the remote control. He was aware of the covenant of peace Casik and Nary had forged at the rock. The Quan-di mentioned it.

"Can we forge a grand and noble alliance between the East and the West? An historic effort for peace. Can we set aside our hatred? Our need for revenge? I've had to do that myself..." Row's voice cracked as he spoke those words.

Suddenly, Qary felt convicted. Guilty. Remembering how much pain he'd caused Row.

"He's talking about me," Qary said to himself. "He had to set aside his hatred for me."

Row's words kept coming, cutting, piercing, like a knife through butter. Row was talking about the need for forgiveness. The need to exchange hate for hope. Pain for peace. We can never be totally free as long as we are fighting to be free. Suddenly, Row's words of forgiveness seemed genuine.

All Qary could feel was pain. Regret. Fear. Was it right for him to kill all those people? Kill Row. His wife and his unborn child. Would Al-Tay really be happy with him?

"We are indeed, and we are today, the last best hope of man on Ven-Us," Row said, the words resounding across the entire planet.

That's true. What have all the wars accomplished? What has all the hate done for anyone other than divide? Separate. Would the fighting ever end? Not until someone ended them. Row was speaking directly to him. Offering him an opportunity to end the wars. End the fighting. End the hatred.

Qary realized at that moment he was a coward. He wasn't the one standing in the crowd about to blow himself up. He wasn't standing face to face with Row, weapons drawn, giving Row a fighting chance. He was going to kill him with a bomb. A surprise. Without a fair fight. He'd kill his wife and child. A child not even born. What would that do?

It would awaken a sleeping giant. The west would avenge his death. The death of the thousands who would die in the square. Tens of thousands of Naryans would needlessly die if he pushed that button. The Naryans would retaliate back against the west. The vicious cycle would continue on for more centuries.

"The future will always be ours," he heard Row say.

What kind of future will we have? Our children have. My wife. My children.

Qary's air-line vibrated. The bomber.

"I'm ready. Al-Tay is great."

The bomber has a remote ability to set off his bomb. Panic pulsed through Qary's veins. "What if he sets off the bomb on his own? I'm not ready. I'm still thinking. Having second thoughts."

Qary sent him a message. *Stand down!*

Did he get it? Am I too late? Will he understand what that means?

Qary looked back at the air-box as Row walked from the podium, his speech over. He saw him sit down next to his wife.

"Don't do it," he shouted, as the networks scanned the crowd, the crowd still applauding, yelling wildly for Row and his speech.

Qary sent another message, *Abort the mission! Do not detonate the bomb!*

He looked up at the air-box in dread as the networks broke away from the scene to an ad for a product.

He sunk into his chair. Was he too late?

24

President Sarah Hatch-Ard was adamant. "I want you to give the speech at the Peace Summit," she insisted.

"Madame President, you should be the one who gives the speech," I retorted.

"I've been President for three years," she said with an exasperated look. "Can't you call me Sarah. I was your student at seminary, for goodness sakes. You made us call you Row even though you were the Dean."

"I made you call me Dean Row," I reminded her.

"That was your choice. I'm the President, so I should determine what you call me."

"Anyway, Madame President—"

Sarah glared at me. "You're so stubborn. I don't know how your wife puts up with you."

I continued, ignoring the comment but not before giving her a wide grin. "You're the obvious one to give the speech. This summit is historical. It's only right for the President to address the crowd."

"I will address the crowd. But you're giving the main speech. It's final. I've already decided."

I started to protest further, but she interrupted me.

"Did you know I heard your speech at the wall thirty years ago?" Sarah asked.

"I didn't know that, although I think all of Ven-Us heard it."

"I was there. In the crowd. It was brilliant. That's why I want you to give this one. You have become a symbol for peace between the Naryans and the west."

"Did you know there was a suicide bomber in the crowd that day?" I asked.

"No!" Sarah said. "I never heard that." She stood up from behind her desk and looked out the window, contemplating that new information.

"There was. We didn't know it at the time, but later we had intercepts between the east and the bomber. Someone called it off at the last minute."

"If a bomb had gone off in the square that day, thousands would have been killed. I would have been killed. You... All of us would've died." Sarah's eyes were distant. She turned away slightly. Maybe hiding tears building up in her eyes.

"It would have been the worst attack in history," I continued. "We went back through the footage, and the bomber was within thirty feet of the stage. According to the intercepts, he was ready to pull the cord and blow himself up and take everyone else with him. At the last minute, a message came through on his phone to stand down. To abort the mission."

"Thank God he did," Sarah said. "Do we know who called off the attack and why?"

"We don't, but I suspect it was Qary."

"Qary? Why would he call off the attack?"

"I don't know. But there hasn't been an attack since. Before that day, there were attacks all the time. Now thirty years later, we haven't had a single attack on our soil. Qary has been in charge most of that time. I think something I said that day might've changed him. Maybe something I said before."

I told Sarah about my conversation with Qary in the interrogation room. I'd never told anyone but Hope about that conversation. Sarah was the President. She'd be meeting Qary face-to-face in a few weeks. The more information she had, the better. That's why I decided to tell her everything.

"All the more reason why you should give the speech," Sarah said, regaining her composure and stating her words more emphatically. "Maybe your speech can bring peace to all of Ven-Us once and for all. It obviously changed history once."

"We don't know that for sure, but if there is something I can do to bring peace between us, I'll do it. The Bible says in the last days there will be talk of peace, but it won't last. We always have to be mindful of that."

"Still, if we can forge a peace at this summit even for a period of time, it will save lives and will secure a longer future for our children and grandchildren. We owe it to them to try."

"I agree. We have to try."

"Happy birthday, by the way," Sarah said, changing the subject. Obviously, I was giving the speech. That subject appeared to be closed for discussion.

"Thank you. I turn seventy years old today."

"Are you doing anything special?"

"My wife is throwing me a surprise birthday party."

"If it's a surprise, how do you know about it?"

"I've suspected it for a while. So, I've been messing with her. I told her I had to work late. Made up all kinds of excuses as to why I couldn't be there. Finally, she had to tell me. She was afraid I'd ruin the surprise."

"You're horrible."

I grinned mischievously. "She's picking me up in a few minutes. We're going out to eat and then back to the house where I'm sure a crowd is waiting."

"Well, you only turn seventy once, so enjoy it. Those people love you. I love you and appreciate you. Everything you do. I don't know how I could do this job without you."

"Thank you. Now that I know it's happening I'm actually looking forward to it. It'll be good to have everyone together. It's been a while since the whole family has been together in one place. If I have to turn seventy to make it happen, so be it."

I suddenly stiffened. A pain shot through my arm. It left just as quickly as it came upon me. Such a short pain, Sarah didn't notice me wince. Or if she did, she didn't say anything.

"Anyway," Sarah continued, "you need to get started working on your speech. The summit is in two months."

I started to say something in protest, to make my case again for her giving the speech, but the pain returned. Only stronger. I couldn't speak for a moment.

Sarah held up her hand to deflect my protest anyway.

"I'm your boss, so you have to do what I say," she retorted. "Your wife may not be able to make you do what she wants, but I sure can."

"Don't worry about Hope," I said as the pain subsided. "She has her ways of making me do whatever she wants. I told her I didn't want a birthday party. In just a few minutes, she's picking me up to go to the birthday party. Between the two of you, I never get to do anything I want."

Sarah laughed.

I smiled, but it was through a grimace. I'd never felt this pain before. It was shooting down my left arm. Intermittently. I felt a heaviness in my chest. Like someone was sitting on it. For a while, I had trouble catching my breath. I actually considered having Sarah call for an ambu-lance. Instead, I left Sarah's office and went to the wash-room. After splashing some water on my face, I felt better.

It's probably nothing.

The doctor had described possible symptoms of heart failure. and these pains matched them but were short in duration. He said when it happened, the pain would be continuous, and I'd need to get to the emergency room right away.

I decided I would make an appointment to see him tomorrow. Besides, Hope had gone to so much trouble to plan this party,

224

I didn't want to do anything to ruin it. If I went to the emer-gency room, they'd run tests, say I'm fine, and then we'd be late for the party. I wasn't going to let that happen over a little bit of chest pain. I'd endured a lot more than that through the years.

A sudden memory of the prison and torture appeared in my mind out of nowhere. I quickly dismissed it as fast as it came. I'd gotten good at ignoring that pain. I'd ignore this pain until tomor-row.

Then it went away on its own.

* * *

I now had a speech to prepare. The words were already starting to come to me. Something about a dream. I want to share that I have a dream about the future of Ven-us and what it can be like.

The first few lines started forming in my mind. "When we were children, we were free to dream. Our imaginations took us to far-away places with gardens, happy creatures, and fairy tales. Where everyone loves each other and is at peace with one another. As adults, we become cynical. Jaded. Our perspective changes. Our dreams are lost. We no longer believe in them. But I still dream. And I have a dream today. A dream of a brighter future for Ven-Us. A dream for peace."

I hurriedly scribbled down the words on a notepad not wanting to forget them, just as Hope pulled in to pick me up. The pain in my arm had subsided to the point that I felt like I didn't need to tell her until after the party. My chest felt better.

I got in on the passenger side. I kissed Hope warmly on the cheek. Since she was already in the driver's seat, I just let her drive.

Good thing.

The last thing I remember was reading her the first few lines of my speech.

* * *

I woke up in a hos-pital room, surrounded by several doctors and nurses, a number of wires protruding from my body connected to a machine with a bunch of numbers on it.

"He's awake," I heard someone say.

"Where am I?" I said groggily.

"You are at the hos-pital," I heard a voice I didn't recognize say. As my eyes cleared, I could see it was a nurse. "You had a heart incident," she said.

"Where's Hope? Is my wife here?" I was still trying to regain my senses. Hope was the last thing I remembered. I suddenly realized I hadn't told her about my heart ailment. *She's going to be mad at me.* She probably knew now. I needed to explain.

My birthday party!

"What time is it?" I asked.

"It's seven."

The party starts at seven.

"I have to go," I said, raising up to get out of the bed.

"Oh no. You're not going anywhere for a day or two." The nurse pushed my chest back down, so I fell back onto the bed.

Why didn't I have the strength to resist?

"My wife's having a surprise birthday party for me tonight," I explained. "I'm supposed to be there. I'll be alright. There's nothing wrong with me."

"You almost died tonight," the nurse said. "Your wife happened to be driving by our hos-pital when you passed out. A few more minutes, and you wouldn't have made it."

"Where is my wife?"

"She went out to the hall to make an air-line call."

She was probably calling everyone about the party. I tried to envision who would be there. Our kids, grandkids. Neighbors. Friends from church. They would all be so disappointed. I'd ruined their evening.

The nurse left and Hope walked into the room shortly thereafter.

"The nurse told me you were awake," Hope said as she took my hand. Fear was still all over her face and in her eyes. She'd been crying.

I squeezed her hand. "I'm okay. I'll be as good as new in a couple days."

"I was so afraid," Hope said, her hand shaking. "I thought I'd lost you. You were talking about your speech, and then your head just drooped down to your chest, and you passed out. The belt in the veh-icle kept you from falling over. I was driving, and I tried to shake you awake. I called out your name, but you didn't respond. So, I drove here."

"You did the right thing. But I'm going to be fine. What about the party? I've ruined it."

"I called Seth. He told everybody. They all send their best wishes for a speedy recovery."

"Who all was there?"

Hope went through some of the list. More than fifty people were in our house waiting for us to get home, so she didn't remember everyone. My heart that was failing felt suddenly warmed by the gesture and outpouring of love from our friends and family who had taken time to come to my party.

* * *

The four days in the hos-pital seemed like two weeks. The President sent her personal physician to take over my care. She said there was some permanent damage. I'd feel weaker. My speech would slur some. I didn't have full use of my right arm. I asked about returning to work. She said I could go back to work on a light schedule in two weeks. I would be fine to attend the summit and give the speech as long as I had the energy.

I still hadn't told Hope that I knew about this beforehand. She wouldn't understand why I didn't tell her.

Hope felt like I should resign.

"I can't," I had insisted. "Not until the summit is over."

"I'm worried about you," she said. "The summit is going to be stressful. You're going to see Qary."

"That's why I have to go. I have to talk to him and look him in the eye. I think there's an opportunity for peace. I've been working on my speech. Let me read you some of it."

Laying in the hos-pital bed for four days gave me plenty of time to work on my speech. Other than getting tired more easily, I felt the same. The medicine took away the pain in my arm and I didn't feel like an elephant was sitting on my chest. The weight of the summit was still on my shoulders. But peace was within our grasp. I believed God had prepared me for such a time as this.

Hope was encouraging. She said the speech was amazing and that I should definitely give it.

After the second day, the doctor had given the okay for me to have visitors.

Our children and grandchildren were the first. At one point, I had three little children under six on my hos-pital bed. The best medicine anyone could ever give me was seeing those kids. I was feeling better by the day.

Eric and Lacy came by. They were celebrating their twenty-fifth wedding anniversary. Both had retired from the V-7 years before. We competed with pictures of grandkids.

While preparing to check out, a knock on the door was a messenger with a cable and a large bouquet of flow-ers. So large it barely fit on the table.

"Who could this be from?" Hope asked, looking at me with a curious grin as the messenger handed her the cable.

"Probably the President," I said. "She's the only one I know who would send such an extravagant gift."

Hope read the card and her mouth flew open. Her eyes widened which peaked my curiosity further. She slowly looked up from the cable.

"What?" I said. "Who's it from?"

"You'll never guess."

"Just give it to me," I said roughly but playfully, the suspense growing from her reaction.

I looked down at the cable, and my mouth was suddenly as wide as Hope's.

Get Well Soon! Best wishes for a speedy recovery. I hope you are well enough to meet me in six weeks. There are things I want to talk to you about. Privately. Qary

The top of the cable read, *From the Office of the Supreme Commander of the Naryan Nation.*

What does he want to talk to me about?

Privately.

25

Four weeks later

My four-day stay in the hos-pital turned into a four-week stay after another major heart incident. The doctor called it a *strike*. A clot in a blood vessel in my neck blocked the flow of blood to my brain, causing me to nearly die a second time. This time the damage was more severe. The blocked vessel was on the left side of my neck and affected the left side of my brain. However, the damage was to the right side of my body. Something I didn't understand, but the doctor said was common.

I lost complete use of my right arm. Now it just hung by my side. The right side of my face was slightly contorted on my cheek and pulled my mouth slightly to the side causing me to slur my words even more than before. I could still walk, but the steps were labored, and I could only sit and stand with help. The doctor performed a surgery and put a small balloon in the vessel, expanded it with air, successfully opening the vessel to blood flow. She didn't anticipate that vessel being a problem anymore but was concerned about oth-ers. She said ominously the same thing could happen again at any time. The next time could be fatal.

I resigned my position as Minister of Defense and stepped out of my participation in the Peace Summit, much to my disappointment. Before the strike hit me, I had basically completed the speech and was looking forward to delivering it and to meeting with Qary. Still utterly curious as to why he wanted to meet with me, I was resigned to the fact that I'd probably never know.

I was shocked when President Hatch-Ard called. Hope was there and handed me my air-line.

"Qary has cancelled the Peace Summit," she said.

"Why?" I asked, not believing what I was hearing.

Advanced teams had gone to the east and met with his advisors and hammered out a basic structure for peace. All that was left was a few minor details. The President was expecting to actually sign peace accords at the summit. Now apparently there was a glitch in the plans.

"Qary will not come unless you are there," she explained. "He knows about your sickness and sends his best wishes, but he wants to postpone the summit until you are well enough to attend."

"Well, that's ridi... c... lous," I said, having a hard time getting out the last word. "That's crazy," I finally said. "What do *I* have to do with it?"

"He won't say. But he won't budge. It's not negotiable, according to him."

"I'll just have to be there then," I said emphatically.

I could see Hope shaking her head no. The air-line was on speaker so she could hear the entire conversation.

"The doctor said you can't go," she whispered.

"I have to," I said so both Sarah and Hope could hear me. "Tell Qary I'll be there. As long as I'm there, I might as well give the speech. It's decided. I'm going."

"Row, what are you doing?" Hope said, after I hung up the air-line. "You know what the doctor said. You could have another strike at any time."

"That's why I need to go. I may not live that much longer," I said gently as Hope winced and tears formed in her eyes. "What's the difference if I die there or here in this hos-pital bed? At least, there I can make a difference. If my presence means there's a chance for peace, then I have to go. I hope you understand."

"I do, and that's why I love you. You're the strongest man I've ever met. And the most stubborn. If anybody can get up out of this bed and go, it'll be you. There's no way I can talk you out of it, is there?"

I shook my head no, trying to seem resolved by contorting my face. Not sure if I succeeded in doing anything other than making myself look like a clown at a circus. Hope didn't seem to notice.

"Then how can I help?" she asked.

"Get my notes. We have a speech to prepare." I said with a wide smile, suddenly feeling renewed energy. A purpose. Something to get me out of my depression.

If Qary wants to meet with me. then he will. I've bested him at every turn. My whole life has been defined by him. Maybe my legacy will as well.

* * *

The Peace Summit, one month later.

Tremendous preparations went into what was the biggest event in the modern-day history of Ven-us. Freed-Om Square was cordoned off, and only security and those with all-access passes could enter the area. A makeshift building was erected to hold the President and her staff. It had three rooms. One for the President, one for staff, and one for spouses of the staff and other aides and dignitaries.

A large, white, open-air tent was in place slightly north of the square where the signing ceremony would take place. Assuming all the terms were agreed to at the summit and there would be a ceremony.

A platform was built for the networks and their crews, and various cameras were placed strategically around the area to get the best views of the event. Qary even allowed cameras on the east side of the wall. The networks frequently panned to the throng of people who'd gathered on that side. Apparently, it was as big an event in the east as it was in the west.

Further north of the square on a hill, a platform was erected where the speeches would take place. From the platform, the speaker could look out over the wall into the Naryan Nation while addressing the masses of people who were on the west side.

Sarah read me some of her speech. Beautifully written, about a shining city on a hill.

Tens of thousands of people in the west camped out overnight just to get a good view of the festivities. Traffic was backed up for mil-eads, and additional security was brought in to control the crowd and organize parking. Thousands of soldiers and undercover agents were stationed throughout the area, and no one could get in without first going through a search of their bags and a search to make sure they weren't carrying any weapons or bombs. So far, there had been no incidents.

I was sitting in a specially designed rolling chair in the room designed for the President. Sarah, Martha, her closest advisor, and Hope and I were the only ones in the room, other than her protection detail. A big screen air-box was in the room so we could see the network feed. From the camera pointed to the east, we could see the road to the Burg-ess Gate that was lined with Naryans on both sides awaiting the arrival of Qary.

The networks estimated that more than one million people were in attendance, and close to a hundred million, what amounted to the entire population of Ven-Us, were watching by air-box.

Martha was going through the final schedule of events. She said my speech would be the last item on the program, and advised that a special ramp was built to get my rolling chair up on the stage. A specially designed chair was placed on stage for me to sit during my speech, but I insisted on standing.

The head of security came in, gave us an update, and then left saying it shouldn't be long now before Qary arrives. He advised that he was only a few mil-ead away.

"Qary is insisting he be allowed to meet with you alone," the President said to me. "I'm concerned about that. What are his motives? What does he want to talk to you about? I must insist that we have one of our agents in the room at all times. For your protection."

The thought had crossed my mind a time or two. Was Qary intending to harm me? Was this his last chance for revenge? He was getting older as well. Perhaps, he wanted to go out as a hero to his people. Maybe it was a matter of pride. I was basically defenseless if he wanted to kill me if we were alone.

"I'll be fine," I said dismissively. "I don't need a bodyguard. What's he going to do? Kill me? I'm already half-dead anyway."

No one chuckled other than me. I could see Hope glaring at me out of the corner of my eye. I imagined steam would be coming out of the top of her body if her head weren't there to contain it. Sarah didn't seem amused either.

"Nevertheless, we're going to have a man in the room. I'll tell him it's for both of your protection. How are you holding up, Row?"

"I'm doing great," I said, mustering as much enthusiasm as I could. The truth was that I was exhausted. Just getting dressed had taken all my strength. The trip there and getting in and out of the chair had zapped what little energy I had. I had no idea how I was going to stand for the duration of my speech but was determined to do so. I believed God had called me to this moment and his strength would get me through it.

I reminded myself of the verse in the Bible, "I can do all things through Christ, who strengthens me." I didn't feel his strength yet, but I knew I would when the time came.

Sarah suddenly pointed to the air-box excitedly.

"That's Qary," Martha said.

We all looked at once. One lone black vehicle was driving down the road toward the gate. It stopped short of the gate, and moments later a man stepped out of the back seat. I recognized Qary immediately. Older. Dressed in a black suit jacket, white shirt, no tie. He waved to the Naryans who cheered his arrival.

"Where are the rest of his advisors and bodyguards?" Hope asked.

"He said he was coming alone," Sarah said. I wasn't surprised. Sounded like something Qary would do. Make himself the entire center of attention.

"We told him we would take care of security," Sarah said. "We weren't going to allow him to enter the west with armed guards. He said he didn't need any advisors. He had the power to negotiate and sign any agreement."

As bad a shape as I was in, Qary looked the opposite. I estimated he was seven or eight years older than me, but he looked trim and fit. Like I remembered him, only slightly older in his face. Same beard. Dark eyes. Bushy eyebrows. Full head of hair. Only difference was slight graying in the hair and beard. A slight grin was permanently affixed to his face. I remembered that grin from as far back as the first time I'd met him. I also saw the mark I'd left on his face, which was still prominent. I wondered if that was why he wanted to meet with me alone. Maybe he wanted to give me a similar mark. An eye for an eye.

The memories flooded back into my mind. A range of emotions spun around inside me like a washing machine spin cycle. Was I ready to see him again? Face-to face. Perhaps for the last time. What would I say? Have I really forgiven him? Were they just words? How I reacted to him today would define whether I really meant it thirty years before.

I felt a sudden pressure. I should tell him why I forgave him. What Christ had done for me. Was the love of Christ strong enough in me that he would see it? Feel it. Know it was real. I know it's real in me. How could he if I still haven't forgiven him? Bible verses I learned as a child started flashing through my mind.

Christ in me, the hope of glory. The verse rang in my ears as I heard my Bible-school teacher reading it to us as a child.

He is my peace, who has broken down every wall. Any lasting peace could only come through Christ.

Then a final verse came in my head. It strengthened me. Emboldened me. Gave me a purpose. Jesus said it.

Blessed are the peacemakers, for they shall be called sons of God.

I was a child of God. A son of God. A peacemaker.

I suddenly knew why God had me there that day. Why he'd let
me live long enough to see this moment.

* * *

We stood on the west side of the gate, waiting for it to open.
President Hatch-Ard stood in front of the rest of us. Her husband
was next to her to her left, dressed in a black suit and a red tie. She
looked elegant in a pleated navy-blue dress just above her knees
with a metallic belt and matching silver shoes. A small thin band of
pearls around her neck. Her hands were shaking slightly. I could
hardly blame her. Anyone would be nervous in this situation.

I'm nervous.

I was proud of her. Regardless of what happened that day. She'd
handled herself with professionalism and grace. The media had criticized her incessantly since the announcement of the summit, saying
it would never happen. That it was bigger than her. Beyond her capabilities. She was proving them wrong, and I was thankful to be
there to see it. The first three years of her term had been met with
constant criticism from a media who hated her and everything she
stood for. The people loved her in spite of all of their attempts to
destroy her presidency.

My attention was drawn back to the large gates as they started to
open. A lone figure stood on the other side. Qary gave a final wave
to the crowd in the east and then turned back to the west and
walked through the gate, giving the soldiers on his side a slight
salute as he entered the west for the first time—legally. I suddenly
remembered seeing Qary walk through that gate more than thirty
years before. Only walking the other direction. During the prisoner

exchange. Ironic that he was now walking toward us, supposedly in peace, this many years later.

Had we really come that far? Was this too good to be true?

A warm smile was on Qary's face as he quickened his steps and held out his hand to greet Sarah and her husband.

Was it genuine? I studied him closely. Only ten steps away. Looking for any sign of guile.

I was in the background, in my rolling chair, with all the other dignitaries and staff. The special service officers were in close proximity, scanning the crowd, looking for anything unusual. Watching Qary closely. Seeing if he was a threat. Was the President a target? A question asked over and over again in preparation for today. They were ready to act in a moment's notice.

The first worrisome part I'd heard them say to Sarah was when the gate opened. It was quickly closed once Qary was well past it. Thankfully, without incident. The second would be when she was alone with him. No one was going to search Qary. No one knew if he had a weapon or not. A chance Sarah determined we had to take. For the sake of peace.

The Vice President was not at the event. Just in case.

Sarah led Qary back to the building we had just come from. Qary kept his head down as he walked. He had to see me there but didn't acknowledge it. We followed them into the building but were led to a room off of the room where they were meeting. One of Sarah's aides pushed my rolling chair behind them. My wife was in another room for spouses, no doubt watching the feed in nervous anticipation. She'd join me on stage later when I gave my speech.

The meeting between the two leaders was scheduled to last twenty minutes. After a few pleasantries, there'd be frank discussions. The final unresolved issues brought up. Hopefully, resolved with a positive outcome. Otherwise, no peace agreement would be signed that day.

I knew this would be the hardest part. Twenty minutes of eerie silence tested my patience. Not knowing was excruciating. If Qary was going to attack Sarah, he'd probably do it in the room when they were alone.

If he was going to attack me... if I was the target, it would happen when we were alone. Sarah had protective service in the room, but I knew Qary. He had skills. If he tried something, I gave the odds at fifty-fifty he could succeed. I only wished I still had the abilities I once had. I was one of the few people who'd ever lived who could've improved our odds.

The meeting continued beyond twenty minutes. Thirty. Then forty. The network commentators were speculating as to what they were discussing. Some were criticizing Sarah. Saying she was incapable of negotiating a deal. She obviously must be having a hard time persuading him to her point-of-view.

The door finally opened. An aide was summoned in.

A few seconds later, the aide emerged and came up to me. He whispered in my ear. "They've agreed to all the points except one. Qary insists on speaking with you alone. He will not sign any agreement until he does. Sarah's resisting. She insists that she be allowed to stay in the room. Or at least her protective detail. For both of us. For our protection. They are at a stalemate."

"I'm going in there," I said as I started trying to roll my chair myself. Frustrated, I tried to stand.

"Help me up," I said to the aide. "Take my arm." I pushed my feeble body up out of the chair with my left arm while the aide pulled me up with my right. I paused to catch my balance. I asked for my cane.

I walked to the door, opened it, and walked in.

I immediately stopped. Not at all what I expected to see.

26

The Peace Summit continued

The room was empty. The President, Qary, and the two protective service detail were gone. Vanished. Into thin air. Like smoke off a grill.

How is that possible?

My one hand was immobile. The other held me up by my cane. Otherwise, I would've used one of my hands to close my mouth which was wide open in total shock.

I looked at the aide who just shrugged his shoulders and said, "They were here just a few minutes ago when they told me to come and get you."

Was this the trap? Was the whole peace summit a ruse? Part of a grand scheme by Qary the master manipulator?

To kidnap the President of the Ven-Us States?

Several possibilities flooded my mind. How would I do it? I'd pull a gun and hold it on her. Before the protective service could react. Then make them all walk slowly out of the room. To the gate. Back to a waiting car in the east. He'd hold her hostage. Then make demands.

To what end, though? Why? What could Qary possibly gain by such a brazen plan? It would never work.

At that moment, a cheer erupted outside. The crowd was going crazy, responding to something that was happening. Likely, Qary and the President had walked out of the room and into view of the crowd. That still fit my scenario. No one would know Qary was in control of her. The gun was probably out of sight in his coat pocket.

The protective service would be in front of him. Not really a good plan. Snipers could take him out. But the gun might go off accidentally. The snipers might not take that chance.

I tried to control my imagination. There must be another explanation. I asked the aide to turn on the air-box. It would show what was happening outside.

The image flickered onto the screen, and I could see Qary and Sarah walking alone toward Freed-Om Square. Everything seemed normal. They were deep in conversation. Sarah didn't seem under duress. Two protective service members were walking nearby. Qary's hands were not in his pockets. He was talking, using his hands for effect.

I breathed a sigh of relief, still not understanding exactly what was going on. I thought Qary wanted to meet with me alone. Supposedly, he wouldn't sign the peace agreement without a private meeting. According to the aide, Sarah had resisted. Now they were out in the square in sight of all the cameras and reporters and our hundreds of soldiers, some of whom were snipers with their guns focused on Qary.

Not sure what to do next, I asked the aide to get my rolling chair so I could sit down. While he was gone, Martha came in.

"What's happening?" I asked with some urgency.

"Qary has agreed to all the terms outlined in the summit with a few small suggestions and changes," she said.

"That's good. What about meeting with me?" I asked shakily.

"He wanted to meet with you alone, here in this room. But the President refused. She wanted her protective detail to be here with you. Qary tried to assure her he had no nefarious intentions and that your life was not in danger from him. Still, she wouldn't budge. So, finally they agreed for you to meet with him in the square—"

"Out in the open," I interrupted.

"Qary would never try anything in front of everyone," Martha said.

They didn't know Qary like I did. If he wanted to harm me, he wouldn't care who saw it.

At this point, I didn't care. I just wanted to meet with him and get it over with. In the room or in the square; it didn't matter to me. I'd meet with him anytime, anyplace of his choosing. I had things I wanted to say, and I'm sure he did as well.

The aide returned with my rolling chair. I struggled to sit down. Once secured, Martha told the aide she would take it from there, and he left the room with my thanks.

"The President asked that we give her a few minutes in the square with Qary alone and then bring you out," Martha explained.

My mind was elsewhere. What would I say to Qary? I needed to be careful what I said. I couldn't do anything to derail the peace process. I couldn't let mine and Qary's thirty-year feud have any effect on the possibility of a lasting peace agreement. Hopefully, Qary felt the same way. So far, every action he'd taken had been magnanimous and seemingly with the same desire to secure peace. He needed it as much as we did. Or at least that's what I hoped.

"We can go now," Martha said, interrupting my thoughts.

As she wheeled me out of the room, I saw Qary and Sarah on the air-box standing by the memorial with the names of the victims.

Mia and Meg.

Anger rose up inside of me again. Why was this so hard?

Forgiveness.

I thought this was settled for me. I suddenly remembered Jesus's words. A disciple had asked him, "How many times must we forgive, seven times?" Jesus said, "Not seven times, but seventy times seven."

The meaning of Jesus's words became clearer in that moment. I had to keep forgiving, until I didn't need to anymore. My forgiveness, thirty years before, had been genuine. I was sure of it. That didn't mean all the feelings were gone. It meant that every time they came up, I had to keep on forgiving. Seven times. Seventy times seven if necessary.

That's exactly what I'm going to do.

A huge cheer rose from the throng of people as I exited the building. Qary looked up at the sudden noise from the crowd. Our eyes met. I nodded. He simply smiled. His hand was on the memorial, moving from top to bottom. Slowly. Seemingly scrolling through the names.

Seventy times seven.

* * *

Sarah left Qary before my arrival and touched my arm with a reassuring smile as she passed me while headed back to the room.

Qary stepped toward us and took Martha's place behind me pushing my rolling chair. "It's been a long time," I said while he pushed me toward the memorial.

"It *has* been a long time," he agreed.

"You look the same," I said with a chuckle. "I saw the photographs of you riding a horse with your shirt off. I wish I still looked that good."

That brought a hearty laugh and eased some of the tension between us. I could hear the cameras of the reporters clicking away at a distance. I tried to imagine what this looked like to the world. Two known archenemies laughing together.

Qary stopped my chair in front of the memorial. He set the brake on my chair and walked around it so he would be next to me. So, he wouldn't be talking to me from behind. Both of us were facing the memorial. I imagined it to be quite a photo op for the cameras and networks. I tried to force a smile.

"Your President is a fine woman," Qary said.

I realized how difficult that must have been for him to say. In his religion, women were second-class citizens. None were ever allowed in leadership. The hard-liners in his country were probably against him even meeting with a woman as if she were his equal. I suddenly had a tinge of admiration for him for the first time in my memory. It took courage to do what he was doing.

"She is," I said. "I'm proud of you as well. It took a lot of guts for you to meet with us today. To seek peace." The words flowed. I never thought in my wildest dreams I'd be saying I was proud of Qary. It was like the Holy Spirit was giving me words to say. Words to defuse any malice or pretension.

"How are you feeling?" Qary asked.

I wanted to be honest. I felt weak. Vulnerable. Insecure. I wanted to be his equal and stand next to him. I couldn't. I was stuck in that chair. Even in prison when he was torturing me, I always felt superior. Like I had the upper hand because God was with me and not him. Now he towered over me. Like he did in prison. The only time I ever had the upper hand was in that interrogation room, and I had refused to act on it.

The words of the Bible suddenly flooded my mind.

I won't boast upon myself, except about my weaknesses.

My power is made perfect in weakness.

I will boast all the more gladly in my weaknesses.

For when I am weak, then I am strong.

I was glad in that moment that I knew so much of the Bible. My Bible teacher had made us memorize so many verses. They had always come to me when I needed them the most. Like when I was being tortured. Like when my wife and daughter died... Like now.

I was fighting an internal battle. The feelings of rage were overwhelming and difficult to control. Yet I had feelings of peace about meeting with him. Feeling like something good was going to come from it.

Rather than answering, I asked, "You wanted to meet with me alone. How come?"

"I wanted to ask you a question I've wanted to ask for a long time."

"What's the question?" I said quietly.

Qary paused as if unsure of himself. I thought I knew what he wanted to ask. Maybe he was struggling with how the question would make him look weak. Vulnerable. He didn't have God's strength to get him through it like I did.

"Why did you forgive me?" he finally asked, his voice cracking. "You know... that day when you captured me. I didn't deserve it."

I could feel the pain in his voice. Genuine searching. For an answer. One that had eluded him for years. I understood. What I did, didn't make sense to someone who didn't know God. Maybe that was really what he was searching for.

God.

"I had no choice but to forgive," I explained. "Well... that's not true. I did have a choice. I didn't have to forgive you. It was the hardest thing I've ever done in my life. But God has forgiven me of my sins. You may not know this, but he has forgiven you for your sins as well. If God can forgive you and he can forgive me, then I can forgive you. So, I did."

"You had a gun. Why didn't you use it? So many times, I wished that you had."

I realized he was dealing with something deeper. Not just searching. Qary had something he wanted to share with me. I also realized that my speech wasn't impaired. God was working in us.

I have put my words in your mouth and covered you with the shadow of my hand.

Remembering the words of the Bible comforted me. Strengthened me.

"You had a bomber at my speech years ago. You called it off. Why?" I blurted.

Qary seemed surprised for a moment, like he was wondering how I knew.

"I think we both did it for the same reason," I continued not giving him a chance to answer. "There was something inside me that knew I had to forgive you. It was the right thing to do. You called off the bombing because you knew the same thing. You didn't know it at the time, but it was forgiveness in a way. You were giving me grace at a time when you didn't have to. The same grace God gives us when we don't deserve it. When he doesn't have to."

Qary was fighting back tears.

I felt totally at peace. Calm. Empowered really.

"I sense there's more," I said. "Something you want to tell me. What is it?"

Qary reached out his right hand on the memorial and scrolled down through the names. His hand stopped near the top.

Mia Church-Well, Meg Church-Well.

"I didn't know about this memorial until President Sarah showed me the names of your wife and daughter," Qary said, his hand noticeably shaking. "Did you know that I too lost a wife and daughter?"

"I didn't know that. What happened?"

Qary looked up to the sky. Took a deep breath.

I changed position in my seat and leaned toward him. Closer. So, I could hear as he began speaking quietly.

Softly. His words were mixed with tears. Qary was no longer trying to hide from the cameras or from the world. The crowd wasn't cheering. Dead silence was evident throughout the entire square. No one could hear what he said but me. Yet the whole world was listening in their own way. Somehow, sensing the solemnity of the moment. Only able to speculate as to why. I imagined Hope watching. Sarah. The commentators of the networks. Schoolchildren. Mothers. People who had lost loved ones. I imagined the entire world was bringing their own pain in their own way to that moment.

"My wife and daughter were in the city," he said solemnly. "They were shopping. My daughter was about the age of your daughter. They were crossing an intersection. A car sped through. The maniac hit them. He killed them both. My wife's body was dragged down the street. I had to go and identify them. I'll never forget their faces."

"I'm so sorry."

"We got the guy. He was in a room. Kind of like the room I was in that night when you came to see me. I was so filled with rage."

I could see Qary's hands balled into fists. He pounded one against the memorial, catching himself at the last minute so he didn't hit it too hard. Probably not wanting to disrespect it.

"The guy was smug. Like I was with you. Mocking me. No remorse at all. I still remember his eyes. He was a young kid. Barely twenty-one. He didn't care that he'd just taken the two most important people in the world away from me. I grabbed him by the throat and started choking him. He tried to resist, but I was too strong. His hands and legs were bound. I can still see his face. Still feel the rage in me. I didn't stop until he was dead."

Qary wiped tears off his cheek. Camera lenses were clicking. A soft murmuring was going through the crowd like a wave. Slowly at first, then gaining momentum as more and more people were becoming aware that Qary was crying. Something intense was happening in the square. They were participating vicariously. In their own way.

Just as quickly as he lost it, he regained his composure.

"That's what I really wanted to ask you. Why were you able to forgive me? You could've killed me that night, but you didn't. I didn't have to kill that boy, but I did. What's the difference between you and me? I showed no remorse that night, when you came to the interrogation room. You had a gun. You wanted to kill me. I could see it in your eyes. What I said about your wife and daughter was cruel. I had taken the two most important people in your life. Your wife and daughter. And I didn't care. I deserved to die. I expected to die. What makes you so much better than me that you could forgive me?"

"It's not that I'm better than you," I began. "We have all sinned and fallen short of the glory of God. Jesus died for all of our sins. The difference between you and me is that I have believed in Jesus, and I've been saved by the grace of God. That allows me to forgive you. Even when I didn't want to."

"Can I be saved as well?"

And there it was.

The question I thought I'd never hear Qary ask me. I'd always believed God could save anyone. Perhaps that belief was about to be tested.

"If you confess with your mouth Jesus as Lord and believe in your heart God raised him from the dead, you shall be saved," I explained with resolve. "All your sins are forgiven, and you can spend an eternity in heaven with Jesus and other believers. If you reject him, you will die and be separated for an eternity from God."

"I don't see how God can forgive someone like me. I've done so many bad things in my life. You know what I've done."

I answered compassionately. "So have I, Qary. I've killed hundreds of people. Look at what I did to your face. I'm sorry about that, by the way. But God has forgiven me of all those things."

His left hand instinctively touched the scar as he wiped away more tears. "Will you forgive me for what I did to you," he said, his words coming faster. With more intensity. More urgency. Like he needed my forgiveness right away. "Can you forgive me for the torture? Your wife and daughter..."

For the first time since we began speaking, Qary looked me directly in the eye. Before, his head was drooped, his shoulders sagged, like he was ashamed to even be in my presence. I could tell he was sincere, then and now. The weight of his guilt had been haunting him all these years. Now he was purposed to get it all resolved.

"I've already forgiven you," I said gently. "Remember. When I said those words thirty years ago, I meant them. I have forgiven you.

God has forgiven you. You just have to accept it. You just have to accept Jesus as your Savior. Then you'll understand."

At that moment, Martha started walking toward us. We obviously weren't going to be able to finish the conversation. I felt like we were so close. Qary was so close to accepting Christ. If I only had a couple of more minutes, he would've given his life to Christ. I just had to accept the timing. I had planted a seed. A seed that someday might bear fruit.

"The President wants to know if you're ready for the signing," Martha asked.

"I'm ready," Qary confirmed, shaking his head yes.

"Can you give us five more minutes?" I asked. "Tell the President we'll be there shortly. Qary can you take me up to the House of the Rock?"

Qary got behind my chair and pushed me up the slight hill, through the entrance, and into the foyer where the rock was encased. We stopped directly in front of it. Qary remained behind me. Both of us stared toward the rock. I could see Qary's reflection in the glass.

"This is a historic spot," I said. "The garden of Eden was here. This is where Jesus was crucified for our sins. Right here at this rock." I paused, giving a moment for that to sink in.

"Also, this is the exact spot where Casik and Nary made a covenant of peace. They even carved their names on the rock so future generations would know what they did here. Qary, this is an opportunity for us to end the wars. End the bloodshed. Keep the covenant of our forefathers. I'm a descendant of Casik; you're a descendant of Nary. We can set aside our differences, in the same way they did, and we can make a covenant of peace."

I motioned for him to come around the chair so I could see him. I reached out with my good hand and took his.

"Casik and Qary shook hands at this exact spot, starting a new era of peace. Let's shake hands on this spot. You and I."

Qary shook my hand vigorously. I maintained my grip trying to match his strength. Somehow, I was able to.

The joy of the Lord is my strength.

"This one thing I covenant with you to do," I said with joy bubbling up inside of me.

"What's that?" he asked.

"Forgetting the past. The things which are behind us." I raised both of our hands in the air. "Pressing forth to the things in the future which are before us. Together, we will press toward the mark of the prize."

I pulled Qary toward me in a hug. Awkward but firm.

I heard shutters clicking behind us. The press had been allowed in and were taking pictures. Air-box cameras were rolling. With some struggle, I turned my chair around to face them. Qary fumbled with the chair to help me, but it was too late. I was determined to do it on my own.

Together, our hands still clasped, we smiled as thousands of pictures were taken. The whole world was watching. It took two thousand years, but a new covenant of peace was formed. Like Casik and Nary, we were two of the least likely people to ever make peace.

27

After my meeting with Qary, Martha took me back to the President's room, and Qary went to the signing of the peace treaty. I asked for some time alone, so she left me to ponder the already-monumental events of the day.

The air-box was still on, and I watched the ceremony and the signing.

The news said the treaty consisted of five points. First and most important was a freeze on the production of all missiles on both sides. We had a hundred missiles for each one of theirs, so the advantage would always be ours, but we had no intention of using ours. Qary didn't appear to want to either, but he wouldn't always be in power, and hopefully, the treaty would constrain future leaders.

Additionally, the missiles they did have would no longer be pointed at the west. Qary had long since acknowledged the danger of a missile penetrating the atmosphere and releasing the water in a cascade that would destroy the planet. Missile technology had been developed on both sides that allowed the missiles to travel along in an arc, rising to an altitude of no greater than 10,000 feet but with enough propulsion to allow it to travel hundreds of mil-ead. Far enough to reach the west. Both sides had enough to destroy the other several times over.

As a second point, Qary would allow inspectors to enter his country and verify the Naryans compliance with the treaty. This was another important concession, in that trust was not very high from our standpoint. Qary could agree to anything. If we had no way to verify they weren't in compliance, the peace agreement wasn't worth the paper it was written on. Agreeing to the inspectors meant he really was serious about complying to the peace treaty. If they were found cheating on the agreement, serious sanctions would fall into place that would devastate their economy.

A third point was a provision for aid and loan guarantees. The west agreed to provide humanitarian aid, and Qary agreed to allow access from our government agencies to distribute it to persons in need. The loan guarantees allowed the Naryans to significantly improve their infrastructure. They could build roads, bridges, schools, and hospitals with much needed funds.

The agreement also opened a channel for trade. The Naryans had many resources the west could benefit from. They had a shortage of oil, technology, and communication infrastructure. The companies in the west could begin doing business in the east which would improve sales and profit in the west and provide much-needed infrastructure to bring the east into a modern society.

The final, and one of the more important points, was that Qary agreed in the treaty to acknowledge our right to exist as a nation. The Naryans had believed from the time of Sal-Am that we were pag-anites and needed to be wiped off the face of Ven-Us. This rhetoric kept tensions constantly high. Agreeing to that point meant we could coexist as nations with mutual respect and cooperation.

The agreement was all we could've ever hoped for and more. Having met with Qary and seeing the change in him and hearing the agreed-upon points left me optimistic that true peace was becoming a reality and the "Deep Freeze" as it had been called to describe our relations, was finally over. We were years removed from the last actual war with military conflict. This treaty meant the strained ongoing tensions between our countries could finally come to an end and peace was possible.

I thought about my speech and wondered if there was more I could do to move the process forward. I felt a sudden weight, as

I didn't want my words to be anti-climactic. I wanted them to be inspiring. Historic even.

I was glad I decided to go to the room and not to the peace signing. I was already exhausted both emotionally and physically. The day was nowhere near over. I still had to sit through the entire program and deliver my speech. I needed this time to recover. If possible.

The doctor had advised me not to attend the summit for reasons that were becoming clear to me with each passing moment of effort. Knowing God had his reasons for me being there, namely, to talk to Qary, and to give my speech, gave me the satisfaction that I'd done the right thing, no matter how hard it had been and was going to be. God gave me the strength to talk to Qary; he'd have to give me the strength to give my speech.

The room was cooled by an air-lightener and after drinking a K-OK bottle of soda and eating a snack, I felt somewhat better. My spirits really soared when Hope walked into the room.

I love her so much.

She was the perfect helpmate in every way. She doted on me and went through her inspection checklist of all my ailments to make sure everything was okay. Satisfied, she sat back to relax and drink her own soda. I could tell the day was taking an emotional toll on her as well. She wasn't only concerned about me physically, but she also knew how emotionally taxing the day would be and was doing everything she could to be encouraging and supportive as only she could do.

I shared with her my conversation with Qary and how close he came to getting saved. She sat on the edge of the couch, listening carefully to every word, her eyes widened in amazement that our conversation had gone so well. Disappointed, as I was, that the conversation was cut off prematurely.

"God knows the timing," Hope said. "Maybe he's just not ready."

"Now is the time of salvation," I retorted. "He may not get another opportunity. I told him as he was leaving that he could get saved at any time. All he had to do was call on the name of the Lord, and he would save him. I just hope he does."

"All you can do is plant a seed. God does the saving," Hope said sweetly, reminding me of what I already knew but saying it in an encouraging way. I didn't need the emotional weight of regrets at that moment. Like I could've said or done more to help him give his heart to the Lord. Hope was wise. I had enough to concern myself with. Second guessing my conversation wouldn't do any good at that moment.

Hope didn't know my thoughts were already elsewhere. I had something I wanted to share with her but wasn't sure if I should.

"Are you doing okay?" she asked as if reading my mind. "Seems like you want to say something. Or ask me something."

I was considering adding a line to my speech. I was torn. Should I do it? If so, when in the speech should I say it. At the beginning? The last line? Should I make it the big finale? I wasn't sure I should say it at all. I'd scribbled the lines onto my notes. I read them to Hope.

Her mouth flew wide open as she said, "Can you say that?"

"I don't know. That's why I'm running it by you."

"Does the President know about it?"

"No. I just thought of it while I was meeting with Qary. I saw all the Naryans standing on the other side of the glass partition, and that's when the thought came to me. I think the Lord might be telling me to say it."

"I don't know, Row. You'd better be really sure it's the Lord. I think you need to talk to Sarah first. It affects her too."

"I would, but I won't get a chance to talk to her beforehand. Anyway, I offered to let her look at my speech, and she declined and said she trusted me. She told me I could say whatever I felt led to say. That sounds like permission to me."

"I don't think she meant this. You need to do what you feel led to do, but I would think long and hard before saying this." Hope just shrugged her shoulders. "I don't have any advice for you. All I can say is that it's very gutsy."

I laughed. "I've never been accused of not being gutsy."

"That's for sure. That's not even what I meant. It could change the course of Ven-Us forever. It could also backfire. Majorly."

"You're right. I probably shouldn't say it." I took out a pen and marked through the words. "But I really want to!" I said.

"It's probably for the best if you don't," she said.

We sat in silence for the next few minutes until Martha came to get us.

"It's time to go," she said. "Time for your speech. Are you ready?"

"I'm ready," I said. "I just hope everybody out there is ready for what I'm about to say." I looked at Martha and Hope with a cautious grin. Martha had no idea what I meant. Hope did and looked at me with a stare.

I decided to say it as a jolt of energy shot through my body like a lightning bolt.

* * *

The day was sunny and warm but not hot. A mild breeze from the south rippled through the trees and created a slight sound and also making the mid-afternoon sun more tolerable. With the atmosphere filled with water, the sky would be a different color on any given day. Some days it was blue. Other days, when the sun was shining at just the right angle, the sky flamed bright fiery red, glowing, the clouds like embers in a fire. Some days, the sun's rays would bounce off the atmosphere and ricochet back and forth like a laser light show. Those were the rarest and most spectacular days that only happened once or twice a year.

Today the sky was an aqua green. Calming and peaceful. Like sitting on a beach looking out at water, except we were looking up at the sky and seeing the water there.

Sarah introduced me to the crowd. I stood from my chair with the help of Hope and Martha and walked slowly to the podium. Sarah embraced me with a warm hug. The crowd cheered, giving me more strength, more energy. The adrenaline was flowing to such an extent that I barely noticed my infirmities.

I began with the acknowledgements of the dignitaries. There were nine of them, along with Hope and Sarah's husband. Fortunately, I remembered all their names. Qary was sitting next to Sarah's husband.

"I'm humbled by the opportunity to speak to you today. I'm proud of our President. I have known her for more than thirty years. I told a short funny story of when she was at our school. The crowd roared in approval. Sarah smiled, slightly embarrassed.

I'm proud of my friend, Qary, who I've also known for thirty years, but under slightly different circumstances." The crowd laughed again and then applauded. Qary seemed embarrassed as well.

"Qary has shown great courage and honor by coming to this summit and seeking peace."

The crowd erupted. I looked at Qary, and he smiled at me, nodding his head. The crowd kept applauding until he stood and waved to the crowds on both sides of the wall.

Should I say it? Now?

Not yet. At the end. If at all.

Sarah said, whatever I want to say.

"I have a dream," I started slowly but with strength and a renewed vigor.

The whole first part of my speech was a blur. I barely remembered it. Interrupted numerous times by applause and cheering. The people hung on my every word. I looked out over the wall to the Naryans. Tens of thousands were gathered. They were able to hear my words by the amplification and the air-box screens that were set up on their side of the wall. My words were resonating. They were inspiring. I could tell. The speech was building momentum.

Save it for the end.

My tone turned more somber. I decided to bring the level of enthusiasm down. A technique I'd mastered over the years. I would start building the momentum all over again. Give the crowd a chance to catch their breath.

"There are many people in the world who really don't understand, or say they don't, what is the real issue between the Free World and the Naryans. I say to them, 'come to this wall.' This wall has become a symbol of the great divide between our two countries. Because of the wall, I respectfully submit to you today, that we can't even see what really divides us. We just assume we are divided because a physical structure says we are."

No applause. An eerie silence had come over the crowd. Just what I wanted.

"We have our differences, to be sure. The west is not perfect. But we don't need a wall to keep our people in. In the west, we espouse freedom. Freedom for all mankind. Freedom for the Naryans. We believe that every person is created in the image of God, and every person has the right to be free."

The crowd applauded and cheered. Not wildly but the appropriate response.

"I commend the Naryans. They are a strong and committed people. You have endured much hardship over the years. But you have not just endured. You have thrived. God promised in the Bible to create a great nation out of your descendant Nary, and he has."

The crowd in the west applauded respectfully. The Naryans cheered more enthusiastically.

"But you have not achieved all of the greatness within your capability. You never can until you are free."

I paused for effect. To let the words, sink in.

"There are those who say the wall is the greatest architectural achievement of our societies. I suggest to you today, that it is the greatest failure of our societies. It is not beautiful as some suggest. It is an ugly reminder of the hatred and bitterness that has divided us for centuries. It is an offense to humanity. It separates families. Divides husbands, wives, brothers, and sisters, and divides peoples who must live separated. We are all descendants of Hamm. Casik and Nary were brothers. I suggest to you today that we are still brothers. Even though we are divided, we have a common purpose. A common destiny. We in the west cannot achieve our full capability as long as we are divided from our brothers and sisters in the east."

The crowd was building in enthusiasm. The cheers louder. The applause grew more intense.

"I take no satisfaction in the fact that this wall is effective in dividing us. I know all of the safety reasons why it's there. Why do those reasons exist? Why does the west have to be afraid of the east? Why can't those in the east come to the west freely to seek a new life if they so choose? Why must they risk their lives and face the barrel of a gun in order to be free?"

The crowd was somber again. That was okay. I was about to bring them to a stunning conclusion. Like the finale of a fireworks display.

"We have come today to promote peace. I say to you that peace is not possible as long as there is a wall between us. When all are free —then we can look forward to that day when our two countries will be joined as one, living in a peaceful and hopeful globe. When that day comes, and it will, then we will know freedom has come to all men. As long as one man is not free, then no man is truly free."

I took a deep breath and built my resolve.

"The Bible says who the son sets free is free indeed."

The crowd in the west cheered wildly. The east joined them.

Here it goes.

I could feel my heart pounding in my chest. I wondered if it could take it. My legs were shaky. My hands were shaking as well as I turned to the last page. I could barely read the words I had marked through. Didn't matter. I had them memorized.

I'm going to do it.

"Do we really seek peace today?"

The crowd erupted in cheers.

I said it louder and more forcefully, "Do you really want peace today?"

The crowd began chanting the word peace over and over again. This went on for several minutes. The crowd was in an emotional frenzy.

"Do you want peace, Madame President? Do you want peace, Supreme Commander?" They both nodded as I turned to each and said it.

"Sarah, Qary," I said less forcefully, more solemnly.

"I understand the fear of war and pain of division that afflicts Ven-Us," I said as a hush came over the crowd. "I commend you both for striving to reduce missiles. You have taken steps today to not just limit weapons of mass destruction, but you have started us on a road to the possibility of someday eliminating them altogether."

Do I dare?

"While peace on a piece of paper is good, there is one sign that each of you could do that would dramatically advance the cause of freedom and peace."

I looked out over the crowd on both sides of the wall.

"Supreme Commander, Qary, if you seek peace, if you seek prosperity for the Naryan people, if you really want peace..."

The crowd was in stunned silence. I left the words hanging in the air. I remained silent. Letting the momentum build.

"Qary, open this gate," I shouted.

"Qary, tear down this wall!"

28

"Qary, open this gate! Qary, tear down this wall!" I'd said.

I hadn't intended on saying the last line. I wasn't even sure where it came from. Open the gate was a powerful line in and of itself. Something that could be easily done. Also easily undone. But "tear down the wall."

How was that even possible? The wall was more than 10,000 milead long. The cost of tearing it down would be astronomical.

Yet, I'd said it. Now it was out there. It couldn't be unsaid. I suddenly realized the horrible position I put Sarah in. How could she respond? Sarah and her leaders would never agree to tear down the wall, even if she and Qary wanted it.

How would the crowd react? Their reaction would tell me how big a problem I had created for Sarah. They seemed stunned at first.

Suddenly, a cheer went up in the distance, on the very far reaches of the east. It started there, then moved toward the west. Slowly at first. Then it began picking up speed and momentum and intensity. Like a swarm of locusts, it became so intense I could feel the earth shaking. As if the crowd could will the wall down merely from their fervor.

By the time the cheers reached the wall, the people of the west had started their own response. Shouting, cheering, clapping, whistling. The two waves of sound met in the middle at the wall and produced the loudest noise I'd ever heard in my life. I now knew how the crowd would react. They were caught up in the emotion. The pressure on the leaders would be intense.

I looked at Sarah. Explaining her look was nearly impossible. She was glaring at me, yet with a hint of admiration at my courage.

Anger was written all over her face, yet understanding. Optimism and fear, both easily recognizable in her eyes. Both. At the same time. If that's possible. All of those emotions mixed with confusion. Uncertainty. Not knowing what to do next.

Qary simply sat there with a thin smile that he'd permanently affixed on his face. As smart as he was, he'd probably already processed all of his options. Thought it all through. I came to realize how brilliant his mind was. He'd probably lived his whole life walking the fine line between insanity and genius.

I walked over to where they were sitting, the crowd still maintaining their enthusiasm. Now chanting, "Tear down the wall." I realized if something wasn't done soon, they might tear it down themselves.

I stood over Qary and Sarah trying to maintain my balance.

"What now?" Sarah asked, looking past me at the crowd.

"I don't know," I said. "I hadn't thought this far ahead."

Sarah's look of confusion became a recognizable glare.

"I like the idea," Qary said.

"We're not tearing down the wall!" Sarah said emphatically. "I couldn't approve that even if I wanted to. The cost would be astronomical. It would take years of construction and tens of thousands of man hours to tear down the wall. We need it for security."

"You don't need it for security," Qary said, angrily. "We pose no threat to you."

"We're not tearing down the wall," Sarah retorted just as angrily.

"Let's take down a mil-ead of it. Just around the gate," Qary said.

"I have an idea," I interjected, realizing this conversation could escalate to a confrontation which was the last thing we needed in front of all these people.

"Let's open the gate. Both sides agree to remove all their soldiers."

Qary nodded in agreement.

"Are you crazy?" Sarah said. "I can't get that approved this fast."

"You're the commander of all the armed forces," I retorted. "You can do whatever you want to do with your soldiers. So can you, Qary. Both of you agree to remove your soldiers from the wall. Even if it's only temporary. Then have the gate opened. Better that you open the gate in a show of peace than to have an unruly crowd open it for you. I suggest you open it together as a show of solidarity. This is a tremendous opportunity for both of you."

"What about the partition in the House of the Rock?" Qary asked. "My people should be free to view the rock any time they want." Qary must have sensed an opportunity to get something done that had been a source of conflict for decades. He would be instantly beloved by his people if he could accomplish that.

I wanted to preempt Sarah's objection.

"I agree," I said. "Let's take down the partition. Keep three soldiers from each side in the building guarding the rock. They should be the only soldiers in the square. Maybe, we'll need a police force eventually. But we won't need a military force on the border anymore. Let people come and go freely."

"I don't know," Sarah said.

"Come on," I implored her. "This is a defining moment for both of you. It's one thing to talk about peace on paper; it's another to put your words to action and bring about a meaningful and lasting peace through your willingness to break down the walls between us, even if you can't destroy all the physical walls."

"Do I have your word that it is safe to open the gate?" Sarah asked Qary.

"You have my word. My people do not seek violence with you. There are still some hard liners, religious leaders who do, but I'll use this as a way to crush their power. We can take it away from them. Look at the people. They want this. We should give it to them."

Sarah sat in her chair thinking, looking out at the crowd. Apprehension clearly ran through her mind as she tried to contemplate all the possible ramifications.

"Sarah?" I said in the form of a question. "What do you want to do? You need to decide. The crowd is getting restless. I could see the Naryans moving closer to the wall.

Sarah stood from her chair and walked to the podium. She motioned with her hands for the crowd to quiet.

"Most have believed for years that peace was impossible," she began. "That the east and the west are doomed to inevitable conflict and war. I reject that view. The problems between us are man-made; therefore, they can be solved by man. Peace has never been beyond our capabilities; it has only been out of the reach of our resolve."

The crowd applauded politely. Like me, they seemed unsure what Sarah was about to say.

"I ask that everyone who is on the wall, please orderly move off of the wall and out into the square. As soon as everyone is off of the wall, I am ordering that all of the soldiers who have been guarding the wall, should leave their posts and congregate over in the square. I ask you to reverse arms. Put them at your side and be at ease."

"Please be careful leaving the wall," Sarah added. "The soldiers who are in the House of the Rock, please maintain your positions. We ask that no one enter the House of the Rock for the time being. We are going to remove the partition so the Naryans can come into the building freely."

A gasp went up from the crowd in the west. The Naryans erupted in the loudest cheer of the day so far.

Qary stood and walked up to the podium. Sarah stepped back giving him an opportunity to speak. He motioned for the crowd to quiet, but it took several minutes. Enough time for everyone to get off of the wall. I saw the soldiers from the west, slowly moving over to the square. Some were sitting. All seemed more relaxed and at ease as Sarah had requested. Their guns were no longer in a forward position.

"I have come to understand," Qary finally said, "the only thing we have to fear is fear itself. Our own prejudice. Our own hatred. Fear is our greatest enemy. Not each other. Not the east and the west. The people of the west are good and decent, a kind and loving people. So are the Naryans in the east. I have fought many battles. In the battlefield, unjustified fear causes a man to retreat when he should move forward. The same is true in peace. Why do we fear peace? Why do we retreat when we should move forward? Let us not. Let us not retreat into the recesses of the fear that has kept us bound for centuries. It is in the front lines of the battle that the battle is won. The battle is won by the courageous. The one willing to take risks. The one who overcomes his fear."

The crowd erupted like a volcano. I couldn't see my face, but I'm sure my eyes were as wide as coins and my mouth open in amazement. I couldn't believe the words I heard coming from Qary's mouth. Brilliant. Eloquent. Impactful. With resolve. Determination. His words commanded and demanded respect. I could see why so many men were willing to follow him to their deaths.

Qary motioned for the crowd to quiet so he could continue.

"To all of my soldiers, go home. You are no longer needed at the wall. I am commanding all of you to leave now. Go to your families and lay down your arms."

Qary chuckled. I had looked over at the soldiers, I quickly looked back at him. Why was he laughing?

"Don't lay down your arms here," he said with a wide grin. "I don't want a bunch of guns laying around. There are kids here. I don't mean it literally. Take your guns with you, to your houses, and put them away. Hopefully, you won't need them again for a long time, if ever."

I could hear the crowd laughing with him, releasing some of the tension in the air in a way that the cheers could not.

Sarah was standing behind Qary. She walked up to the podium and stood next to him.

"Qary and I have reached an agreement," Sarah said. "The Burgess Gate is to be opened and kept open until further notice."

A gasp went through the crowd. I saw several of Sarah's leaders get up and walk away.

She motioned for Qary to follow her as the protective service detail scrambled, not sure what she was doing. They walked together to the gate. Side-by-side. The crowd appeared stunned by the sight. Yet cheering. Like all of us, not fully able to grasp the full gravity of the moment.

When they reached the gate, Sarah motioned for the operators to open it. The large gates swung open, and Sarah and Qary stood in the roadway staring out into the east. No one moved right away. Unsure of what to do.

I went back to the microphone and said, "To those of you in the west, stay on this side of the wall for the moment and let those on the east who want to pass through the gate... let them go first. To those in the east, please enter the gate in an orderly fashion. Not all at once, for safety reasons. From all of us in the west, I want to say welcome to our friends from the east!" I lifted my good arm as a gesture of hospitality.

The protective detail swiftly moved Sarah and Qary back into the building and probably into the President's room. Hope helped me into my rolling chair and wheeled me off of the stage. Rather than going to the building, I asked her to push me over by the gate. I sat in my chair watching as thousands of Naryans came through. Most cautiously, like they were doing something wrong, but orderly.

They were greeted warmly by those in the west. Given water. Food. People who didn't know each other and had never met were hugging excitedly, kissing each other on the cheeks, introducing friends and families. I saw some loved ones reunited with family members they had not seen for years. Some were crying. Some laughed. All were relishing in the moment.

Hundreds of well-wishers made a point to come up to me and give me words of encouragement. Shake my hand. Touch my shoulder. Naryans and westerners alike kept coming up to me, congratulating me on my speech and thanking me for my courage.

After nearly an hour, I was so tired I asked Hope to take me back to the building. As she did, I saw Qary. He'd come back out of the building and into the crowd. He walked around and greeted people, smiling broadly. Something I'd never seen before and never thought I'd see in my lifetime. He seemed genuinely happy.

I wasn't sure exactly how Sarah would greet me. Would she be happy, or would she be angry with me? At that point, it hardly mattered. What was done was done. She would certainly be criticized and confronted by her leaders.

There were those in the west who made their living on continuous war. Production of missiles, arms, ammunition, defenses were their livelihoods. Those so called "ravens" profited by keeping peace at bay. They wouldn't be happy with Sarah or with me. They'd question who gave me the authority to make such a bold statement. They'd question why I was even giving a speech.

I was relieved when Sarah stood from her chair and greeted me warmly as soon as I came in the room. She didn't seem to mind what I'd done. If she did, I couldn't tell. She was thrilled by the day's events. From a political standpoint, the day had gone as well as it possibly could. As beloved as she was before, her popularity would soar.

This would definitely be a good political move... as long as there wasn't a terrorist attack. The opened gates would make it easier for someone to strike the west. Something I prayed wouldn't happen.

"I'm sorry, Sarah," I said sincerely. "I should've talked to you first. I didn't think of it until just before my speech."

"You called me Sarah instead of Madame President," she said with a grin. "That's progress."

"I shouldn't be surprised. No one has ever been able to control you. What's that saying you have that's famous over at the V-7? The one up on the wall?" Sarah asked.

"It's easier to ask forgiveness than permission," I said.

"That's the one. I think you did it on purpose," she said with a smile.

"I don't know. I sort of felt led by the Lord to it."

"So, blame it on him," she said jokingly.

"Or give him the glory. Seems like everything's going well. Look at all the people," I said pointing to the air-box. "They're all so happy. This is a good thing."

"You know there's no way we can tear down the wall," she said.

"I know. I'm not sure why I said that. That was unplanned."

"It was powerful," she said. "I'll give you that. But not practical."

"Opening the gate is a good start," I said. "You can worry about the wall later."

Sarah opened her mouth to speak but never got the words out.

Suddenly, the earth shook.

A roar filled the room. Cracking. Violent shaking.

Screaming.

Inside and outside. Hope let out a loud scream. Sarah gripped her chair with both hands.

We could see people running from the wall. Terrified.

"Dear God," Sarah said. "What's happening?"

Ven-Usquake.

The temporary building tilted back and forth. The makeshift floor moved like a wave under my chair.

Hope lunged to try and hold me in place, so I didn't tip over. I almost fell out of the chair.

The protective servicemen stumbled, trying to catch their balance and get close to Sarah.

The air-box swayed back and forth as was the picture on the screen as the cameras in the square shook and moved wildly. I tried to focus so I could see what was happening in the square.

The people who'd been milling around before were now running for their lives. Grabbing their children. Some frantically looked for their children and loved ones. The cameras panned into the House of the Rock where the partition between the Naryans and the west was laying on the ground, shattered in a thousand pieces. The soldiers in the room were holding on to the railings along the wall across from the destroyed partitions, unwilling to leave their posts.

Are we all going to die?

A violent shake.

The strongest tremor yet.

I didn't know how our building was still standing. Anything on a table had fallen to the floor except the air-box, which was bolted in place. We could still see the wall, the gate, and the square from the network cameras still focused on the horror unfolding before us.

The ground around the wall suddenly separated.

A huge fissure appeared in the ground. The crack grew to more than a hundred feet wide.

We could hear the groaning of the wall. The stones separating.

Rumbling.

Hope squeezed my hand tightly.

"I need to go out there," I said.

"There's nothing you can do."

Suddenly, a loud crashing sound.

The wall disappeared.

Gone.

The Burg-ess gate was on the ground.

One last violent shake, and the ground closed where the wall once majestically stood.

Sudden calm. No more shaking.

We all stared at the screen in utter disbelief.

No rubble. No stones. Only a misty dust floated from the ground into the air.

The Great Wall of Ven-Us was no more.

29

Five months later

Hope's air-line rang. She clutched her husband's hand with her left hand as he lay in the hos-pital bed. The other was holding what was left of a tissue falling apart and drenched in tears. If it hadn't been the President's name that appeared on the screen, she wouldn't have answered it.

"He's gone," Hope said, her voice cracking as she fought back the tears.

"I know. I just heard. I'm so sorry, Hope," Sarah said in a somber tone. Hope could tell from her voice that she had been crying as well. "Row was a great man and a good friend," Sarah continued. "I'll miss him desperately. The whole world will miss him."

"He died about ten minutes ago. The kids were here. He didn't seem afraid at all. You know him."

"I do. I can't imagine him being afraid of anything. Including death. You have my deepest condolences."

"Thank you," Hope said. "He loved you like a daughter." Hope paused to take a deep breath. "It's going to be hard not having him here. I don't even know what I'm going to do."

"If there's anything I can do, don't hesitate to call me."

"Thank you."

"Are you still fine with the funeral arrangements we discussed earlier this week with Row?" Sarah asked.

The doctor had advised that the end was near and that Row should get his affairs in order. Row, Sarah, and Hope had a call earlier in the week where they discussed a formal state funeral.

Row had resisted, but the two of them had persisted until he finally gave in.

"I'm good with everything we talked about. Of course, Row didn't think we should go to so much fuss. He thinks we should just find a pine box somewhere and throw him in the ground." Hope chuckled half-heartedly. "You know how he is."

"There's nothing he can do about it now. We can do whatever we want."

Hope released some tension with another laugh. She looked at Row. His face was peaceful with a slight smile as if he really did approve of their plans.

"The whole world is going to want to pay their respects," Sarah continued. "I think he's more popular than I am. If he had run for President, I don't think I could've beat him. I think he could even win a Naryan election. He's more popular there than Qary."

They both laughed. "I can't see Row being a politician," Hope said. "He's too blunt. He would make too many people mad."

"Every time he gave a speech, no one would know what he was going to say," Sarah said jokingly. "Don't I know that all too well? I never asked you, but did you know he was going to say '*Tear down this wall?*'"

That saying had become famous throughout Ven-Us.

"I knew right before that he wanted to say open the gate. I advised against it. I told him to talk to you first. I don't know where the tear down the wall came from. I think he thought of it right before he said it."

"I think you're right. Now, I'm glad he said it. At the time, I wasn't so sure."

"Trust me," Hope said grinning, "He said a lot of things over the years that I didn't think he should say. Something about Row though... he's like the non-stick coating they put on pans. Nothing sticks to him. Look at everything he went through in his life and, yet he survived all of it. Thrived even. I don't know how he did it."

"God had a plan for him, and he was perfect for it. I know I've never met anyone like him. I already miss him."

Hope dabbed at her eyes again, not able to put words together to respond. Afraid that if she did, the tears would start flowing again. She wanted to be strong while talking to the President. Not that it mattered. Sarah was like family to them. They could talk and grieve without any pretense.

"I'm sending a heli-copter over there as we speak," Sarah said, re-gaining her composure and drawing on her leadership skills. Like Row had done when he faced adversity. "It's already on its way," she continued. "There should be two soldiers outside your room right now standing guard. You can expect the press to be all over this soon if they're not already. We'll bring his body back here and pre-pare it for his funeral. He's going to lay in Freed-Om Square for one week so people can come through and pay their respects. I also have another idea I want to run by you."

Sarah explained her idea for Row's funeral. Hope was in total agreement and thought it was the perfect tribute.

"Let me run it by the kids," Hope said. "You get the approval from whoever you need to."

"I don't think it'll be a problem on my end."

"Great!" Hope said. "I'm sure the kids will think it's an amazing idea. Row would think it's too much. He'd say it's over the top. But like you said, he doesn't have a say anymore. I say we do it."

"I'll get to work on it."

"Thank you for calling, Sarah. It means a lot."

The air-box tuned to the VNN Network suddenly had a banner across the bottom of the screen that read in big red letters, *Breaking News.*

"That didn't take long," Hope said to herself as she turned up the sound.

"Rowan J. Church-Well," the VNN reporter said, "died peacefully in a local hos-pital just moments ago, according to a hos-pital spokesperson. His wife Hope and their children and grandchildren were said to be by his side. He was seventy years old. Church-Well is most noted for serving our country as a V-7 operative and then as Minister of Defense. He is credited for discovering that the garden of Eden was at the same location as the House of the Rock. He's also noted for discovering the meaning of the writings on the rock. His speech at the Ven-Us Peace Summit is said to be the greatest speech in the world's history, and his efforts at the peace summit ushered in a new era of peace and tranquility between the east and the west."

The news anchor paused for a moment and put his hand to his ear as if listening to a producer or someone giving him important information.

"The President of the Ven-Us States has just issued a statement," he said as he began reading it.

"It is with great sadness that I learned of the passing of my good friend, Row Church-Well just a few minutes ago. We join the entire nation in mourning and expressing our deep condolences to his family and friends during this difficult time. Our hearts and prayers go out to you. Ven-Us has lost a great patriot, friend, statesman, and he will be greatly missed. I am ordering that all flags be at half height in honor of Row. Minister Church-Well's body will lie in honor at the Capital for two days and then will be moved to Freed-Om Square at the House of the Rock for one week so that the entire world—Naryans, and Christians—can pay their respects. God bless Row Church-Well, and God Bless the United Ven-Us States."

Hope's air-line rang, so she pushed the mute button on the remote.

Unknown Caller.

"Hello," Hope said.

"Mrs. Church-Well?"

"Yes. This is Mrs. Church-Well."

"This is Qary. I just heard the news and wanted to call and express my sincere grief over Row's death."

"Thank you for calling, Qary. That means a lot to me and would mean a lot to him. He really enjoyed talking with you a couple days ago."

Qary and Row had talked for more than an hour. Joking. Ribbing each other. Having the best time. The call had perked Row's spirits, and doctors had some optimism that he might pull through this latest heart strike. When he took a turn for the worse this afternoon, the doctor told Hope she needed to call the family to his side. He didn't have long to live. As it turned out, he only had a couple hours.

Hope had never left his side since he had been hos-pitalized four days before. The kids had been in and out and had arrived a final time shortly before his passing. Row was still coherent enough for them to say their goodbyes. They were all down at the café getting something to drink.

"I wanted to ask if you would mind if I came to his funeral," Qary asked hesitantly.

"I wouldn't mind. I'm sure Row would be pleased for you to be there. You can say a few words if you want."

"I would be honored."

"Qary, I'm sorry, but I have to go," Hope said. "They're coming for his body. Let's talk again in the next few days. I'm looking forward to seeing you at the funeral. I mean it. I want you there."

The whirring of the heli-copter landing on the lawn of the hospital grew louder as she hung up the air-line. She knew she only had a couple minutes left before they arrived. This would be her last chance to be alone with her husband.

She stood from her chair and leaned over and kissed Row on the forehead and then lightly on the lips as her tears dripped onto his face. She wiped them off with the sleeve of her shirt.

"I'll miss you so much," she said, still gripping his hand. "I'm glad you're no longer suffering. You've been the best father and husband a woman could ever ask for. Rest in peace, my love."

A knock on the door interrupted her as two soldiers entered. Hope quickly regained her composure, determined to be strong. She'd have to be strong over the next few days. For her kids. For the nation.

The men asked Hope if she was ready for them to move his body. A sudden overwhelming pain in her heart created uncertainty. She had known they were coming. That was the plan. Now that it was actually happening, the weight of the loss was suddenly crushing her heart.

"I can't let him go. I'm not ready," she wanted to shout. Instead, she just sat at the side of the bed, stunned, unable to move.

The soldiers walked to the bed, one on each side, but Hope was blocking one of them. Her hand was still locked to Row's like a vise. The one soldier on her side stopped, seemingly unsure what to do. The other reached over and slowly, gently, separated her hand from Row's. It was like someone was ripping her flesh apart. Hope understood at that moment what the Bible meant when it said she was one flesh with her husband.

Holding hands had always been something special to Row. They'd sit on the couch watching the air-box, and he'd hold her hand for hours. In the car, Row almost always had his hand on hers or was holding it no matter how long they drove. When they walked side-by-side, he almost always reached for her hand. Like he was protecting her or simply wanting to be one with her. She'd often wondered why he always wanted to hold her hand, thinking that it hadn't meant as much to her as it did to him. Suddenly it did. She'd never hold his hand again. Never touch him again. Never kiss him again. Never feel his body next to her... again.

He was her rock. What would she do without him?

Hope suddenly felt numb. She started reacting out of instinct. She stood from the chair and walked to the other side of the room. They pulled out a black body bag, and she looked away. How they would move him had never occurred to her. When she heard the zipper open, the sound ripped open a hole in her heart. She wanted to yell for them to stop. The numbness was gone. She now felt everything.

He really is gone.

They placed Row's body into the bag and then zipped it closed. The blow to her gut, stole all of her air as she struggled to catch her breath. She had seen him for the last time. The casket would be closed. The soldiers covered the bag with a flag. Hope felt a sudden urge to get out of the room as soon as she could. She bolted out and ran into the kids who were just about to enter.

She explained to them that their father and grandfather had passed. That the soldiers were there to take his body away. The soldiers stopped in the hall to give the kids one last chance to say goodbye. Her boys were trying to be strong. Probably for her. Rowan Jr., especially. He was the oldest. The man of the family now. Their daughter was sobbing, unable to hide the grief. Trying to be strong for her kids but the tears overwhelmed her resolve. The kids were not sure how to react. They all just had blank stares on their faces. Some had tears rolling down their cheeks. They loved Papa, the name they called him.

The family followed the soldiers out of the hos-pital and onto the lawn and watched as they placed Row's flag-draped body onto the heli-copter and flew away. Several soldiers stood at attention, saluting. Reporters and cameras were already in place to report on and capture the images, no doubt broadcasting them across all of Ven-Us.

Hope was certain the cameras were on them at that moment. No one moved. They stood frozen in place, their eyes affixed to the helicopter until it finally was out of sight.

* * *

The day of Row's funeral was sunny and warm. A cool breeze blew from the south. Row's body had lain in honor for two weeks in the House of the Rock next to the rock. It was scheduled to lay there for one week, but the crowds were so large and kept coming that Sarah extended it by an extra week and rescheduled the funeral.

The funeral lasted about an hour. Several dignitaries spoke along with Rowan Jr. Hope could see a lot of Row in their son. His was an emotional, heartfelt speech, and there didn't seem to be a dry eye in the entire crowd after he spoke. He shared some funny stories of his memories of his dad in his childhood and then talked at length about the character he'd instilled in him.

Sarah spoke and gave a rousing eulogy on country, love of God, and the sacrifice Row had made for the pursuit of peace.

Qary spoke before Sarah, and his words were brief but powerful.

"Row Church-Well was a great man. I'm honored to be here today to speak a few words. I aspire to be half the man Row was. I am humbled, knowing it is an impossible task. He was a man of principle. Courage. Valor. A determined enemy. Impossible to defeat. It was also impossible to overcome his goodness. To exceed his compassion. To overtake his ability to see the good in others. To see the good in me. He brought out the best in me. He brought out the best in our two nations. He is a westerner by birth. But I can tell you on behalf of all Naryans everywhere, he is one of us. Our loss is just as great. I hope to see you again, my good friend."

* * *

The statisticians estimated that more people attended Row's funeral than were at the Peace Summit. The entire square was unrecognizable compared to what it had been like five months before. The wall was completely gone. God had removed in three minutes what it took man more than five hundred years to construct.

Some skeptics said that it was just the natural phenomenon of the quake that removed the wall. Row always said it was the providence of God. The precision in which the wall was removed could not have been a random act of nature. The entire wall, more than 10,000 mil-ead, starting from the gate and going all the way to the north and to the south, was completely gone. There was no evidence it ever existed. The entire monstrosity was swallowed up by the ground.

However, the House of the Rock was still standing. It sustained no damage at all, except for the partition that had kept the Naryans out, which came crashing to the ground during the quake. Another act of God, Row insisted. Symbolically and physically, God was removing the barrier between the Naryans and the Christians.

Remarkably, only one person died in the quake. Again, Row claimed it was God's providence that led Sarah to ask everyone to leave the wall. Otherwise, thousands would've died. As it was, the only fatality was a Naryan who was crushed when the gate fell on him. Turned out he was wearing a suicide vest and was armed with a gun. God protected everyone from the bomber by killing him before he could kill anyone. More definitive proof to Row that God's hand was all over the peace summit.

Five months later, significant resources had been invested in the square. Trees were planted, fresh flowers had started to bloom. The building housing the rock was expanded so the Naryans had access and could come through and view it.

And a new monument was constructed specifically for that day.

Sarah's idea was for Row to be buried in the square, a monument constructed, and a flame attached to his grave that would burn continuously. The gravesite would be guarded by soldiers twenty-four hours a day, and the guard would be changed every four hours. It would become a permanent memorial on the square only steps from the other memorial with the name of Row's wife and daughter. Hope would be buried next to him when she died.

Hope stood with Qary at Row's final resting place.

"Your words were very touching," she said to him.

"I meant everything I said," he stated soberly.

"Row treasured your friendship."

"I still can't believe we became such good friends. I still can't believe he forgave me. I didn't deserve it."

Hope touched Qary's arm.

"None of us deserve forgiveness," Hope said. "But God gives us all forgiveness freely from his grace, if we just believe in Christ."

Qary nodded as if he understood.

"I have to go now," Hope said, as she hugged Qary. "They are wanting me up at the rock. It was so good to see you."

Hope turned and walked swiftly away from Row's grave. She looked back before she entered the House of the Rock.

Qary was on his knees in front of the grave. His head bowed. His lips mouthing words.

Saying something.

EPILOGUE

While people are saying, "Peace and safety,"
destruction will come on them suddenly.
—1 Thessalonians 5:3

30

Sometime in the future

Eventually, a new Naryan Supreme Commander came into power who knew nothing about Row or Qary.

* * *

Heaven, where there is no time

Heaven is nothing like what I expected when I was on Ven-Us.
It's Better.
I'm still called Row. Everyone here somehow knows each other's names. I have a new body. All the aches and pains of the old body are all gone. Just like the Bible said, no pain, no tears, only constant joy and peace. We strived so hard for peace on Ven-Us. No need for striving in heaven. It all comes naturally. Joy and peace are constant. Like air was on Ven-Us. Just always there. Taken for granted even.

When a loved one is about to come to heaven from Ven-Us, we are told about it so we can meet them at the Pearly Gates. Mia and Meg met me. So did my mom and dad. My grandparents. Some friends. The reunion was indescribable. I knew I would see them again, and it would be joyous, I just had no idea how great it would actually be. I wondered why I grieved their loss so much on Ven-Us. They were better off in heaven as I came to learn. And it wasn't that long until I saw them again anyway. Now I would be with them forever.

Since I came here, I've been told to meet a number of people. Hope many years after my death. My children and grandchildren years later although we had no real concept of time. Sarah. Her husband. Eric and Lacy. I am as happy to see them as they are me. We all have so much fun together. There is no marriage in heaven. So, nothing is weird between Mia and Hope. We all always get along. They are like best friends.

Conflict, anger, war, disagreement—none of those things are present in heaven. Everyone is happy all the time. It's nothing like it was on Ven-Us.

There is no concept of time. So, I can't tell you how long I've been here, or how long it was between the time I got here and others started arriving. I have a sense that time is passing, but I have no perspective on how to gauge it. I have nowhere I have to be. Nothing I specifically have to do. I have an understanding that I'm here for an eternity. Other than the specific time I go to greet people arriving from Ven-Us, there is no perspective that time is passing.

One of the misconceptions I had on Ven-Us was how long it would take to get to heaven. I thought it would be a process. I would die. Get in a line. Go through processing. Orientation, maybe. Then I'd find out if I made it.

It wasn't like that at all. The moment I was absent from my body, I was in the presence of the Lord. Immediately. On my knees, bowing before him. If there was any time between my death and being present with the Lord, I didn't realize it. He is the first person I saw and the one I continually see all the time. I am never outside of his presence. I see my friends and family a lot, but not all the time. Jesus, I see all the time. I find myself worshiping God all the time.

Jesus actually greets everyone upon their death. Believers and nonbelievers. The believers are led into heaven. The nonbelievers are cast into the outer darkness where they perish. Jesus greets both so even the unbelievers know he died for their sins. I guess, in a way, everyone eventually believes. Everybody bows their knees and then confesses Jesus as Lord before they meet their fate. But for some, it is too late.

One of the highlights in heaven is that I get to see and meet people from other planets. I learned that God created many planets. He put on them an Adam and Eve, a garden of Eden, and a tree of the knowledge of good and evil. All the planets eventually ate of the tree and brought sin and death into their world. After meeting the Adam and Eve from Ven-Us, I had a better understanding of what they went through in the garden. They told me all about carving on the rock. The ones from the other planets told me their stories.

It's interesting to meet people from other planets. I get to talk to some from the beginning of the creation of the planet to some who lived in the last days. Every generation of every planet is represented in heaven. One of the things I learned is that all of the planets eventually ended in various violent and destructive ways. They all eventually destroyed themselves. I hope Ven-Us can avoid the same fate.

It's been quite an experience meeting everyone from Ven-Us and hearing their stories. I've met all the apostles. I've actually met all of the biblical characters who made it to heaven. Casik and Nary. The prophets. Jesus's father and mother. Brothers and sisters. It is interesting getting to know them. They are real people, with real stories to tell. Not just print on paper.

We all remember what happened on Ven-Us, but we have no regrets. It's not like that. We can remember the good and the bad, but we always are able to see how God used it for our good, so the memories are never bad.

Speaking of memories, Qary is here. One day I was told there was someone for me to meet who was coming from Ven-Us. I have to say I was shocked when I saw him. Of course, I wasn't the first person he saw. That was Jesus. After he saw Jesus, then I was the first to greet him, after his daughter. The one who died from the car. I had already met her. I told her all about her father. Children automatically make it to heaven as long as they haven't reached the age to where they are accountable and reject Jesus as their Savior. Even children of unbelievers make it.

Qary explained that he gave his heart to the Lord and got saved at my funeral. He knelt down on one knee and prayed for God to save him. And God did. His wife and family all got saved later. He would get to greet them when they arrive, I explained to him.

On Ven-Us things were always awkward between Qary and me. Even after we became friends. We had a lot of history that we put aside on Ven-Us, but it was always there. It's not here now. There is nothing but love and friendship between us. I am so happy he's here and that we get to spend an eternity together.

Something I never thought would happen.

**

I am told to go to the Pearly Gates. In fact, everyone I know from Ven-Us is told to go there. Someone is arriving today from Ven-Us. That much we knew. We just weren't sure who. Everyone I knew was already here.

When I arrive at the gate, a large crowd has gathered. It seems like only people from Ven-us are here. I don't know for sure, but it might be everyone who ever lived on Ven-Us who made it to heaven. It seems like that many people.

There is a sudden commotion as the clouds part and a throng of people come through the clouds. They are immediately greeted by Jesus and they all fall to their knees in unison. Shortly thereafter, we see a large number of them enter into the Pearly Gates, and the rest are cast out into the outer darkness.

We rush to greet them. Some are my descendants. Hope is here and we greet them together. We learn they are several generations removed from us. They lived a hundred or so years after us.

"What happened on Ven-Us? Hope asked. "Why did everyone arrive at once?"

One of the young men, I think our great, great grandson explained. "The Naryan Supreme Commander shot off a missile toward the west which hit the atmosphere and pierced it. All of the water in the sky came crashing down to Ven-Us, and we all drowned. We all died at once."

"Just like all the other planets," I thought to myself. "They all eventually destroyed themselves. Ven-Us did too."

What a shame!

THE EDEN STORIES

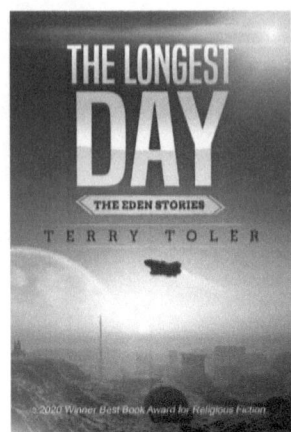

About the Author

TERRY TOLER is the author of *The Eden Stories* series, along with the Alex Halee and Jamie Austen book series. He is a minister, public speaker, counselor, and retired entrepreneur. Impacting the lives of people worldwide through storytelling has become one of his passions in life. He can be followed at terrytoler.com.

www.ingramcontent.com/pod-product-compliance
Lightning Source LLC
Chambersburg PA
CBHW020235260626
47156CB00002B/688